JO BARNES

As a student at Leeds, Jo specialised in mediaeval English, the language that developed from the Anglo Saxons and the Normans who defeated them at the Battle of Hastings. Before she became a writer, Jo taught children and young people in London schools from age three to 19.

This book brings together three worlds that fascinated Jo: the real historic world of the Anglo Saxons which the Normans brushed aside after they invaded; the myth worlds of the Anglo Saxons and the Celts before them; and fantasy worlds of authors such as JRR Tolkien, CS Lewis, Philip Pullman and JK Rowling. Jo was also a fan of Buffy the Vampire Slayer and liked to joke that, unlike Buffy, her hero Wulf doesn't have to save the world 'a lot' – once is enough.

This is the second of Jo's books to be published. Her first, *Odd Fox Out*, is a thrilling adventure about a fox who decides, rather inconveniently, that he can no longer eat meat. It is also published by SilverWood Books and available from booksellers and online.

ALSO BY JO BARNES

Odd Fox Out

WULF
AND THE POWER OF
THORN

JO BARNES

SilverWood

Published in 2024 by SilverWood Books
SilverWood Books Ltd
14 Small Street, Bristol, BS1 1DE, United Kingdom
www.silverwoodbooks.co.uk

ISBN 978-1-80042-288-9 (paperback)

British Library Cataloguing in Publication Data
A CIP catalogue record for this book is
available from the British Library

Page design and typesetting by SilverWood Books

For Thomas and Anna

CHAPTER ONE

WULF

I grinned across the table at Oz. Everyone was shouting and laughing and my hands and face were smothered with fat from the roast venison. And the ale! It was like drinking liquid gold. Perhaps I'd died and gone to heaven. Not the heaven they talk about in church, with choirs of angels and all that. Boring. This was more like the stories my mum told, where the warriors go to feast in Valhalla when they've died. Because that's what we were. Warriors. Even me and Oz. Even though we were only thirteen. We beat them! We beat the Normans and chased them back across the sea!

Oz grinned back at me and lifted his tankard.

"Good stuff, this," he said. "Not like that gnat's piddle they usually give us."

It was good stuff, a lot stronger than our usual watered down ale. I'd probably had enough, but I didn't care.

"D'you know, Oz," I said, "I don't think I've ever felt this happy in my entire life."

My eyelids were drooping and the hall seemed to shimmer with gold. The blazing fire in the middle, all those gold armbands and necklets on the nobles, gold cups on the high table, even the golden ale I was drinking. Yes, I was definitely in heaven and I turned to look at the man who'd brought me here.

There at the high table, far away, right at the other end of the hall, sat the king. And he was gold too, with his crown and his golden brown hair and moustache, just his black eye-patch spoiling the picture.

"I reckon," said Oz, tipping his tankard up and draining the last drop, "d'you know what I reckon?"

"What do you reckon, oh wise one?"

"I reckon we've been part of history," said Oz. "Like – people'll always remember 1066, you know what I mean? They'll sing songs and teach kiddies about it – the two great English victories."

Someone on the next row of tables started a chant.

"Ingerland! Ingerland!

"We beat the Normans! Ingerland!"

We thumped the table and joined in.

And then the king stood up and everyone was quiet in an instant.

King Harold One-eye, performer of miracles. My hero. Who else could have raced his army up north, thrashed the Norwegian army, then raced his men back down south and walloped the Normans? It was practically impossible, but Harold had done it. He lost his eye to a Norman arrow, but he won the battle.

The King raised his goblet. You could hear the silence.

"To you," he began quietly, looking round the hall with his good eye. Looking at each and every one of us. "To you, my faithful warriors. Without you we would be groaning now under a foreign yoke, slaves in our own land. Men need a king, one they can trust and follow into battle. But a king needs brave and faithful followers to fight for him." His voice was rising now. "And this I have, a hundredfold, a thousandfold."

He paused, then his voice rang out, and the birds in the rafters jumped and twittered and the dogs under the tables leapt to their feet.

"I raise my cup to you, my warriors, to England and the English!"

Everyone cheered and whooped and I yelled myself hoarse, and so did Oz and so did the dogs, barking to see who could yelp the loudest.

Harold beamed round at us all like one of the old gods in his glory. Like one-eyed Woden, king of the gods.

Oz must have been thinking the same thing, because as we slumped back on to our benches he said, "D'you reckon it's true, what they're saying?"

"What?"

"About him being under Woden's protection."

I went quiet. My hand reached inside my shirt for my lucky charm. It was a rune-stone on a leather thong and my mum gave it to me when we went off to fight. Lord Aelfric had come galloping back from the battle up north needing fresh men because some of them were dead or wounded or just plain knackered. So his brother Guthrum rounded up us boys that he'd been training and we went as replacements. Oz and me were about the youngest. Scary, but exciting too.

"May Woden protect you," my mum said and she hung this rune-stone round my neck. Well, it certainly brought us luck. I liked the feel of it. It was smooth, but you could make out the shape of the rune carved on it. It felt warm now. It did that sometimes, as if it had a life of its own.

My mum could read the runes. I didn't have a clue. Of course, the priests said you shouldn't have anything to do with the old religion, but most people did. Went to church on Sunday and the wise-woman when they were sick or in trouble. And why not? Christ and Woden too, what was wrong with that?

My mum said this stone was very old – maybe one of Woden's original runes, given to him when he'd hung on the World Tree for nine nights and nine days. She laughed when she told me that.

"If you believe that, you'll believe anything," she said. "But still – keep it safe and it'll bring you luck."

"Well?" said Oz impatiently. "What d'you reckon?"

I shrugged. For some reason I didn't want to talk about it.

I was saved by the arrival of Caedmon, the minstrel. Oz groaned.

"He's written a song about the battle," I grinned. "So at least it'll be a bit more cheerful than the usual."

"I hate those old songs," moaned Oz. "They're so miserable! All about how glorious it is to die with your lord, even when you're having your arms and legs hacked off."

I did an impression of Caedmon's warble and quite a good take-off of the sort of stuff he usually sang.

"They're gonna win, we're gonna die.

"We're in a right mess.

"But our courage grows greater

"As our strength grows less."

"Yeah!" said Oz. "At least this one'll be,

"Let's kick their teeth in! Yes! Yes! Yes!"

9

I snorted some ale up my nose and had to stifle my coughs as Caedmon sat tuning his harp, but when the singing began my eyelids gradually closed. Cheers and clapping woke me up, so I was lucky and missed the song.

And then I saw someone I knew. Sort of, though she wasn't that easy to get to know. It was Bronwen walking by with a jug brimful of ale. She had her dark hair in two long plaits, so long she could sit on them. I liked her hair. I liked her, actually, but I had no idea what she thought of me. Anyway, she wasn't looking at us. She was gripping that jug like her life depended on it.

"Ah, it's Bronwen, come to fill up our tankards," smirked Oz.

I smiled at her sleepily.

"Give us a drink, Bron," I said, "We've run out."

She stopped and let her eyes glide from the jug to my face.

"I'm not your servant," she said haughtily. "This is for my Lady Rhiannon."

"What, all that?" said Oz. "She's got a thirst on her!"

"Well, *obviously* she's not going to drink all of it personally," said Bronwen, "but I was asked to fetch a full jug and I'm not going back with a half-empty one!"

"Oh, go on, Bron," I wheedled. "They won't miss half a cup."

"I wouldn't give you any, Wulfstan, if I had gallons to spare," said Bronwen. "You've had more than enough already."

And she moved off, carefully steering the jug round staggering bodies.

"She likes you," grinned Oz. "Girls always act like that when they like you – all stuck up."

BRONWEN

I heard that. I stopped walking, but carefully, and glanced back. Oz had both elbows on the table, a silly grin on his face under his messy fair hair. Had he heard of such a thing as a comb, I wondered? And Wulf wasn't much better, with his brown head sinking back down on to his folded arms. He really had drunk enough. It was annoying, but I did quite like him. Why, though? Wulfstan and Osric, what a pair of idiots! Typical English louts, even more insufferable now they'd won this battle. Would I ever be able to go home to Wales? At least the louts there were Welsh.

And then time stopped.

An icy breath was freezing me rigid.

There, on the other side of the hall – a stranger with a black cloak drawn round him, in all that heat. A piece of black cloth was wound round his head and his beard was just as black. And his face...his face was darker than any I've ever seen. A girl was offering him a drink, but he shook his head. He was looking at someone. He couldn't take his eyes off him. Wulf! He was staring at Wulf.

It wasn't a gift, having the sight, it was a curse. And I couldn't even tell what it meant, this sudden wintry draught, this stopping of time. Nain would have known. My grandmother could always tell the meaning of my waking dreams. But she was back home in Wales. I couldn't ask her. She said I'd grow into it, but I wasn't sure I wanted to.

Who wants to know when something bad is going to happen?

CHAPTER TWO

WULF

Next morning, I knew I wasn't in Heaven after all. I had a thumping headache. There was straw sticking through my mattress cover. Hang on, there wasn't any cover, just straw. Where was I? But my eyelids were stuck together and I couldn't be bothered to prise them open.

Something warm and breathy pushed at my side.

"All right, Mum," I mumbled.

Another shove, then, "Mooooo!"

Oh no, it was a cow and she was starting to eat my bed and I felt… oh, this was horrible. I leant over and…eurgh! I was sick all over the floor. Eurgh…there it went again. There couldn't be anything left in my stomach.

"Sorry, Winfrith," I gasped. "Don't look at me like that. Couldn't help it."

But it wasn't Winfrith, our old cow at home. This one was a darker brown and she looked much younger. Where was I? The light was quite dim in here – thank God – but I wasn't on my own and I knew some of these people. They were from our village. There was Oz. Sleeping with his mouth wide open like he always did.

And then I remembered. I shuffled away from the cow, who was trying to eat my bed. Then I lay down again and smiled to myself, because…I remembered it all now. The battle. That terrible, empty feeling as Harold went down when the arrow grazed his eye, and all the rejoicing when the reinforcements arrived. And then the king staggering to his feet to show us he was still alive and then…

I lay there grinning my head off, thinking about those Normans running for their lives. And after that, days later, the feast! Most of my share must have been in that disgusting puddle on the floor.

Oh, yuck – Winfrith, or whatever her name was, had just added a steaming pile of dung to my vomit. Eugh, I had to get up...the smell! I didn't want to be sick again. But my head! I couldn't go anywhere near that barn door. It was too bright, I couldn't bear it.

Suddenly a dark shape loomed in the door, blocking out the light.

"Ha! Wulfstan and Osric!" boomed a voice. "Just the pair I was looking for!"

I winced as this voice thumped in my head. It was Guthrum, larger than life and with a bull's bellow to match. He strode over, shoved the cow out of the way, looked at me and Oz and roared with laughter. I winced again.

"Can't take your drink, eh?" he said cheerfully. "I know the best remedy for that."

He grabbed my arm in one great fist and Oz's in the other and hauled us both upright.

"Wha...wha's goin' on?" mumbled Oz, his legs buckling under him. "Gerroff! I'm goin' back to sleep."

And then we were both dragged towards that blinding light in the doorway. I screwed my eyes tight shut and the next thing I knew was a shock of icy water, and I couldn't breathe! He'd dunked our heads in the animals' drinking trough.

"Gerroff!" spluttered Oz when we were pulled up again. "S'not fair! Wanna go back to sleep!"

I didn't say anything. I was too busy coughing. When I managed to open my eyes they were staring into Guthrum's, crinkled up with laughing. He'd bent down to our level and thought it was a huge joke.

"Sorry, lads," he grinned, "but I couldn't wait around all day for you two to recover. I've got a job for you. Go into the hall and get yourself some porridge. That'll settle your stomachs. Then come and find me."

He shoved us towards the great hall, the scene of all the carousing the night before. Inside, the light was blessedly dim, and after a helping of porridge from the big iron pot I did begin to feel more human. At least, I reckoned I could walk around without my head falling off.

Oz suddenly turned as white as the porridge, clutched his stomach and leaned forward. I dodged out of the way and a sharp-faced old woman rushed over.

"If you're going to be sick, get outside!" she scolded. "I'm trying to get this hall cleaned up."

Oz staggered to the doorway, but didn't make it any further. As he doubled up and spewed out the contents of his stomach, the old woman descended on him with a bucket of water.

"Get out, get out!" she shrieked, throwing the lot over Oz.

I sauntered after him, feeling a lot better now.

"We are having a good wash today, aren't we?" I grinned.

Oz flung himself at me, and by the time we'd rolled in the dirt a few times, I was just about as wet and dirty as him. Suddenly we were grabbed and pulled upright. It was Guthrum again and he wasn't laughing now.

"I've had enough of you two! I told you I've got a job for you. Have you got any clean tunics?"

We shook our heads.

"You'd better come with me then."

He marched us to a hut on the edge of the settlement. I'd never been in here before. There was a pile of shields and helmets and a big wooden trunk of clean, new-looking tunics and breeches. Who did they belong to? I had one spare set of everything, with more darns than cloth, but it was all at home.

"You smell disgusting, the pair of you," said Guthrum. "Strip off and I'll find something that fits you."

I pulled my tunic over my head and found Guthrum gazing at my chest with a funny expression on his face.

"That's a pretty trinket," he murmured, reaching towards my rune-stone on its leather thong. His hand stopped just as he was about to touch it.

"Pretty?" I said. That's the last word I'd have used to describe it.

"Hm, not pretty exactly, but it looks…very old," said Guthrum, eyeing it almost greedily. "It must be valuable."

I laughed. "You're joking. We haven't got anything valuable. My mum'd sell it like a shot if she thought we'd get anything for it. I'm only wearing it for luck, because she told me to."

"Ah, yes," said Guthrum. "Very sensible. Wouldn't do to disobey the village wise-woman, especially when she's your mother."

His hand was still hovering, as if he wanted to touch it but didn't quite dare. I shrank back. I preferred the old bullying Guthrum, even when he was angry with us. Then – was it my imagination, or was my stone starting to tingle and grow warmer? No, I wasn't imagining it – it was almost burning me.

Guthrum suddenly looked sheepish.

"Well!" he said abruptly. "No time to lose."

He fished in the wooden chest and handed Oz a green tunic and me a dark blue one.

"These should fit you. You'll find breeches in there as well. I'll see you outside. Oh, and – er – remember your mother's advice. Don't lose that rune-stone."

He grinned at us as if nothing had happened and ducked through the doorway. Me and Oz looked at each other. The rune-stone was back to normal too.

"What was all that about?" said Oz.

I moved to the door and watched Guthrum stride across the yard and greet a man I'd never seen before. The place was full of strangers. Nothing odd in that. But there was something about this man, standing in the shadow of one of the guesthouses – a sort of stillness. He was tall, with dark hair, a pale face and high cheekbones. His clothes looked good, but not showy. I felt as if – not sure how to put this – I felt as if he'd rather be the watcher than the watched. Although it looked like someone else was watching *him*. In the shadow of another building stood a big blond man, very upright, like a soldier, and he had his eyes on Guthrum and this stranger as well.

There was a quick conversation and the dark haired man handed Guthrum a leather purse and what looked like a scroll of parchment. Guthrum nodded and went on his way, tucking it all into the front of his tunic. Then before I could move the man turned round and looked straight

15

at me. He smiled and I could feel myself blush. This was embarrassing. I ducked back into the outhouse.

"Who's that?" said Oz, coming to the door.

"I dunno," I said, "but he's just given Guthrum a purse full of money and I've got a funny feeling about it." I peered round the door and nodded towards the other stranger. "See that bloke over there? He was watching them like a hawk. There's something going on."

CHAPTER THREE

BRONWEN

I was in a black mood that day. The bags were heavy and I didn't want to go back. Not yet, anyway. We'd rushed down for the celebrations and now we had to rush away. My lady wanted to be home with the baby so I had to collect a whole load of loaves and cheeses for the return journey. But I wanted to stay and enjoy myself! I felt like throwing the bags at her.

Oh, I knew I shouldn't think like that. I did love Lady Rhiannon – she was my only link with home. But since we'd left Wales three years before, when I was ten, I'd been stuck on Lord Aelfric's estate and then... my first chance to do something interesting, and my lady was missing the baby!

It had been quite exciting at first. I'd only just gone to work for Lady Rhiannon when the English won those battles in Wales, which was why my lady married Lord Aelfric, which was why we came to England, which was why I ended up in the same bit of monotonous flat countryside for three years.

The whole point of coming to England had been to travel, to see some of the wide world. I'd been on at Nain ever since I was tiny. "What's over the mountain, Nain?" "Take me to the next village, Nain!" "What would happen if we followed the river? Would it lead us to the sea?" And then I'd left the river and the beautiful mountains and my Nain. For what? A boring English manor.

And now they'd won this other stupid battle. I supposed I was glad. I didn't really want the Normans over here. But actually, I couldn't get very worked up about it. What I really, really wanted was to go home to Wales and see Nain again. She'd been mother and father to me since my parents died and I missed her so much.

Oh no, it was those boys.

"Well, if it isn't our friend who was so mean with the ale," grinned Oz.

"Good morning, Osric," I sniffed. "I didn't expect you two to be up yet. In fact, I didn't think you'd be showing your faces till tomorrow."

"What *do* you mean by that?" said Oz, widening his eyes.

Wulf smiled, but kept quiet.

"Cat got your tongue, Wulfstan?" I said, and started to move round them.

"What you doing with that lot?" said Oz, nodding at my bags.

"We're leaving today," I said. "This is for the journey."

"Already?" said Wulf.

"Ah, you *have* got a tongue," I teased him. "Yes, my lady's missing young Aelfwin." I started to roll my eyes, then stopped myself. I wasn't going to criticize Rhiannon in front of these boys. "I must go and help her get ready. I'll see you in a few days, I suppose?"

"Yeah, whenever," said Oz. "We don't know when we'll be back, do we, Wulf."

Wulf shook his head. I raised my eyebrows.

"Goodbye, then," I said, and made my way, frowning at the ground, to Lady Rhiannon's quarters. Hadn't something happened last night, something to do with Wulf and that dark stranger? I'd had a little to drink myself, everyone had, though not as much as those boys, and I couldn't quite remember.

WULF

Me and Oz snapped to attention when Guthrum came striding back with a 'don't mess with me' air about him.

"Right, you two, I've got a letter for you to deliver."

So this was what he'd been paid for, to get us to deliver a letter. But this was Guthrum, Lord Aelfric's brother. He'd known us all our lives, taught us to fight, joked around with us. There couldn't be anything fishy about it. I couldn't think of anyone more straightforward than Guthrum.

He held a scroll of parchment out to me. It had to be the same one that stranger gave him. Then he frowned and took it back.

"I've seen you at that priest school, haven't I?"

We both nodded.

"Can either of you two read?"

"A bit," I said.

"Waste of time if you ask me," grunted Guthrum. He looked suspiciously at the rolled up parchment. "Ah, but I think this is in Latin. Can either of you read Latin?"

"Only a bit of the church service," I said.

Guthrum's face cleared. "That's all right, then," he grinned. "I don't think there's anything holy about this little message. Anyway, d'you see this seal?"

He held out the purple wax seal for us to inspect. We nodded.

"If this seal's been tampered with in any way whatsoever, I shall personally hang you upside down from a gibbet and let the crows peck your eyes out."

"Oh, we wouldn't touch it, would we, Wulf," said Oz.

"'Course not," I agreed, nodding like mad, and then shaking my head instead.

"Right," said Guthrum, returning to his usual good humour. "Here's what I want you to do."

A couple of hours later we'd mounted two fine horses, on loan for the journey. I had a chestnut mare and she seemed sweet-tempered enough, though the ground looked a long way down. At home we didn't ride much and when we did it was ponies much smaller than this or the odd plodding workhorse. What was I going to do if she decided to gallop?

"This is the life!" grinned Oz from the saddle of his grey, and started trotting ahead.

Did he ever have doubts about anything? Oz always seemed to plunge into things while I hung back pretending not to be scared.

Lady Rhiannon's party looked like they were ready to leave. Their horses were snorting and shifting around, and their only cart was loaded up with all kinds of stuff. Edric was in charge, one of Lord Aelfric's housecarls. He said something to her ladyship and she nodded.

"Right, let's go!" he called, and they started to move off.

"Hey, wait for us!" yelled Oz.

Everyone pulled on their reins and stared as we rode up.

"We're coming with you, Guthrum's orders," I said, feeling my face grow hot.

"Yeah," said Oz. "He reckoned you needed a bit of protection."

The men all roared with laughter, and even Rhiannon and Bronwen smiled.

"Shut up, Oz!" I muttered, feeling even hotter.

"Well, come on then," said Edric. "We should be home by tomorrow evening. We'll spend tonight at Thorsham. Let's get a move on, or it'll be dark before we get to the inn."

Me and Oz caught up with Bronwen and our horses broke into a steady trot.

"We're on a mission," said Oz importantly.

"I know, to protect us," she smirked.

"Nah, I was just kidding about that."

"Oh, you surprise me!" said Bronwen, wide-eyed. "I'm so disappointed. I thought you were going to give us a display of your marvellous swordplay, show us how you defeated the Normans. Oh no, I forgot. It was stones you were throwing, wasn't it?"

"Only when the arrows ran out!" I said. I liked Bronwen – I liked her a lot – but that wasn't fair.

"Yeah," said Oz. "We gave them a few good showers of arrows first. And we didn't give up when the arrows were gone. That's why the English'll never be defeated. We don't give up."

"Oh, and I suppose the Welsh do!" said Bronwen hotly.

"Stop it, you two, this is stupid," I said. "Nobody was talking about the Welsh."

Bronwen glared at us.

"I'm going to see if my lady's all right," she said, and pulled her pony away.

"You are an idiot, Oz," I sighed. "You know how touchy she is about anything to do with that Welsh defeat."

"I never even mentioned it," said Oz. "She's just got a chip on her shoulder."

"Well, you can sort of understand it. She was dragged away from her home, couldn't even speak the language. I mean, if Harold hadn't won all those battles in Wales, she'd probably still be back there."

"That was three years ago," said Oz. "She should get over it."

I shook my head.

"Oz, I really like you. You're my best friend and all that, but sometimes I think you've got the understanding of a...turnip."

Oz leant sideways, took a swipe at me and nearly fell off his horse. I snorted with laughter and galloped ahead, with Oz chasing after. The mare ran like a dream, sensitive to every tiny pull on the reins or pressure of my knees. What had I been worried about? It was a good open road, a sunny afternoon and I felt like I was riding the wind. I glanced back at Oz, slowly gaining on me and grinning like a maniac.

"Truce!" I called.

"You wish!" yelled Oz.

"Oi! You two!" bellowed Edric. "Get back here!"

Oz skidded to a halt, once again almost slipping off his saddle, while I gently slowed my mare and turned her back.

"That's enough messing around!" growled Edric. "We've got to get to this inn before dark. I want you two to go ahead and warn the innkeeper we're coming. Tell him how many's in the party, make sure he's got enough supper cooking, that sort of thing."

"We've never been there before. Is it a straight road?" I asked.

"Pretty well," said Edric. "There's a crossroads, but with a signpost, so you can't miss it. Thorsham, it's got a reasonable inn, big enough for us lot. You should be there in about half an hour. I'm sure you two won't mind sleeping in the stables."

"Great!" said Oz. "Cows last night, horses tonight."

As we were talking, Lady Rhiannon drew her horse alongside.

"I've asked Bronwen to go with them, to get a room ready for me," she said to Edric.

"Very well, my lady," nodded Edric, while Bronwen looked coolly on.

Without a word she trotted off with us, ahead of the rest of the party. Oz looked at me and rolled his eyes.

"Girls!" he mouthed.

But a few minutes later she started to thaw.

"What's in your bag?" she asked, looking at the leather satchel slung over my shoulder.

"A letter we've got to deliver," I told her.

"Yeah, that's our mission," said Oz, "and we've got to guard it with our lives. We're going home first, and then on to deliver this. It's all hush-hush, so don't tell anyone."

Bronwen gave us an amused smile.

"I like your horses," she said.

I smiled back. "Wish they really were ours," I said, stroking the mare's neck.

"Come on," grinned Oz, "let's get to this inn!"

We galloped away, leaving the rest of the party to trot sedately at the pace of the horse and cart. Me and Oz had to slow down a bit so that Bron could keep up, but her little pony could go surprisingly fast.

By the time we reached the crossroads we were long out of sight of everyone else. The forest, which had been hanging back on the horizon, seemed to have crept closer to the road. A clump of bushes and small trees squatted opposite the signpost.

"I think it's that way," said Bronwen, pointing straight ahead, where the road was still fairly clear of trees.

"No, it's not," I said. "Look, the sign says Thorsham that way."

The sun was low in the sky by now and we all gazed uneasily at the path, which led directly into the woods.

Bronwen frowned. "I'm sure that's not right. We came this way and we didn't ride through the forest."

"Well, what are we gonna do?" said Oz. He yawned and stretched. "You know what, adventures and battles are all very well, but I'm beginning to look forward to seeing the old village again. Who do we believe, Bron or the signpost? I just wanna get home."

While he was talking I got down and peered at the foot of the signpost.

"There's something funny here," I muttered. "Feel this." I prodded the ground around the wooden post. "The earth's loose. Somebody's moved the sign!"

There was a muffled scream and a grunt. I spun round, but my view was blocked by a barrel chest and a pair of burly arms. Then something rough and smelly was jammed down over my head and a cold sharp point was at my throat.

"Clever, ain't you," sneered a voice, "but you worked that out a bit too late. And as for you, my little homesick friend…"

I heard a thump and a groan.

"It's a pity, ain't it, that you're never gonna see your village again."

CHAPTER FOUR

WULF

Gradually, I came to. Dark, unpleasant dreams had me in their grip and they didn't want to let me go. I felt like a swimmer breaking the surface of the water, being sucked down and then struggling up again. Where was I? This had happened to me before, hadn't it? I'd woken up not knowing where I was, with the mother of all headaches. There'd been a cow, and then Guthrum, dragging me out into the blinding sunlight. I opened my eyes. No sunlight this time. Nothing. It was as black with my eyes open as with them shut. There was something over my face, that was why. When I breathed in I sucked it into my mouth and nose. I started to panic. I was going to suffocate!

I tried to put my hand up to pull it off, whatever it was, but I couldn't move my arm. Both my hands were behind me and there was something tight round my wrists. The panic grew worse.

Then there was a noise. A door creaking open. Feet and heavy breathing. Then a voice, which I'd heard somewhere before.

"Ah, look at 'em. The little babes are sleeping peacefully. Must be that knock on the head. Works better than ale, that does, to get the kiddies to sleep. I'll have to tell the missus."

There were shouts of laughter.

"You better take them sacks off their heads," said a different voice. "They might go and suffocate."

Yeah, I thought.

"Nah," said the first voice. "There's plenty of airholes. It's only sackin'."

"I dunno," said the other voice. "I heard of someone who was sick and drowned in his own vomit. That's more likely to happen if there's somethin' tied over your head."

"Look, who's running this job, you or me?"

"Well, you are, Ed. It was only a suggestion."

A third voice chimed in, a cold, sneery voice that chilled me as I lay there listening.

"What are we keeping 'em alive for, that's what I wanna know. We got the letter. Let's just slit their throats and be done with."

"You think you know everything, don't you," hissed the man called Ed. "It was the letter and *something else*."

"There's nothin' else on 'em," spat the sneery voice. "We searched 'em well enough. Only that little cross round the girl's neck and that ain't worth a groat. You're goin' soft, you are."

"There was that stone thing round the boy's neck," said the second voice.

"Well, it weren't worth nickin', anyway," said sneery. "I vote we cut their throats. We could have a bit of fun first."

No, don't listen to him, Ed!

"Oh, you're so clever," said Ed, his voice rising. "It could be a piece of information he's after, have you thought of that? And we don't know which one's got it."

"Yeah," said the second voice. "We gotta keep 'em alive till the boss gets here. That's why I reckon we ought to take them sacks off their heads."

Yes, yes!

Ed sighed. "You're obsessed with that, you are. Go on then, take 'em off. Who's for some more ale?"

The door creaked again and I felt the sack pulled, none too gently, over my chin. It got stuck and the man cursed and fiddled with a knot. I kept my eyes tight shut and resisted the urge to say *ow!* as the sack caught my nose. Then I listened carefully as the man did the same to Oz and Bron and stumped outside, pulling the door shut behind him.

Only then did I dare to open my eyes. Not that it made much difference. I stared round in the darkness, trying to make sense of my surroundings. We seemed to be in some sort of hut, quite small, and the floor felt like rough earth. Under the door there was a space of a few inches, and the only light was coming from there. Firelight – it was night-time and a chill autumn night at that. I shivered. Gradually my eyes adjusted and I could make out the other two, lying a foot or so away. I could hear the murmur of voices and the occasional burst of laughter, but from Oz and Bronwen – nothing. I might as well have been on my own. *Oh, wake up, you two!*

Then one of them started to stir and moan, and I panicked again. It was Oz. Painfully I wriggled over – my feet were tied, as well as my hands – and hissed *shhhh* in Oz's ear.

"Don't say anything," I whispered. "We're prisoners, and for God's sake stop moaning!"

Oz opened his eyes and looked at me stupidly, then he tried to move. He looked down at his tied ankles, looked back at me and nodded.

"Bron's still out cold," I whispered. "I hope she's all right."

A horrible thought occurred to me. Men like this, they did things to girls, didn't they? Unspeakable things. Slowly I wriggled over to her. All her clothes seem to be in place, that was something.

Then another thought occurred to me, this one much more cheering. I shuffled back to Oz and whispered, "Let's try and undo each other's hands. You'd have thought they'd have tied us to something, so we couldn't move. Wonder why they didn't."

Oz looked around the hut. "Perhaps because there's nothing to tie us to," he said.

"Remember to keep your voice down!" I hissed. "There's a bloke out there itching to cut our throats."

"Charming!" muttered Oz as we awkwardly manoeuvred ourselves back to back.

Some minutes later I was still struggling with the knots at Oz's wrists. My hands were numb and the knots were very tight.

"This is useless," I grunted. "We need something sharp to cut them and my dagger's gone. A stone might do it."

But despite the unevenness of the ground there didn't seem to be any sharp stones around.

"You have a go at mine," I puffed.

Perhaps my knots weren't quite so tight, because after a bit of a struggle Oz managed to work one loose. The rest came easily and suddenly my hands were free. Oz flashed me a triumphant grin.

"You should be able to do mine now," he whispered, as I wiggled my fingers, stretched my arms and moved my shoulders in circles.

"Yeah, give us a minute," I muttered.

"We haven't got a minute," Oz hissed back. "What about the bloke who wants to slit our throats?"

"All right, all right."

With my hands free I could lie facing the knots and – more or less – see what I was doing. Soon Oz's hands were free as well and we both managed to untie our own ankles.

"Keep the ropes there and be ready to look as if we're still tied up," I whispered. I'd been listening anxiously to the murmur of voices outside. There'd been one or two patches of silence and now I thought – I really, really hoped – that I could hear a faint snoring sound, as well as the occasional spit and crackle from the fire.

Then there was a low moan from inside the hut and we both shot over to Bronwen.

"Quiet, Bron," I whispered in her ear. "Our lives depend on it."

"What…what's going on?" she said in a slurred voice.

I put my hand over her mouth and her eyes shot open in terror.

"It's all right, it's only us, but you *must* be quiet," I whispered. "Untie her ropes, Oz," I said unnecessarily – he'd already started on her feet. "I'll take my hand away, but you've got to be quiet, right?"

Bronwen nodded and whispered, "Where are we?"

"We were captured, don't you remember? We're in some kind of hut in the forest and there's three men outside waiting to kill us." My earlier worry came back to me. "Are you all right?" I murmured. "They didn't…I mean, have you got any pains anywhere?"

"My head's killing me," she whispered, " and I sort of ache all over."

"But no real pains anywhere apart from your head?" I muttered, embarrassed.

"I don't think so," she whispered. "Actually, my wrists hurt where they were tied. Thanks, Osric, that's much better."

"What are you on about?" hissed Oz. "You didn't ask me all that."

"Never mind," I hissed back. "I think they're asleep. It might be now or never."

We all listened. The snoring had grown louder and seemed to be coming from more than one open mouth. I tried to look under the door, but all I could see were some feet and the fire, now dying down. Could I open the door without being heard? A thin crack of light showed what must be a wooden latch on the outside, but I couldn't get my hand through to lift it.

"We need a stick or something," I whispered. Luckily the hut had more sticks than sharp stones and I soon found one thin enough to poke through and under the latch. There was a creak and it started to shift. I stopped and we all froze for what seemed like an age. The snoring carried on. At last I plucked up the courage to try again. The latch shifted so slowly with a slight scraping sound and then – the door creaked open. I grabbed the edge to stop the creaking and we all crouched in terrified silence.

The fire spat and one of the men shifted and grunted, then there was more snoring. After another age I let the door open slowly, slowly, until we could all see outside. Empty ale pitchers lay on their sides and the three men were sprawled senseless on the ground. Me and Oz looked at each other and smiled.

Bronwen nudged me and pointed. A leather bag lay half open by the nearest man, its contents spilling on to the ground. It was the bag I'd been carrying, with the scroll inside, and there was the letter, with the seal still intact. How pleased would Guthrum be if we not only escaped but rescued the scroll and delivered it?

As noiselessly as I could, I crept the few yards to the bag and slowly lifted it. The men snored on. This was too good to be true!

It was too good to be true.

A hand reached out and grabbed my wrist.

"Sneaky little bastards!" said the cold, sneery voice. "I knew we should have cut your throats."

CHAPTER FIVE

WULF

I found myself staring into the eyes of the man who was so itching to kill us. The firelight played on his face, making his cold slits of eyes glitter. Suddenly I believed in devils and hell. His lips curled back in a leer.

"One of us had to stay half-sober. Oh, the boss'll be pleased with me. Not so thrilled with them," he spat.

I didn't move or say anything. It was useless to plead with him. But if I could just catch him off guard? I could smell ale on his breath, so he wasn't completely sober. I was half kneeling, half crouching. I tensed myself and suddenly sprang backwards, pulling him with me, and then kicked out at his stomach. Useless! I fell backwards with him on top of me. I felt as if I'd been caught underneath a falling tree, but a tree with eyes mocking my pathetic efforts to get away.

I could hardly breathe with his heavy weight pressing on me and his foul breath filling my nostrils, and the other two men were stirring now, mumbling and shifting around. *Where on earth was Oz?*

The man gritted his teeth. "Little bleeder!" he growled and grabbed the leather thong round my neck. His hand closed round my rune-stone and the thong cut into my skin as he twisted and tugged it. Then… slowly…his flinty eyes widened, his mouth dropped open and a look of horror came over his face. He let go of the rune-stone, pushed himself up and backed away, waving his arms in front of him and shouting, "No! No! Leave me alone!"

As I tried to get my breath back I thought I glimpsed a shadow slipping round just outside the circle of firelight. Then I heard a thud. The man fell in a crumpled heap on the ground. Over him stood Bronwen, the remains of an ale pitcher in her hands, staring in amazement at the broken shards of the rest of the pitcher and the blood seeping into the man's hair. Her expression clearly said, *did I do that?*

I sat up and at last saw Oz, methodically smashing two more pitchers on to the heads of the other two men. The second pitcher wasn't empty and there was a gush of ale all over the kidnapper.

Bronwen shuddered. "Oh, Diew!" she said. "I couldn't do it in cold blood when they were just lying there."

"Well I could," said Oz, cheerfully wiping his hands down his front. "That's nothing to what they'd have done to us."

And I just sat on the ground trying to take it all in.

"I wondered what had happened to you," I said to Oz.

"We were making plans, weren't we Bron, in sign language."

"Yes, but what happened to that man in the end?" said Bronwen, frowning. "He looked as if he was staring into the gates of hell. We were going to try and knock him out when you were fighting, but it wasn't easy without him seeing us. And then he sort of went mad."

"He grabbed my rune-stone," I said.

"Your what?" asked Bronwen.

"My rune-stone," I said, "that my mum gave me, to bring me luck."

Oz looked at me seriously. "She knows a thing or two, your mum. I wouldn't want to mess with her." He paused. "Anyway, let's get out of here. I wonder where the horses are."

"Tie them up!" ordered Bronwen, pointing at the three bodies. "Get those ropes they tied us with and bind their hands and feet."

Me and Oz looked at her with respect and I went back into the hut to collect the ropes. Oz nudged the nearest man with his foot. He didn't move.

"Oh!" gasped Bronwen. "They are still alive, aren't they?"

She put her ear to the chest of each one in turn and nodded.

"I don't care if they're not," said Oz.

"Well, I don't want to be a murderer," said Bronwen.

"Look, Bron," explained Oz as we each tied the hands and feet of one senseless body, "it's not murder, it's self-defence. Even if we'd killed them we wouldn't have done anything wrong."

"And if we don't get a move on," I added, "this boss man'll turn up, probably with some mates, and it'll all have been for nothing."

"Boss man?" said Oz.

"Yeah, they were waiting for their boss. That's why they didn't kill us straight away."

"Now he tells us," said Oz. "Let's move."

"Wait!" said Bronwen. "Are these yours?"

She held up two short daggers, which had been lying in the shadows.

"You've got a cool head," said Oz, taking his and handing the other to me.

"Thanks," I said, smiling sheepishly at her. I couldn't believe I'd been about to leave without my only weapon! I tucked the knife into its sheath and slung the leather bag over my shoulder.

While all this was going on the sky had gradually lightened and a cold grey dawn was breaking. A whinny told us where the horses were tethered and when we got there we found three, but all belonging to the outlaws. Neither Bronwen's pony nor our two mares were anywhere to be seen.

"I hope they didn't do anything bad to them," said Bronwen.

"Nah," said Oz. "They'll just have turned them loose."

"I wonder if we could borrow these," I said, going up to a black stallion.

The horse neighed, showing the whites of its eyes, and reared up menacingly. I backed away quickly.

"Perhaps not," I said. "Looks like we'll have to foot it."

"But which way?" said Bronwen.

We looked at each other. We had no idea where we were.

"Right," I said, feeling that someone had got to take charge and that if I didn't, Bronwen would, and then I'd feel even more stupid. She was, after all, a girl. "Let's think. Which way was the sun setting when we were attacked?"

"In the west?" said Oz helpfully.

Bronwen burst out laughing and I gave him a withering look.

"Very funny. I mean, was it behind the woods or on the road straight ahead or to our backs, or what?"

"It was more behind the woods and a bit ahead," said Bronwen. "And that's right, because we were riding north and a bit west…towards Wales," she added.

"More to the point, towards Aelfric's estate," I said.

Oz was looking at Bronwen in amazement. "How did you remember all that?" he said. "You didn't even have to think about it."

"My nain taught me always to notice the world around. The birds, the animals, the plants, the sun, the moon. You should always know where you fit into things."

"Your nine?" said Oz.

"My grandmother," explained Bronwen.

We were both staring at her now, till I suddenly blinked.

"For God's sake, we'll hear about your nain when we've put a safe distance between us and them. Look, the sky's lighter over there, so do we go back east that way and try to find the road we were on, or do we carry on roughly northwest, the way we were heading?"

"If we go back to the road," said Bronwen, "that is, if we can find it, Edric might have some men out looking for us. Poor Lady Rhiannon. She'll be worried sick."

"We don't know how far they brought us though," said Oz. "And for all we know there'll be more outlaws around. It might be better to stay under cover."

"We'll be undercover for a bit anyway," I said. "There don't seem to be any paths round here. Though they can't have ridden the horses too far through these trees." I paused and braced myself. It was decision time. "The main thing is to get going. I vote we strike roughly northwest, the way we were originally heading. There must be a path somewhere."

But there didn't seem to be. With the rising sun on our right and just slightly behind us we struggled through undergrowth and ducked beneath low-growing branches. Bron was the worst off. More than once we had to stop and help her disentangle her skirts from the bushes.

"This is hopeless!" she said, when we'd freed her dress for the third time. Then she pulled her underskirt just above her knees and wound her overdress around, between her legs, finally tying it in a big knot.

It was a bit embarrassing at first, seeing her white legs above her leather shoes. I tried not to look, but it was hard. Of course, I knew that girls *had* legs but you didn't often see them when they were as old as Bron. But in the end I got used to it.

"That's better!" she said. "Well, come on then. What are you waiting for?"

And we struggled on, with still no sign of a path, let alone a proper road.

"I'm starving," moaned Oz at last. "I was looking forward to a good supper at that inn. D'you realize we haven't eaten anything since midday yesterday?"

"But I can hear water," said Bronwen. "That's something."

They stopped and listened to the faint, welcome trickle of a stream.

"You've got good ears," said Oz.

"I told you," said Bronwen. "My nain taught me always to be aware of the world around."

We headed in that direction and after a while found a small, shallow stream flowing downhill, but nothing to eat, not even some late blackberries.

"That's a bit better," said Oz when we'd gulped down mouthfuls of water. "Now I'd like some nice crispy bacon and then I'll be ready to carry on."

"Oh, shut up," I said. "You're only making it worse." My stomach felt as if was being gnawed by a rat.

It was decision time again, so I said, "Let's follow this stream uphill. It's going in roughly the right direction, and when we get high enough, one of us can climb a tree and see if there's a road around."

No-one else had a better plan and it was good to have the stream to follow, instead of having to keep trying to decide which way was northwest.

"So what more did you find out about those blokes who captured us?" said Oz as we puffed uphill.

"Not a lot," I said. "They were waiting for their boss, who wanted

Guthrum's letter and something else, but they didn't know what the something else was. And one of them, the one in charge, was called Ed."

"Ed," said Oz. "Could be Edward, or Edgar, or Edmund."

"Or Edric or Edwald," added Bronwen. "It's probably the most common name in England. But what's so important about this precious letter? Where were you taking it?"

"Well, we were going home first," I said, "and then the next day we had to carry on, about another two or three days' ride west..."

"Or Edwin or Edred," said Oz.

"Shut up, Oz," I said again, "to the estate of a bloke called Sigelac. We had to give it to him. That's all. But the way Guthrum was going on about it – we had to guard it with our lives, he'd personally murder us if anything happened to it – it must be really important."

"*I* reckon," said Oz, "that old Guthrum got well paid for getting us to deliver it."

"Well, I worked that out ages ago," I said.

"A pity he didn't chuck a few coins our way," muttered Oz.

While we were talking the trees were thinning, and we suddenly found ourselves on a bare hilltop, blinking in the sunlight.

"They must have galloped a good way with us last night," I said. "I never noticed this hill in the distance yesterday."

"Well, I'm sure our friend here did," grinned Oz. "The one whose 'nine' taught her to notice everything."

Bronwen looked at him coolly. "I didn't, but I'll tell you what I notice now." She walked a few paces ahead and looked down, where the hillside dropped almost vertically. "A road. Over there."

We looked in the direction she was pointing and couldn't help smiling when we saw the road snaking along in the distance. Looking over the edge we could see that it wound directly below the hill. But not just that.

A solitary rider was cantering along it towards us.

"It could be Edric, or one of his men," I said hopefully. "He'll be near enough soon for us to see."

"Or it could be that boss man the outlaws were waiting for," said Oz.

"You're right," I said, "and the whole world could see us up here. Let's lie down. We can still keep our eyes on the road."

We lay on our fronts and strained to see the rider, shielding our eyes from the sun. But the closer he got, the less he looked like an English soldier, or anyone English at all. From a black dot on the horizon he gradually grew to a man swathed in black from head to toe, riding a black horse.

I was already growing uneasy when Bronwen suddenly groaned and covered her face with her hands.

"What's the matter, Bron?" I said, alarmed.

"Oh, stupid, stupid!" she moaned. "How could I forget?"

"What?" said Oz. "What are you on about?"

"I've seen him before," Bronwen half sobbed, "at the feast. And when I saw him I knew something bad was going to happen. He's evil! But I forgot about it! With getting kidnapped and everything, I forgot!"

She closed her hands into fists and hit the sides of her head.

I looked back at the rider. His horse was slowing down. The man raised his hand to shield his eyes and looked up. The horse stopped. No doubt about it. The rider was looking at us.

"Run!" I gasped.

CHAPTER SIX

WULF

We scrambled up and dashed back to the trees, Bronwen half sobbing as she ran. But a little way into the forest I grabbed the others and stopped them.

"This is stupid!" I panted. "We're just going back the way we came!"

"Got any better ideas?" said Oz. "Where else are we going to go? We've got to get away from him!"

"Oh, hurry!" said Bronwen, clutching my arm.

"Well, we don't want to completely lose our direction," I said. "Let's stay in the woods but close to the edge, and keep going north. He's on a horse, which'd be no good up here. And it wouldn't be easy for him to get up that hillside. It was more like a cliff."

"And hang on," said Oz, "now we've got our breath back, how do we know that was the man Bron saw at the feast?"

Bronwen put her hands on her hips and glared at Oz.

"That's the stupidest thing I've ever heard, Osric! How many men have you seen dressed like that, like the angel of death? Of course it's him, and even if I'd never seen him before, haven't we been attacked by outlaws? And aren't we being careful not to be seen in case we're attacked again?"

"She's right, Oz. Wait here. I'm going back to have a look. He might have just ridden on, and then the best thing to do would be to try and keep roughly in the right direction."

"I'm coming with you," said Oz.

Bronwen sighed. "And I suppose I am too."

We crept back to the edge of the wood and me and Oz wriggled on our bellies until we could see the road. Bron hovered anxiously just inside the trees.

The black horse was standing patiently, riderless but untethered, cropping the grass by the roadside.

"Where is he?" muttered Oz.

I shook my head. "I'd really like to know," I muttered back. "We can't just go running blindly into the trees."

Then from below we heard a scrabbling sound, the sound of someone climbing the steep hillside. We leapt up and ran blindly into the trees. What else could we do?

After a bit I tried to stop panicking and get my head round it.

"This way!" I gasped, grabbing them both. "The trees are closer together over there!"

We stopped for a few seconds to catch our breath and look back. No-one.

"Where is he?" panted Oz.

There was no sign of him.

"Do you think we've lost him already?" said Bronwen doubtfully.

"I don't know," I said. "That's why I think we should go over there, where the trees are thicker."

"What happened to, 'the most important thing is to keep in the right direction'?" said Oz, sounding more like his old self.

"Oh, forget that!" I said. "We've got to stay alive. We can worry about directions later."

"That's the most sensible thing you've said for a long time," said Bronwen. "Well, come on then."

And she started to walk into a thickly overgrown part of the forest. We couldn't run – the trees were too close together – but we felt far more hidden. Bronwen stopped to retie her skirts, which were coming undone.

"Suppose he catches up with us," said Oz as we walked. "We've got our daggers. I mean there's only one of him and three of us."

"Two and a bit, I'm afraid, if it comes to a proper fight," said Bronwen. "I haven't got a weapon and I'm not exactly trained. I'd have a go, though, if one of you has got a spare."

I grinned at her, the first time I'd smiled in ages.

"Thanks, Bron," I said. "Let's hope it doesn't come to that."

Then I looked back over my shoulder and froze. Not more than a hundred yards behind us strode the figure in black, a bow slung over his shoulder and in his hand a vicious-looking sword.

"Oh Diew!" whispered Bronwen and crossed herself.

Me and Oz grabbed our daggers, but Bronwen said, "No, run!"

But we couldn't run. We could only scramble through the undergrowth and over low-lying branches, while this man seemed effortlessly to gain on us. Suddenly we came into a clearing and, racing across it, I tripped. My dagger flew out of my hand and Oz stopped to drag me up on to my feet.

"It's no good," moaned Bronwen, and then she did the most surprising thing. She calmly untied the knot holding up her dress and let her skirts fall once again around her ankles. Then she stood up and looked straight at him. Her expression seemed to say that if she was going to die, she wanted to do it with dignity.

After that, everything happened in slow motion. Somehow my dagger was back in my hand. I pushed Bronwen back and Oz and me stood tensed and ready to attack, but it didn't seem real.

The man reached the clearing, stopped and smiled. The sword glittered as he flourished it in the air and laid it at our feet. Then he swept a low bow.

"I am Abdul Mutazz ibn Haroun…at your service," he said.

At first neither Oz nor me moved. Then Oz reached out with his foot and hooked the sword behind him. The man laughed and Oz leaned forward, raising his dagger slightly higher. Almost before you could breathe, the man produced a knife out of nowhere, knocked Oz's dagger from his hand, caught it by the handle and stuck both knives in the ground, point downward. Then he turned to me.

"Your turn, I believe," he said.

"You're taking the piss," Oz spat at him.

"Shut up, Oz!" I said. There was a pause while we all eyed each other, then I went on, "Are you trying to tell us you're on our side?"

"Ah, one of you has some brains," said the man.

This was too much for Bronwen.

"I don't believe you!" she said, and we turned round astonished as if we'd forgotten she was there.

The mocking expression left the man's face and he inclined his head towards Bronwen.

"I can understand that, my lady. My methods may have given the wrong impression. I apologize."

"I'm not your lady, or any kind of lady at all," said Bronwen. "I'm a servant girl, but I have my honour and I don't like the way you're playing with us. Besides, I've seen you before, in the great hall, and I knew then you were bringing evil."

The man narrowed his eyes and looked at her keenly.

"Yeah," said Oz, "what's the game, if you're on our side? How hard would it be to call out and tell us not to run?" He turned to me. "And don't tell me to shut up!"

"Sorry," I said, "but I was trying to…make up my mind about him."

"And have you made it up?" said the man. "You still hold your dagger as if ready for a fight."

"But my friend's right," I said. "Why chase after us with a sword in your hand if you're on our side? But then, why lay it down if you're not?"

"Ah," said the man, "people can be difficult to read, can they not, and you must get used to that. If I were a foe, pretending to be your friend, I would have done the opposite – called after you telling you not to worry and then produced my sword. Perhaps I wanted to test you."

He bent down, pulled the two daggers out of the ground and handed Oz's back to him, hilt first. Then he tucked his own into the side of his boot.

I nodded slowly. "All right. I sort of believe you."

The man started to reach behind Oz for his sword, but stopped.

"May I?" he asked.

Then he stooped down, picked it up, wiped it on his robe and sheathed it. I noticed that it had an unusual curve on one side at the tip.

"This is mad," said Oz.

"You may call me Abdul," said the man, "but I am afraid I do not know all of your names, except that one of you is called Wulfstan."

I nodded. "That's me."

Abdul smiled. "I thought it might be. And you are?" he said, looking at Oz and Bronwen.

"Oh yeah, let's all be best mates," said Oz. "I'm Osric, and I still think this is mad."

Bronwen said nothing.

"Well, Wulfstan, Osric and lady with no name, you must be hungry and perhaps also in need of a rest. And I must return to Noor, the light of my life. I have deserted her for too long."

"Who's that?" said Oz. "You were on your own when we saw you."

"I left her grazing by the roadside," said Abdul.

"Oh, your horse!" said Oz.

"Come, we must go and find her," said Abdul.

Bronwen stood like a statue.

"I'm not going anywhere!" she said. "I knew you were evil when I saw you at the feast. Why should I trust you now?"

"Lady," said Abdul, inclining his head. "I believe you may be one of those who sees things which most of us do not."

"Perhaps," said Bronwen.

"Then let me ask you," Abdul went on. "When you saw me, did you know that *I* was evil, or merely that something evil was coming and that I would be involved in some way?"

"Oh," said Bronwen and she blinked rapidly. I thought she was struggling not to cry. "That's exactly the sort of question Nain would have asked me! I should never have left her!"

Abdul smiled at her. "And how would you have answered her?"

"I'd have to say I wasn't sure," said Bronwen. "But I'd have to say, as well, that you don't feel evil now."

Abdul bowed. "I thank you," he said. "There is evil in the air, and we must all fight it together. Now shall we go?"

He turned and led the way back.

A few hours later, as dusk turned to dark, we were sitting round a fire burning our fingers, tearing at grouse and partridge roasted on a spit. As well as being expert with a sword and dagger, it turned out that Abdul was an ace marksman. Noor the black mare was standing peacefully by, finishing her supper of grass. We'd all agreed on a site to set up camp, some way off the road and shielded from it by a clump of trees, but not actually in the forest. Abdul had bread in his bags, a bit stale, but it tasted wonderful to us. We stuffed it hungrily into our mouths while the meat was cooking, and took a few swigs from his two leather water bottles.

Sprawled by the crackling flames as the first stars came out, I felt myself relaxing – the first time for ages. What a difference from last night! No would-be murderers around the fire, just friends. Food instead of empty stomachs, and someone else to help take difficult decisions. Yes, and to fight for us if need be. I gazed sleepily at this strange-looking man, ripping meat off a bone with his teeth, and somehow I just trusted him.

Oz took another swig from a bottle.

"Are you sure you haven't got any ale?" he said.

Abdul laughed. "Ah, no, I never drink that disgusting stuff."

When I'd finally had enough, I licked my fingers and picked up Abdul's bow.

"This is beautiful," I said, running my thumb along the curves. "Is that *bone* inside the wood?"

"It is," said Abdul. "It takes a year to make a bow like that."

"It's a pity we haven't got our bows with us," said Oz. "We'd have been a bit more help with the hunting."

"Yes," agreed Abdul. "We must get you some weapons. But now tell me where you were going when you were attacked."

"Don't you think," said Bronwen, still chewing, "that you should tell us a bit more about yourself? Like how you knew Wulfstan's name. And what you're doing here at all. I come from Wales, but I bet you come from a lot further away than that."

"I do, my lady," said Abdul with a mock bow. "But how could you tell?"

"You're always laughing at us," said Bronwen, "and I'm being serious. And don't call me 'my lady'. It sounds as though you're mocking me. I've told you, my name is Bronwen."

Abdul sat up and crossed his legs. "I apologize, Bronwen. I am a visitor to this country, a guest of a friend whom I met on my travels. I was making the Hajj, our great pilgrimage to Mecca and Medina, and I decided also to visit Jerusalem. I come from Cordoba in Andalusia and it seemed a good idea to see as much as I could of the east before returning home. In Jerusalem I met an Englishman, making his own pilgrimage, and we became good friends. We travelled together. He taught me English and I taught him Arabic and he invited me to his home in England. Is that enough for now?"

"Wow!" said Oz, and I looked at Abdul in awe.

"That's enough for now," I said, " but you've got to tell us a story every time we stop, as payment for chasing after us with your sword."

Abdul roared with laughter.

"You drive a hard bargain," he said, "but now you must tell me where you were going, and why."

"What about how you knew Wulfstan's name?" said Bronwen.

"All in good time," said Abdul. "Now it is your turn to answer my question."

"Well, I was going home," said Bronwen, "or at least, back to Lord Aelfric's manor, but these two were on some sort of a mission."

"We had to take a letter to someone called Sigelac, that's all," I said, "two or three days' ride on from Aelfric's estate."

"And may I see this letter?" said Abdul.

I shrugged. "There's nothing to see," I said, unfastening my bag and taking out the scroll. "It's just a scroll with a seal on it, which mustn't be broken till we hand it over to Sigelac. Guthrum said we'd got to guard it with our lives and he'd kill us if it got tampered with. Anyway, it's in Latin."

Abdul held out his hand, but I hesitated.

"Don't you trust me?" said Abdul.

"Well, yes, but…"

Abdul reached over and took it. He peered closely at the seal, then before I had time to react he slid his dagger under the wax and opened the scroll.

I cried out and sprang up.

"What did you do that for?" yelled Oz. "We're done for now!"

"I trusted you!" I shouted. "We'll be outlaws now! We can never go back to Guthrum, or to our homes. He'll kill us!"

Visions of our future lives flashed through my brain. Fleeing in terror from Guthrum or his men, taking refuge in distant parts of the country, far from Aelfric's lands, homeless, with no lord and protector, finally hunted down and killed. Without your lord you were nothing.

Abdul was calmly scanning the letter, tilting it towards the light from the fire.

"Can you read Latin, as well?" said Bronwen, big-eyed with shock, but still curious.

"Enough to understand this," said Abdul grimly. He looked at me and Oz, both with our daggers out, ready to attack him.

"Sit down, sit down," he said, "I have something to tell you."

"You can tell us while we're standing up," I said, feeling utterly betrayed and stupid for trusting a man we barely knew.

"This letter that you're guarding with your lives," said Abdul. "It is your death warrant."

CHAPTER SEVEN

WULF

At first there was complete silence. Then me and Oz started talking at once.

"I don't believe you!" Oz exploded.

"You're making that up!" I yelled. "You know you shouldn't have opened it in the first place and you're making it up as a cover story!"

But then came Bronwen's voice, calmly cutting through our shouting.

"Be quiet, you two," she said softly. "Listen to me. I was watching his face as he read that letter. I never took my eyes off him. I saw his expression change. He's telling the truth."

Oz's jaw dropped as he turned to face Bronwen.

"Oh right," he said. "Let me get this straight. First of all he's this evil monster who we had to run away from because you'd had some vision or something. Then it turns out you might have been wrong about that after all. But now we're supposed to believe you because you were looking at his face when he was reading the letter. Well, *I* was looking at him too, and I never saw anything to make me believe him."

"You weren't looking at him properly," said Bronwen, in the same calm voice. "You and Wulf were too busy leaping up, waving your daggers around to really pay attention."

Abdul stared at her in surprise and a half-smile played around his lips.

"What an interesting person you are," he said, ignoring us.

"And I'm sorry I got it wrong before," Bronwen went on, looking down at her lap. She twisted a piece of her skirt round her fingers and took a deep breath. "It's not easy having these…feelings…and I'm not very good at it yet. But this isn't the same as that. It's just *noticing* things. And that's something *you're* not very good at, Osric!" she finished tartly.

"And we've got no way of knowing," I said bitterly. "None of us can read enough Latin to understand the letter…It is *in* Latin, isn't it?"

Abdul nodded and handed it to me. I crouched in the firelight, scanned it and shrugged.

"About the only word I recognize is *corpus*. I know that means 'body'."

Abdul nodded again.

"*Your* body," he said. "It refers to a treasure which you have on your body." He got up and moved across to me. Bending over my shoulder, he followed the closely written script with his finger and translated. "'And when the treasure has been handed over, his body will be of no more use and can be disposed of, and that of his companion.' They obviously were not expecting more than two of you."

"But I haven't got any treasure!" I said.

Bronwen gasped. "The thing round your neck!" she said excitedly. "What did you call it? That thing your mother gave you!"

"My rune-stone?" I said, bewildered.

"That's it! That's the treasure! It's magic!" said Bronwen. "That outlaw, you said he touched it, and then he went mad!"

I slumped to the ground. This was all too much to take in.

"But Guthrum gave me this letter. I mean, I know he got paid for giving it to me, but *Guthrum!* He's taught me everything I know about fighting. He's Aelfric's brother, so he's practically my lord. He's…"

I hid my face in my hands and fell silent. Oz was still standing, looking at me in amazement.

"Am I the only sane one around here?" he said. "Are you telling me you're gonna believe *him*," pointing at Abdul, "rather than the bloke who's been training us up for the last couple of years? The bloke from home, who we've known all our lives?"

"I don't know," I said despairingly. "That's what I'm saying. I don't know what to believe. I might trust *Guthrum*, but what do we know about the bloke who paid him to give us the letter? I don't think Guthrum thought he was doing anything wrong, but perhaps he's not a very good judge of character."

45

"I did not know that he was paid to give you this," said Abdul. He looked at the letter again. "The writer calls this Sigelac 'my lord', and says, 'I have used your English name to allay suspicion.' So the person it is addressed to has another name, which is not English. The writer signs himself 'your faithful servant Madoc'."

"That's a Welsh name," said Bronwen. "Perhaps this other person has a Welsh name as well as an English one."

"Perhaps," sighed Abdul. "It is a riddle. And then, where does your Guthrum fit in? Can he read Latin?"

"That's a point," I said, suddenly slightly more cheerful. "I don't think he can read at all. Perhaps he didn't know what was in the letter. Perhaps Aelfric had told him to do a deal with that man and he was just obeying orders. Which is what soldiers are supposed to do, you know," I said pointedly to Abdul. "Not go round opening letters they're meant to be guarding with their lives."

"Well, if you had obeyed that order," said Abdul, "you would have ended up dead."

Oz suddenly dropped to his knees with an expression of shock on his face.

"No, he did know," he said quietly. "Sweet Jesus, he knew…Guthrum knew something."

"What? How?" I said, shaking my head in confusion.
"Don't you remember, when you took your old shirt off, when we were getting changed, how interested he was in your rune-stone? Kept going on about how it must be valuable? Bron's right. It's the rune-stone."

My mind flashed back to the hut with the chest of clothes. Guthrum staring at the stone. Guthrum's face, with the slightly greedy expression, almost like a different person from the bluff soldier we were used to. Oz was right and Bron was right. It fitted. It all made sense…But actually, it made no sense at all. I stared blankly at the flickering flames of the campfire. I didn't want to think. It was too painful.

No-one said anything for a while, then Bronwen looked at Abdul.

"I think we all believe you," she said, "so what do we do now?"

"Well, we can't go home, that's for sure," said Oz gloomily. "So what the hell *are* we gonna do?"

I tried to shake myself out of my dazed state.

"We don't have a clue what's going on," I said. "So how can we decide what to do?" I looked accusingly at Abdul. "*You're* the only one who seems to have any idea what's going on, so come on, let's have a bit of help here."

"You are angry with everything," said Abdul, "and so you take it out on me. I actually know little more than you."

"Well, how about sharing what you do know!" said Oz. "And don't talk in riddles!"

Abdul put his head on one side, spread his arms wide and smiled.

"I will be as straight-talking as a Saxon," he said, settling himself into a comfortable cross-legged position.

I felt myself settling down too, as if I were going to be told a story, and so did the others

"As I told you," Abdul began, "after our journeying, I was staying with my good friend and travelling companion…"

"Whose name is?" interrupted Oz.

Abdul raised his eyebrows. "Who is telling this, you or I?"

"Look," said Oz. "I just want everything laid out fair and square. When you mentioned him before, you just kept calling him, 'my friend'. I thought it was a bit fishy, not letting on what he was called."

I was on the point of telling him to shut up, but I thought better of it.

Abdul sighed. "It is not always wise," he said, "to bandy people's names about unnecessarily. Nevertheless, if you had waited more than a heartbeat I would have told you. Also, I am known as a patient man, but my patience is not endless."

Despite everything, I couldn't help being amused.

"I will begin again," said Abdul. "I was staying with my good friend and travelling companion, Godwin, at his manor north of here."

"Godwin!" I exclaimed. "Is he any relation of…oh, sorry, I didn't mean to interrupt."

"No, go on," said Abdul. "I welcome *sensible* questions."

Oz's mouth dropped open, but he didn't say anything.

"I wondered if he was related to the king. I mean, his father was called Godwin and names often run in families."

"He is," replied Abdul, "though not closely. As you know, your king is an aristocrat, but not actually of royal blood. My friend Godwin comes from a different branch of the same family. Perhaps it was this relationship which made, shall we say unsavoury people, approach Godwin with a proposition."

He paused, and we all leaned forward slightly.

"They came by night, two men with an urgent request to see Godwin. I had just retired to bed, but I was not asleep. I heard raised voices and was ready to intervene to protect my friend. It was not necessary, however, and although Godwin bade them stay the night, they left in bad humour. I heard one of them call out that he would regret his decision. The next morning he told me. It was a very strange story, which at first I found difficult to believe."

By now we were totally absorbed, all our eyes on Abdul's expressive face, lit by the glowing fire, all our ears straining to catch what he was saying.

"It seems that a group of your English noblemen were trying to acquire some ancient stones – rune-stones, they called them – in order, they claimed, to help the king against his enemies. Godwin believes that the king himself has no knowledge of this, but I am not sure. They said – and I laughed when I heard this – that they were the actual stones given to the god Woden when he hung on the world tree for nine days and nine nights. They had some of these stones and they wanted Godwin to help them recover the rest. He is a pious man, rightly named God's friend. He would have nothing to do with it and they left. But they had told him the name of one who might have such a stone. It was Ertha, a wise-woman who lives in the manor of Aelfric."

I froze. My mum! She'd laughed as well, when she told me about the rune-stone.

Bronwen had sat in silence through all this and now she couldn't contain herself any longer. "But there's no such god as Woden!" she said. "That's all just stories!"

"Interesting that you say that," said Abdul, "when you yourself have a little experience of things that others might not believe in."

"You mean my feelings, my waking dreams," said Bronwen. "That's completely different. I'm a Christian, and Nain says it's a God-given gift."

"Ah," nodded Abdul, "I believe you are right, but there are some in your church who would not agree. Did your grandmother not warn you of that?"

"She did," said Bronwen quietly.

"And do *you* believe Woden exists?" said Oz. "If that's a sensible enough question."

Abdul roared with laughter. "It is, Osric, it is!"

"Well?" Oz went on. "What's the answer, then?"

"The answer is – maybe."

"You believe in our old gods then," I said excitedly.

"I do not think that they are gods," said Abdul. "There is only one God, who created everything, but I believe they may be djinn."

"What?" we all said together.

"Allah – our name for God – created many beings. Not just humans and animals, but also spirits, such as angels and djinn. The angels are good and exist to do His will. But djinn are like humans. Some are good, some are bad, some are mixed. Some of the djinn wanted to be like Allah and have people worship them. They called themselves gods. I believe this Woden, if he exists, may be a djinni. And the stone you wear, Wulfstan, may be a thing of great power."

I stared at Abdul and a shiver ran through me. We all sat in silence – stunned, I think. At last Bronwen spoke.

"Excuse me, Abdul, but somehow this doesn't seem to make it any easier to decide what to do."

"Well said, Bron!" Oz chimed in. "I dunno about you lot, but I'm finding it hard to keep my eyes open." As if to emphasize his point, Oz gave an enormous yawn. "I vote we sleep on it and decide in the morning."

"But you haven't finished your story!" I said. "How did you find us, for instance? And what about my mum? Is she all right? If they knew her name, something might have happened to her!"

"Your mother is safe," said Abdul, "or was, when I saw her a few days ago."

"You've seen her?" I gasped.

Abdul nodded. "These men had visited her and tried to frighten her, but I believe she is not easily frightened."

I grinned. "You can say that again."

"They left her once they realized that she no longer had the stone. Also, I believe they had a certain respect for her. Her own beliefs fitted in with theirs. Nevertheless, she did not tell them your name or where you were. They found that out from asking around the village. She only told me when I persuaded her that I wanted to protect you."

"How did you do that?" I said incredulously. "I mean, I'm not being rude, but if somebody looking like you turned up at our cottage, my mum wouldn't turn round and tell you her life story."

Abdul smiled. "I had a letter from Godwin, which the priest read to her. As you say, there was little point *my* reading it to her. By good fortune, the priest knew of Godwin and told her that he was an honourable man. Reluctantly she told me your name and that you had gone to fight with the king. And so I found you easily at the feast."

"So why didn't you say something then?" I said. "And where was Godwin? Was he at the battle?"

"And why did he decide to get involved?" put in Bronwen, stifling a yawn. She was dead tired but really curious. "You said he wanted nothing to do with it."

"One question at a time," said Abdul, looking grave. "Firstly you were in no fit state for me to talk to when I saw you at the feast, Wulfstan, and I did not expect you to leave so soon the next day."

"Nor did we," agreed Oz.

"Secondly, my friend was not at the battle because he is gravely sick. An affliction came on him the very night that these men visited. He believes they have cursed him and that is why he asked me to try to stop them getting this stone. They say they want only to help the king, but he believes they are evil and should not have access to the sort of power the stone might give them. And there you have it."

I nodded slowly. Despite everything we'd been through I felt wide awake. Suddenly I seemed to be living in a different world, where I didn't know the rules and where anything might happen. Fighting the Normans had been the most important and exciting thing in my life so far, but it was what I'd trained for. It fitted with what I expected from the world. But this...

"Sleep now," said Abdul. "Decisions are for the morning. I will build up the fire and take the first watch."

He added two branches to the smouldering embers and, using another branch, packed them into a neater pile.

"No, I'll take the first watch," I said. "I couldn't sleep yet."

"As you wish," replied Abdul, and curled into a ball with his back to the fire. "Wake me if there is anything suspicious, and wake me anyway in a few hours. You must get some sleep yourself."

Oz and Bronwen said nothing. They were already asleep.

"Oh, Abdul," I said. "What shall I do with the letter?"

"Burn it," replied Abdul, without turning round. "It has told us everything it can and you will be safer without it."

I threw the scroll on to the flames and watched it flare up, then sink to ashes. The wax seal sizzled as it melted. Then I turned around and sat staring out into the blackness. There was no moon and the darkness was so deep that I couldn't even see the edge of the forest, about thirty yards away. Nothing seemed to exist outside our little circle of firelight. But there *were* things out there, even though I couldn't see them. An owl hooted. A breeze sprang up and leaves rustled. Somewhere a creature screamed its last high, thin scream.

I strained my eyes, trying to make out any shape in the dense black. Then I realized that I wasn't looking for just anything. I was looking for a cloaked figure, a one-eyed man with a broad-brimmed hat. Woden, disguised in his travelling clothes. Not long ago I'd have laughed at myself for doing that, but now I knew that Woden might really exist. The rune-stone under my shirt might really have belonged to the king of the gods. I'd always felt it as a comforting presence, a protective charm, even when it did strange things. Now it seemed alien, tingling with an unknown power. As I stared into the darkness, it was no comfort at all.

CHAPTER EIGHT

BRONWEN

I woke up in the dark with a crick in my neck. *What's happened to the bed?* I thought irritably. *I'll have to put some more straw in the mattress.* A faint glow through my eyelids told me that the brazier in Lady Rhiannon's room was still burning. But when I opened my eyes it wasn't a brazier. It was a dying campfire. And I wasn't in my tiny room leading off Lady Rhiannon's bower. No wonder my neck hurt. For the second night in a row I was sleeping on hard ground with no cover but my cloak wrapped round me.

Now my eyes were open I remembered everything. There I'd been, the day before yesterday, grumbling to myself about leaving the celebrations. Not wanting to go back to my humdrum life in Lord Aelfric's manor, longing for something different. I smiled ruefully to myself as I tried to ease the crick in my neck. "Be careful what you wish for," Nain used to say. "You might get it!"

Surely I could get back to Rhiannon somehow. I'd lost Nain, though of course I hoped to see her again. I didn't want to lose Rhiannon too – my last link with home, the only one I could speak my own language with. Surely Abdul could take *me* back to the manor, even if Wulf and Oz couldn't go home.

But these men, the ones who were looking for them, they'd know I'd been with the boys. They'd try to make me talk. What would they do to me if they found me?

I stared at the faint orange glow of the fire. A figure was slumped on the other side of it, sitting, but obviously asleep. It didn't look quite big enough for Abdul and I could see Oz a foot or two away, mouth open, fast asleep. It must be Wulf. Then out of the darkness, a shape crept up on him. I tensed. But it was only Abdul, putting his hand on Wulf's shoulder and murmuring something that I couldn't hear. Wulf curled up into a ball and Abdul arranged his cloak over him, then sat, looking this way and that, obviously keeping guard.

Where had he been? I thought I knew the answer, because I realised now that it wasn't only my stiff neck that had woken me. My bladder was full to bursting. This was a definite problem when you were travelling with boys. They'd been good about it yesterday, walking slowly ahead while I ducked behind a tree, taking a long time with my tied-up skirts. I looked out into the dark and wondered if it was safe. At least I wouldn't have to go far before I became invisible to anyone round the campfire. There was no help for it – I couldn't wait till morning.

As soon as I moved, Abdul spun round. I mouthed, "Won't be long", and he seemed to understand. I had to wait with my back to the fire until my night eyes were good enough for the dark, then a few careful steps brought me to a small bush. With my nerves on edge, looking around me all the time, I squatted behind it.

I turned to hurry back to the camp...and then stopped. The picture before me was like a tableau in church. Abdul sitting, the boys curled up asleep and the fire bathing them all in a beautiful golden light. How bright it was, much brighter than any light the dying fire should have shed. I didn't want to move. I just wanted to stand and look. Despite the danger, despite the discomfort, I was suddenly filled with the sense that this was where I was meant to be, that it was right somehow for me to be part of this.

Then Abdul turned his head and looked in my direction. How long I'd been standing there I had no idea, but I walked back with a feeling of deep peace inside me. I smiled at Abdul and he nodded and smiled at me. Then I settled myself on the uncomfortable ground, pulled my cloak around me and went back to sleep.

WULF

The next morning Abdul made us scatter the dead remains of the fire, and make it look as much as possible as if no-one had camped there.

Then we went inside the forest to breakfast on cold leftovers of grouse and partridge. The bread was too hard to eat.

Oz asked the inevitable question, "So what are we going to do?"

"First we must buy at least one more horse," said Abdul. "I know of a settlement where we may, if we are lucky, buy three, but it is about a day's walk from here."

"And then what?" I said.

"You obviously cannot return to Aelfric's manor. Not even you, I am afraid, Bronwen. You were all three together when you were captured, and they may be searching for you as well."

"I know," said Bronwen. "I'd already thought of that. Though I'd love to get word to Lady Rhiannon. She'll be so worried."

"Then I wish to visit my friend Godwin," continued Abdul, "to see if he has recovered. We must be cautious, but when we reach there we can provide you boys with weapons and other things we shall need."

"I can use a bow," said Bronwen.

Abdul raised his eyebrows. "Really?" he said. "That may be useful."

"But what are we going to do after that?" I said. "We can't just keep creeping round the countryside trying to escape whoever's looking for us."

Abdul leaned towards me. "This is where you will be helpful, Wulfstan. I want you to think of everything you know about these rune-stones. The next time we stop you can tell us about them. I hope it will help us work out what our enemies are trying to do, and therefore how we can stop them."

I laughed. "You want me to tell you about the runes? Well that'll take a long time, 'cos I don't know anything."

"You do," said Abdul seriously. "You know more than you realize. You have grown up with a woman who uses these things. They are completely foreign to me. You must know more than I."

I was amazed and a bit pleased to think that I might know more about something than Abdul. Abdul, who seemed to know everything about everything. I couldn't help feeling, though, that they'd all be disappointed when they found out quite how little I did know.

"You know what?" said Oz, as we started off. "Where we were supposed to be heading wasn't far from the Welsh border, according to Guthrum. What with the bloke who wrote the letter having a Welsh name, I vote we stay well clear of Wales." He grinned. "No offence, Bron."

She glared at him and went to walk beside Abdul.

We made our way north, keeping to parts of the forest where the trees didn't grow so close together. But it was slow going, all the same. We dare not use the road, and sometimes we ended up going in the wrong direction till we found a bit where the undergrowth was thin enough for Noor to manage.

"This is taking us twice as long as it should," grumbled Oz. "We keep going the wrong way."

"And what do you suggest, Osric?" asked Abdul. "That I risk my priceless steed becoming lame?"

Oz said nothing.

"She is not only beyond price," Abdul went on. "She is my best friend also, are you not, my beloved?"

He stroked the mare's nose and she seemed to nod her head in reply.

"But are we sure we're going the right way?" I said. "I'm getting confused with all this doubling back."

As soon as the words were out of my mouth I knew what Bron would say.

Sure enough, she smiled in a superior way and said, "Oh, it's easy, Wulfstan, if you follow the sun's path across the sky."

Oz smirked. "You asked for that one," he muttered.

Then came a time when the trees grew so thickly together that it was impossible for Noor to get through safely.

"I think we are not far from the road," said Abdul. "We may have to risk using it for a little while. Not for long. I am sure we are not far from the settlement I spoke of. The trees must thin out before that."

"Well, it's this way then, isn't it?" said Bronwen, pointing left. "But oh, we must be careful!"

We walked as quietly as we could in the direction that Abdul and Bronwen both felt would lead to the road. Sure enough, the ground sloped downwards and there it was – a track broad enough for two horses, and at this point not much lower than the woods.

"I think I can lead Noor down there safely," said Abdul. "But first, look and listen."

We stood for some time, all ears and eyes alert for horses' hooves or human voices. A crow cawed, a few leaves rustled to the ground and our own breathing began to sound loud to me.

"Come on, if we're gonna do it," whispered Oz. "Me and Wulf'll creep out first. If we still can't see anything, you follow."

Abdul nodded and we dropped to our hands and knees. I didn't like it out in the open, but we still couldn't hear or see anything. We looked back at Abdul and nodded. I started to beckon to them, but my arm froze in mid-motion.

Horses' hooves, faint but coming this way! We scrambled back the few yards, which seemed like a mile, to join the others, and all of us backed further into the woods.

"Wait!" whispered Abdul. "Let us see who it is!"

I felt something digging into my arm and realized it was Bron clutching me, with a panic-stricken look on her face.

"Sorry!" she whispered, turning a bit pink and letting go.

The clop of the hooves grew louder and then slowed to a halt.

"It's no good, Ed," complained a familiar voice. "They could be anywhere."

I felt sick.

"You give up too easy, you do," said another familiar voice. "What's the boss gonna say?"

Then that third chilling, sneering voice said the words that I was dreading.

"Well, *I* ain't givin' up, after what they done to me!"

CHAPTER NINE

WULF

"What you gonna do then, Bert?" said Ed. "The boss won't be pleased, but Wilf's right. They could be anywhere and there's only three of us. We need to report back. He said if he wasn't there by morning we should go straight back with 'em. He's got loads more men. They can comb these woods and then there's no way they'll get away."

"I told you we should have killed 'em in the first place!" hissed Bert. "Well, I'm gonna be there when he gets 'em and I'm gonna make 'em suffer...I'm gonna pull out their fingernails and cut little bits out of 'em... when the boss's got whatever he wants. An' I reckon it's that stone he wants."

"You keep sayin' that," said Wilf.

"I told you," growled Bert. "I only touched it and it made me see things...things like...I thought I was in hell. Anyone who had that stone..." He tailed off.

"Well, we ain't even got the letter now, nor the kids," said Ed. "The boss is not gonna be pleased, oh no."

"No, he ain't," said Wilf thoughtfully. "P'raps we should have one more look after all."

"Let's go up this bank," said Ed, "and have another look in the woods."

Listening to this conversation I'd felt paralysed, but now I turned to run. Then I saw what Abdul was doing. He'd slipped three arrows from his quiver, fitted one to his bow and was carefully taking aim, holding the other two in the hand that pulled back the string.

"These *are* the men who kidnapped you?" he whispered.

We all nodded, and while the outlaws were getting off their horses Abdul let fly one arrow after another, so fast that I could scarcely see his hands moving. There were three strangled cries and three bodies slumped to the ground. The horses neighed in fright and galloped off down the road.

"A pity," murmured Abdul. "We could have used their steeds."

Me and Oz looked at each other open-mouthed.

"Wow!" said Oz. "I've never seen anyone do that before."

"When we get bows, Abdul," I said, "you'll have to show us how to do that. I mean, we're not bad, but…" I shook my head in admiration.

"Oh, but the men," said Bronwen, putting her hands to her mouth. "Was that fair? I mean, they didn't know you were there."

"You're nuts, Bron!" shouted Oz, while I groaned.

"What would *they* have done to you if they had caught you?" smiled Abdul. "Should I have waited till they saw me and attacked them with my sword, one armed man against three?" Abdul shook his head. "Come, we must drag the bodies into the trees on the other side of the road. There is no time to bury them properly; the ground is too hard. Then I think we should set up camp, and Bronwen and I will go on alone to this settlement tomorrow, while you boys stay under cover."

"You know what?" said Oz. "We were stupid. We left them with their weapons."

I nodded. We'd have to get better at this sort of thing if we wanted to stay alive. I cringed to think that we'd almost left without our own weapons. Oz knelt by one of the lifeless bodies and drew a heavy sword from its scabbard.

"I don't think we want those now, though," I said.

Abdul nodded. "Godwin will find you something more suited to your size."

Oz shrugged and put it back.

We hauled the bodies into the trees and covered them with broken off branches and leaves. Then we retraced our steps and found a clearing out of sight of the road and big enough for our overnight camp.

"You light the fire," said Abdul, "while I find us something to eat."

I had my flint in the bag that had carried the letter and after a little while scraping it with my knife I'd got a fire smouldering. Before long Abdul was back with more grouse.

"These woods are thick with them," he said.

We were all used to plucking birds and soon there were several small bodies roasting on spits. I was starving. The brief moments of terror and then the sheer relief of Abdul's killing the outlaws seemed to have left my insides hollow. I turned the browning grouse on their spits, willing them to cook more quickly.

"Excuse me," said Oz, gathering a handful of leaves. "I'll enjoy my supper all the more if I go and fertilize the ground first."

I grinned as he disappeared into the bushes. Oz could be annoying, but he did brighten life up a bit.

The light was dimming by the time we'd finished gnawing the last scrap of flesh from the birds' legs and wings. Abdul insisted we had to save some for breakfast and I settled down to gaze into the fire. Yellow flames were flickering and dying, but its orange heart glowed steadily. My mind emptied and my body relaxed.

"Let's have a riddle," said Oz, making me jump. "What's the cleanest leaf in the forest?"

I groaned. "Oh, not that old one!"

"Well, I don't know it," said Bronwen. "What *is* the cleanest leaf in the forest?"

"The holly," crowed Oz. "Because nobody wipes their bum on it!"

Abdul roared with laughter, and Bronwen picked up a bone and threw it at Oz.

"That's disgusting!" she said, but she was laughing too, and so was I, though I'd heard that joke about a thousand times.

"So, Wulfstan," said Abdul, when they'd calmed down. "What have you remembered about the runes?"

I sighed. "Absolutely nothing," I said flatly. "I told you, I leave all that stuff to my mum."

"You know, I've been thinking," said Oz, sitting up.

"That's a first," I said.

Oz ignored me. "That stone can't be one of the originals that was given to Woden."

"Why not?" we all said together.

"Well, it wasn't like that," said Oz, looking round at us all, obviously enjoying having an audience.

We were all sitting up now instead of lolling around the fire.

"And what *was* it like?" I asked. What did Oz know about this?

"Well, Woden was hanging there for nine nights and nine days, sacrificing himself to himself and all that."

Oz put his head on one side, stuck his tongue out and crossed his eyes, in imitation of a hanged man.

I sniggered, in spite of myself, but Bronwen said, "Oh, don't, Osric! That's horrible!"

"That is enough, Osric," smiled Abdul. "Go on with your story."

"And didn't he pluck out his eye and give it to someone?" I said suddenly, "In exchange for the runes? Or was that some other time?"

"So you *do* know something!" said Abdul eagerly.

"Yeah!" said Oz. "It was Mimir at the well of knowledge! And either in exchange for his eye, or because he'd hanged himself – I can't remember which – Woden got the runes. But the point is, I don't think he got a load of little rune-stones. It was more like knowledge in his head."

I pulled my rune-stone out and examined it in the firelight.

"That makes sense," I said. "But this *does* look very old."

"Perhaps Woden made the stones after that, so he wouldn't forget," suggested Oz.

"Don't be daft," I said. "If he was a god, he wouldn't forget." I traced with my finger the faint outline of the rune etched into the stone. My mum had told us this story, sitting by the fire in our little hut.

"No, I remember now," I said softly. "I don't know anything about how the runes work, but I used to love those old stories about the gods. It wasn't Mimir and the well of knowledge, and Woden giving his eye for a drink from the well. That was another time." I sat up straight and half-closed my eyes. The firelight became the cooking fire at home, with my mum stirring the pot.

Then as if someone else was using my voice, I chanted, "He hung from the World Tree for nine nights and nine days, pierced by a spear. No-one gave him anything to eat or drink. He stared down into the abyss, into chaos, and then he saw them, the runes. He reached down, howling, and snatched them up and then he fell back. He'd done it. His ordeal was over. He'd got the runes."

Everyone sat in silence, the only sound the crackle of the fire.

"Weird stuff," breathed Oz at last.

"I'm not sure that I like that story," said Bronwen quietly. "Though it sounds a bit like Jesus, too. Not the bit about the runes, of course."

"It is indeed a very strange story," said Abdul. "Much to think about. But anyway, it is time to sleep. Tomorrow we find some more horses."

I had an uneasy thought as we settled down for the night. Suppose the ghosts of those men came to haunt us? I clutched my rune-stone tightly and it tingled in the palms of my hands, warmer than a cold stone should be. Tonight it felt comforting, not alien, the way it had the night before. *I'm not sure where you come from, but you'll protect us, won't you?* I whispered, staring out into the darkness and gripping the stone in both hands. I was still holding it when I went to sleep.

CHAPTER TEN

WULF

After a second breakfast of cold grouse, this time minus the partridge, we once again kicked away the remains of the fire and tried to leave the clearing as we'd found it. When Abdul was satisfied, he murmured something in Noor's ear. She whickered in reply and he stroked her nose. Then he turned to me and Oz.

"You boys must stay in the woods, with Noor. Bronwen will come with me. I shall say I have need of a horse for myself, one for Bronwen and one for baggage. If I can only buy one we will have to make do. Bronwen can ride behind me and you two must ride together." Me and Oz nodded. "You must be all eyes and ears," Abdul went on. "You are still not out of danger. I would like to leave you with better weapons than your daggers, but my bow would not be much good in these trees if you were suddenly attacked. I shall need my sword to protect Bronwen, and besides, I do not think you would have the skill to wield it."

I was a bit sorry about that, but I nodded. I might not have been any good with Abdul's sword, but I'd love to have had a go with that beautiful bow.

"Wait a minute, Abdul," said Bronwen. "Shouldn't we have a story to tell these villagers? I mean, what am I doing with you? We're obviously not father and daughter."

"Father and daughter?" smiled Abdul. "Do I look so old?"

Bronwen blushed furiously, but Oz roared with laughter.

"I know!" he shouted. "You've just got married! You were taking her home to Andalusia when you were attacked by outlaws and lost your...ow!"

Bronwen had picked up a branch and whacked Oz, who staggered, missed his footing and sat down with a thump. She turned to Abdul.

"I'm sorry if I offended you," she said.

63

Abdul bowed deeply. "No offence was taken," he said. "And I have seen thirty-two summers, so I could, I suppose, be your father. But you are right about a story to tell."

"You've both got the same colour eyes and hair, judging by Abdul's beard," I said, "but your skin's way too pale, Bron. Couldn't you rub it with berry juice or something, and then you'd look like relations."

"Oh, this is getting ridiculous!" said Bronwen.

Abdul laughed. "I am sure all this will not be necessary. I am simply a friend of a family for whom Bronwen has been working. She has to return to Wales because we have received word that her mother is sick. I am accompanying her to keep her safe and to extend my knowledge of your beautiful island."

He turned to Oz, who was brushing himself down and muttering, "If you weren't a girl…"

"But your idea was a good one, Osric, about our being attacked. That would explain our need of more horses."

Oz grunted.

"Look after my beauty," said Abdul, stroking Noor. "No need to tie her up. I never tether my beloved when she is among friends. But be sure to keep all three of you out of sight."

"One more thing," I said.

"What is it now?" sighed Abdul. "It will be nightfall before we even reach the settlement."

"If Bron can't go back to Lord Aelfric's because she might be recognized, why is it all right for her to go to this village?"

"They were looking for two boys, Wulfstan. Word may have got out that a dark-haired girl was accompanying you two, but no-one is as yet looking for me or anyone with me. I believe she will be safe. Now, we will be as swift as we can. Come, Bronwen."

BRONWEN

Abdul and I turned and left the trees and made for the road. The land here had levelled out again, so there was no steep climb down. When

64

we reached the road, I turned back and looked into the forest, but the boys had hidden themselves so well that I could see nothing. Just endless autumn trees, some with red, gold or brown leaves still clinging to their branches, some already bare.

I glanced up at Abdul, who was striding along lost in thought, taking only one step for every two of mine. Without the boys I felt suddenly shy, but luckily he didn't seem to expect me to talk.

After about half a mile the road curved and I saw the place we were making for. Abdul stopped and frowned. Men were working all along the edge of the village, digging a ditch and using the earth to build a stockade wall. No-one had yet put a gate across the road, but posts for a fence were being stuck into the top.

"I did not expect this," said Abdul. "I passed through here briefly with Godwin, some time ago. Come, let us talk to these men."

I didn't say anything, but followed him, all my senses alert. As we got nearer, more and more of the men stopped working and stared at us.

"Good morning, friends," said Abdul. "May I enquire what is going on here?"

A burly yellow-haired man sauntered over to us.

"I should have thought it was obvious," he said. "And may *I* enquire what business it is of yours?"

The other men laughed.

Abdul smiled at him. "Curiosity merely," he said. "I wonder why you are building a stockade now, when your king has just won two great battles. Do you not feel safer, with such a king on the throne?"

The man's eyes narrowed.

"We started this before them battles was won," he said. "And besides, there's always enemies. Plenty of queer-looking foreigners around." He looked Abdul up and down and paused as if waiting for a reply. He didn't get one, so he went on. "There's Norwegians to the north, Danes everywhere, Normans to the south, pesky Welsh to the west."

When he said that I couldn't contain myself.

"I never heard of the Welsh coming this far into England," I said hotly. "I thought it was usually the English attacking the Welsh!"

There was a roar of laughter, and the man bent down to my level.

"Oh, we've got one of 'em here!" he crowed. "Proper little firebrand, ain't she?"

Abdul put his arm round me and pulled me closer.

"Hush, Bronwen," he whispered, then louder, "Enough! We wish to buy some horses. Could you tell us where we might do this?"

The men all looked at each other.

"There's no horses for sale round here. Specially not for people looking like you," said one.

"Shut up, Cuth!" said another. "He can't help what he looks like any more than you can help your big nose."

There were more roars of laughter and the man who'd made the joke grinned cheerfully at Abdul and me.

"Never mind this lot," he said. "The only place you might find riding horses round here – and I reckon that's what you're wanting, not dray-horses – is in the thane's stables. The stable-master might be able to sell you one, but I ain't promising. Just follow the road."

Abdul bowed. "I thank you for your help," he said and, still with a protective arm round me, walked past the stockade into the village.

The first thing that hit me was the smell. Of course, I'd been in villages many times before, but after two days in the fresh country air the reek made me gag. Perhaps it was because my nerves were on edge, but this seemed particularly bad. Pigs, chickens, humans and even cattle were all living side by side. Children stopped running round and stared at us. One or two started to follow us until they were called back by their mothers. Women feeding animals or stirring food in pots over smoky fires all stopped to stare at us. Abdul smiled at them and bowed his head slightly in greeting. I tried to do the same, but it was hard when we got so few smiles back. Why had we come here? We could do without horses! This was madness.

Suddenly, as if out of nowhere, two soldiers appeared in front of us. They wore chain mail and iron helmets and carried spears. One of them spoke to Abdul.

"Our thane wants to see you," he said.

"Ordinarily, I would be delighted to pay my respects to your thane," smiled Abdul. "Today, unfortunately, I am in something of a hurry."

The soldier lowered his spear and pushed the point under Abdul's chin.

"No, mate," he said. "I don't think you understand. That ain't a request – it's an order."

CHAPTER ELEVEN

WULF

I hope they're not gonna be long," I said.

I was sitting under a tree, feeling edgy but at the same time bored.

"Give them a chance," said Oz, frowning as he whittled at a piece of wood with his knife. Whatever he was trying to make wasn't working.

Noor was delicately nibbling the leaves of various scrubby bushes and deciding she didn't like any of them.

Oz threw the botched carving away in disgust and leaned back against his tree. Noor jumped, whinnying softly, then went back to her nibbling.

"So, my friend," said Oz, "oh expert in all things to do with rune-lore, have you decided what nuggets of wisdom you're gonna impart to old Abdul?"

"If only!" I groaned. "I wasn't kidding when I said I didn't know anything about it."

"Come on," said Oz. "You must have learnt something in all those years of watching your mum peering at the runes and muttering charms."

"Nope," I said, "not a thing. For the simple reason that I always keep well out of the way when she's doing that stuff."

Oz shook his head. "You're nuts," he said. "I'd love to have had the chance to find out about all that." He paused and took a breath as if about to say something else, then thought better of it. Picking up another small branch he began some more half-hearted whittling. Finally he said, "If you really want to know, I've always sort of envied you, living alone with your mum. Not only have you got about ten times more space than we've got in our cottage, but you could be, like, an apprentice – learn all that weird stuff."

I looked at him, startled. Was this really Oz, talking about something personal? Jokey, tactless, thoughtless Oz, saying he wanted to be a wise-woman's apprentice? I shook my head and laughed.

"You can swap places if you like," I said. "I think my mum's a bit disappointed in me. She accepts it because she says it's your fate, being the sort of person you are, but I bet she'd love to have a son who was interested in all that."

Oz sat up and grinned.

"Tell you what," he said, "if we ever get out of this and go home, I'll ask her to teach me some of it."

I leaned against the tree and looked at him in a new light.

"If you want to know the truth," I said, hesitantly, "*I've* always sort of envied *you*."

"Why?" said Oz. "What's to envy? Apart from my incredible good looks and superior brain power, of course. Plus my expertise with the sword, the bow and arrow and any other weapon you can think of. I mean, what's to envy?"

I paused. I could have told Oz that I envied his cheerfulness and the way he was so ready to jump into things without worrying about danger. But I didn't say any of that.

"Well, you're so *normal*," I said, "you and your family. It's *normal* to have so many kids they're falling out the door. It's *not* normal to have the priest looking at you all suspicious, as if you're gonna cast a spell when his back's turned. It's *not* normal to have people muttering behind your back if something bad happens, and making the sign of the cross when your mum walks by."

"Ah," said Oz, "but they all beat a path to your door when they want something, don't they? And they know she can heal, your mum, as well as harm. That's power, that is."

I sat up straight and clapped my hands.

"Ah, now we have it!" I whooped. "It's the power he wants! And there was me thinking you were coming over all mystical!"

Noor suddenly let out an ear-splitting neigh and reared up in the air. We leapt to our feet.

"Calm down, girl, calm down!" I said. "I didn't mean to frighten you."

She backed away, her eyes white with terror. Oz walked carefully towards her from the front, his hand cupped as if he was holding a treat.

"Come on, Noor," he murmured. "It's all right. It's only Wulf being an idiot. Come on old girl."

But Noor carried on snorting and backing away from us. Suddenly she reared up again, turned tail and galloped off through the trees.

"Oh, shit!" I yelled.

"Well, come on then!" said Oz. "She hasn't got a clear run. We can catch her!"

We raced after her, vaulting over fallen trees, which Noor cleared with ease, deeper and deeper into the forest. Soon we were panting and losing sight of her. The ground started to slope downwards, making it hard to run without losing your footing.

"Abdul'll kill us," I gasped. "She could fall and break a leg!"

"Hang on, I've got stitch," said Oz, doubled over.

"We've lost her anyway," I said, collapsing on the ground. "I *knew* we should have tethered her! All that stuff Abdul said about her staying where he told her to stay: '*I never tether my beloved when she is among friends!*'"

Oz straightened up, rubbing his side. "Come on, we've got to try and find her. Noor, Noor, where are you?" he called.

I looked around uneasily. The forest seemed to be closing in on us.

"You know what?" I muttered. "She's not the only one who's lost. We are too."

"We'll find the way back," said Oz, "though it's a shame we haven't got Bron with us. She'd know exactly where the sun was when we started."

"No, there's something weird about this," I said. "Why did Noor go like that? It can't just have been because I clapped my hands and shouted."

"Don't," said Oz. "You're giving me the creeps, and the main thing is just to find her. *Noor, Noor!*" he started calling again.

"And this isn't easy ground for a horse to cover," I went on. "It's as if she was led by something."

A whinny sounded from further down the valley, not too far away.

"Good girl, Noor!" called Oz. "Good girl, stay there!"

We ran in the direction of the whinny.

"She sounds all right," said Oz. "She doesn't sound frightened or hurt or anything."

I didn't answer. I couldn't shake off this uneasy feeling. How could a horse gallop at speed through woods like these without stumbling and injuring itself? Noor had been frightened and driven away, I was sure of it, but then she'd been *led* through the forest. And we'd been led here after her. Who was playing games with us? A cloaked figure was watching us, I knew it. A one-eyed cloaked figure with a broad-brimmed hat. Woden.

"There she is!" whispered Oz.

At the bottom of the valley was a stream, and on the other side, calmly drinking, was Noor. She looked up at us and snorted quietly.

"Don't move," said a deep voice behind us. "Now, hands in the air and very slowly turn around."

CHAPTER TWELVE

BRONWEN

Abdul calmly pushed the spear to one side with the back of his hand, though his other arm was still protectively wrapped around me.

"There is no need for that," he said in a friendly voice. "Of course, it was remiss of me not to pay my respects to your thane, however great my hurry. Please lead the way."

The soldier looked as if he wasn't sure what to make of that and I smiled to myself. One thing I was learning about Abdul: he never reacted the way you expected.

"Erm...all right, then. Follow me!" said the soldier gruffly. "Ecgwin!" he barked at the other soldier. "You bring up the rear!"

And so we continued in the direction we had been walking, but this time with an armed guard. I realized that we must already have been making for the hall. Probably the stables were close by. I tried to ignore the tight ball of fear growing in my stomach and just kept my eyes on the back of the soldier we were following. After all, if anyone could talk his way out of a tricky situation, it was Abdul.

Soon I could see the roof of the great hall, covered in wooden tiles instead of thatch. The thane who lived here must be wealthy. We stopped in front of the doors and the soldier stood to attention. Two more men at arms were standing guard and Abdul and I looked at each other. This wasn't usual in peacetime.

"Two prisoners to see Lord Grimwold!" barked the soldier.

Before either of the guards could go anywhere, Abdul leaned forward.

"Excuse me," he said. "I was not aware that we were prisoners. We have, after all, come willingly. Could you change that announcement to visitors?"

The guards looked at the soldier, who shrugged and then smirked.

"I dunno if I'd say they came willingly," he sneered. "He's got delusions of grandeur this one. Seems to think he's some sort of lord instead of a heathen. But go on, let's humour him."

I felt Abdul's grip tighten on my shoulder, but his expression didn't change. One of the guards went inside and left us with a clearer view of the carved doorposts: dragons, painted red and green. Like the dragons in the Welsh story about Merlin, I thought, except that those were red and white. In some strange way this comforted me.

In a few moments a figure appeared in the doorway. Not the returning guard, but an impressive looking man in a blue tunic hemmed with braid. His hair and beard were light brown and his eyes were as blue as his tunic. He held out his arms in greeting.

"Welcome, welcome, strangers," he boomed at them. "Never let it be said that Grimwold is inhospitable to his guests. Please introduce yourselves."

Abdul bowed low. "I am Abdul Mutazz ibn Haroun of Cordoba," he said. "And this is my ward, Bronwen of Wales."

I curtsied and our host bowed in return. "I am Grimwold, thane of this borough. Welcome to my hall! Please come inside and refresh yourselves."

For the second time in a few minutes the soldier who had led us there seemed nonplussed. I looked sideways at him as we walked past, and couldn't resist a tiny smile.

And then we were in the great hall. Although the shutters were open, the windows were narrow and high up, so it took a few moments for my eyes to adjust. I looked round at the wall-hangings, whose woven pictures seemed to be telling a story, though not one I knew. Down at one end of the hall was the usual bustle of servants cooking, but Grimwold led us away from this, to the high table at the other end. He gestured toward a fine carved chair for Abdul and a more simple, but elegantly made one for me. I hung back.

"I'm not...I mean I don't usually..." I stuttered.

Grimwold looked at me with raised eyebrows.

"My ward means that she has been a servant, although one very close to her mistress, and she is unused to sitting at table," explained Abdul. "But since accompanying her on this journey, I have come to regard her as a daughter. I should prefer it if you would allow her to sit with us, as you are so kindly suggesting."

"Certainly, certainly," boomed Grimwold, and I sat down looking gratefully at Abdul.

Grimwold beckoned a servant and muttered something to him. So you *can* talk quietly, I thought, but nothing more sinister came than bread and cheese on wooden plates, a pitcher of ale, and three finely decorated earthenware beakers.

"Ah," said Abdul. "I hope you will not take it amiss if I refuse your ale. I am sure it is very fine, but I am afraid it is against my religion."

Grimwold raised his eyebrows. "What can I offer you, then?"

"I shall be happy with water," said Abdul, and Grimwold roared with laughter.

"You heathens take your life in your hands every time you drink!" he chortled. "Perhaps the water is sweeter in southern lands. But our well is clean spring water. If that is what you wish…unless…my cows give good rich milk. Perhaps you would care to try it?"

"Thank you," said Abdul, inclining his head.

"And your fair companion?" said Grimwold to me.

I looked at him sharply to see if he was mocking me, but his smile seemed to be genuine. Although…I definitely didn't trust this thane. Still, there was nothing to be done but play along.

"Milk, please," I said. At least that way I'd keep a clear head.

The servant went to fetch a second leather pitcher, this one filled with creamy milk, which Grimwold personally poured for us. He looked serious for a moment.

"I must apologize for the misunderstanding," he said. "I have told my man that I wish to see everyone who passes our gates, but I certainly did not mean you to be treated as prisoners. He is a good man, Leofric, but a little over-zealous. I shall have words with him."

Abdul inclined his head again. "Interesting that you feel the need to see everyone who enters your lands. Does that include every passing cart driver and pedlar?"

"Ordinarily, no, of course not. But these are not ordinary times," said Grimwold, lowering his voice. He paused, and then added, "We both know, do we not, that strange things are afoot."

Abdul narrowed his eyes. "Do we?" he said. "I am not sure what you mean."

"Are you not?" smiled Grimwold. "But please, eat some bread and try our cheese, from the same herd that produces that creamy milk."

We ate and drank in silence for a few moments and I studied the tapestry nearest to me. The picture was of an enormous tree, from its leaves possibly an ash. An eagle sat in its branches and a squirrel was running down the trunk toward the three great roots at the bottom. Twisting in and out of those gigantic roots and gnawing at them with its fangs was a huge serpent.

"I see you like my wall-hanging," said Grimwold.

I nodded. "Very much," I said. "It's beautifully embroidered. I almost feel I could climb the tree, though I wouldn't like to meet that serpent. But I don't know what it's all supposed to be."

"Ah," said Grimwold. "You are Welsh, so you do not know our old legends. That is Yggdrasill, the World Tree, which supports everything in the universe. Ratatosk the squirrel runs up and down the trunk carrying messages and gossip between the wise old eagle at the top and Nidhogg the serpent. If Nidhogg ever succeeds in gnawing through the roots, that will be the end of all the worlds, and us as well."

"Oh," I said. Something clicked in my brain. The World Tree. Wasn't that something to do with Woden and the runes? I looked warily at Grimwold, not knowing what to say. Eating and drinking seemed to be safer, so I took a sip from my beaker.

"This milk is very good," I said.

"I hope to offer you more of our hospitality," said Grimwold. "Please stay and join us at our evening meal."

"That is very kind," said Abdul, "but I fear we cannot. We are in a hurry to reach Wales, where Bronwen's mother is sick. We were ambushed on the road, luckily not hurt, but our horses were taken. Our purpose in coming here was to buy some horses to speed us on our way."

"This is terrible!" said Grimwold. "I shall look into it. Of course, we shall visit my stables and choose whatever you need. But where would you sleep tonight? Far better to set off fresh and early in the morning."

"We really should not stay," said Abdul.

"But you must taste my carp, fresh from our ponds," said Grimwold. "No meat, of course, it being Friday. Old habits die hard."

Old habits die hard? What did he mean? Surely everybody...I felt sick as his words sank in. Friday! And I'd had meat for breakfast! I'd completely lost track of what day it was. To have eaten flesh on the day Our Lord was crucified! Would God forgive me? There'd been nothing else to eat, but that was no excuse. I should have fasted rather than done that. *O Lord, forgive me!* I started to pray. *I didn't know what day it was. I'll never, ever do it again!*

But my prayers were suddenly cut short when I realized what Grimwold was saying.

"And we have so much to discuss, you and I," he was murmuring to Abdul. "Matters of great interest to both of us."

"Indeed?" said Abdul.

"Indeed," smiled Grimwold.

I went cold as I saw that the smile didn't reach his eyes.

"Matters such as a certain wise-woman called Ertha, on the estate of Lord Aelfric. Have you heard of her?"

Abdul shook his head slightly and looked as if this were a really interesting subject that he knew nothing about. How could he keep so cool?

"Someone went to see her, to ask about an immensely valuable object in her possession. An object which she no longer has."

Grimwold paused, but Abdul carried on looking as if he knew nothing about it.

"Someone," Grimwold continued, "who looks exactly like you."

CHAPTER THIRTEEN

WULF

This was it. I was going to come face to face with the rightful owner of my rune-stone. In a way it was a relief. I could just give it back and hope that Woden would let us live.

Slowly, slowly we turned round. But where we looked for a face there was nothing. Below that, though, about three and a half feet high, was a grinning brown person. Brown hair, brown face, brown clothes and brown, flint-tipped arrow pointed straight at my heart.

The small brown person shifted his bow slightly so that it was now pointed at Oz. Then his grin became even wider until he doubled up with laughter.

"Yous should see your faces!" he cackled, in a voice completely different from the one we'd first heard.

Me and Oz stared at him with our mouths open, and then looked at each other.

"Uh, oh!" said the person, with his bow instantly at the ready again. "Don't move! Did I say you could move? I don't remember sayin' it – so don't!"

He started to saunter round us, looking us up and down, still with his bowstring taut.

"Well, here's a fine pair of fellows," he sniggered. "Lost your horsey, did you? Don't you worry about her, she be fine. In fact, I'd like to know what a couple of nogoods like yous be doin' wi' a fine horse like that."

"We're not nogoods!" said Oz, indignantly.

"Uh, oh!" said the person. "Don't talk! Did I say yous could talk? I don't remember sayin' yous could talk!"

"Well, you asked us a question!" I said.

77

"I did not!" said the small brown person. "I said I'd like to know. That ain't a question, is it, Toadstool?"

Another small brown person clambered down from a branch. He looked very like the first one: snub nose, slanted eyes and enormous pointed ears.

"No, Pooka," he said. "That ain't a question."

"Well, it be *sort* of a question," said yet another of the creatures, appearing from behind a tree. How many of them were there, for God's sake? This one had longer hair than the others, in a wild curly bush sticking out all round her head. Somehow I knew it was a her, though she didn't look that different.

"I didn't ask you, Chickweed!" said the first one. "Go and find the girls!"

"They be right *borin'*, Pooka," said Chickweed. "All they does is comb their hair and giggle. I wants to be in your lot."

"You *be* in my lot," said Pooka. "We's all in the same clan, ain't we, but that don't mean I wants you hangin' round all the time."

As he was speaking Pooka looked at Chickweed and lowered the bow slightly, and I started to drop my hands. Instantly, Pooka let an arrow fly. It skimmed past my ear and thudded into a tree trunk behind.

"I didn't miss!" said Pooka. "That were just a warnin'."

My hands shot back up in the air and Oz froze.

Toadstool and Chickweed hooted with laughter and clapped their hands.

"Nice one, Pooka," chuckled Toadstool.

"Do it again!" squealed Chickweed. "Spike one of 'em ! Do it in his hand, if you wants to keep 'em alive!"

Pooka started circling round us again.

"Now, *does* I want to keep 'em alive, that's the question," he said thoughtfully. "I could kill 'em now, or..."

"Or we could have a bit of fun wiv 'em, an' then kill 'em," said Chickweed.

"Or we could just let 'em go," said Toadstool.

I found that I was praying, which wasn't something I did a lot. *Let Toadstool win*, I prayed. *Please, God, let us get out of here.* We'd lived through the battle against the Normans, and escaped kidnappers. With all the worries about dangerous men, and even gods, it seemed crazy to be killed by these…these…what on earth were they? They couldn't really be…*elves*, could they? And why couldn't Abdul come back and find us?

"We'll have a meetin'!" announced Pooka suddenly. "Nobody can say as how I throws my weight around. We'll *all* decide."

Still with his bow trained on us he threw back his head and, in a curious yodelling voice, called a series of names.

"Spider! Mugwort! Beetle! Dandelion! Nettle!"

There was a shift in the light, the sound of a breeze, and there, standing in front of us, were five more of the creatures. Two of them were girls, much more obviously than Chickweed, as their long greenish brown curls flowed down past their waists.

"Jesus," whispered Oz. "They *are* elves!"

The newcomers looked us up and down. One of the girls swayed over to Oz, her ragged green skirt swishing as she walked. She put her arms round his waist and laid her head against his stomach.

"Ooh, I likes this one," she simpered.

"You can have that one, Nettle," giggled the other girl. "I likes this one."

She minced across to me and ran her hands down one leg.

"Hello, human," she breathed. "My name be Dandelion. What be your'n?"

"Typical!" snorted Chickweed, and spat on the ground.

It was difficult to keep my hands in the air while someone else's hands were slowly stroking my legs, and I lowered mine for a second. Then I remembered the arrow and put them up again.

"He's learnin'," nodded Pooka.

Dandelion smiled up at me, showing pointed little teeth. She abandoned my legs and reached up to run her fingers over my chest.

"Ooh, what be this?" she cooed. "He've got somethin' round his neck. Somethin' pretty, look. A necklace. I wants it…ouch!" She shot back.

79

"What did he do to you, Dandelion?" said one of the others, putting an arm round her.

"Nothing!" I said. "I didn't touch her!"

"He did!" Dandelion stamped her foot. "He did, Mugwort. He's hurt my hand and I were only bein' nice to him. I doesn't like him any more!"

"I didn't mean to!" I protested. "It's the rune-stone. It doesn't seem to like people touching it."

Oz gave me an alarmed look. Should I have kept quiet about it? But what was the point? Dandelion had found it. They already knew. All the elves, if that's what they were, were looking uncomfortably fierce now, and several had bows and arrows trained on us. Pooka marched up to me and tore the top of my tunic, leaving the rune-stone exposed.

"It be one of them rune things," he announced. "Where did you get this?"

"My mother gave it to me, to bring me luck," said Wulf. "She's a wise-woman," I added, before Pooka could ask me what she was doing with such a thing.

Mugwort suddenly looked interested. "I'll have a look at that," he said.

"Tie 'em up!" said Pooka abruptly, waving Mugwort away. "Beetle, you tie this one to that tree. Spider, you tie the other one to that tree."

Practically before we could blink, me and Oz found ourselves sitting with our backs to a couple of young oaks, bound with something fine but extremely strong. Oz suddenly found his voice.

"Please," he said. "We didn't mean any harm."

"*Please, we didn't mean any harm*," mimicked Pooka in an uncanny imitation of Oz's voice.

All the elves doubled up with laughter.

"We were only trying to rescue the horse," Oz went on.

Noor! I'd forgotten about her! I looked over to where she was still standing, on the other side of the stream, browsing the bushes there. *She doesn't care about us*, I thought bitterly.

"And we've got to get back to our friends," pleaded Oz.

"What friends be those?" asked Pooka, swaggering up and down in front of us.

"The man who owns the horse, and a girl, a friend of ours," said Oz.

"Outlandish looking chap, were he?" asked Spider. "All dressed in black?"

Oz and me looked at each other. These creatures hadn't done anything to Abdul and Bron, had they?

"That's right," I said.

"Me and Beetle seen him," said Spider. "Him and a girl, goin' into Grimwold's place."

All the elves leaned forward, wide-eyed.

"He be a crony o' Grimwold's, be he, this friend o' yourn?" asked Pooka.

We shook our heads.

"We don't even know who Grimwold is," I said.

"And I don't think our friend did, either," added Oz. "He just said he thought there was somewhere nearby where he could buy some horses."

Some of the elves started laughing. They clapped their hands and clutched at each other.

"Be quiet!" ordered Pooka.

"Oh, come on," chortled Spider, wiping his eyes. "They be only humans."

"Yous mean to say," said Pooka, "they just went wanderin' into Grimwold's place when they didn't know him?"

We nodded. Shrieks of laughter followed, Beetle even rolling on the ground gasping for air. As we looked at them in disbelief, Pooka shook his head.

"Well, I shouldn't worry about meetin' up wi' your friends," he said. "If they be visitin' Grimwold, you ain't likely ever to see 'em again."

CHAPTER FOURTEEN

BRONWEN

"Perhaps we should stop playing games," said Abdul quietly.

"Excellent idea," said Grimwold, just as quietly.

"I mean," Abdul went on, "perhaps *you* would like to stop playing games with *us*. My request was honest. I need to buy horses."

Grimwold laughed and took a sip of ale. "And why do you need to buy horses, I wonder. Were you really robbed? I see little sign of it."

"They were horse thieves," said Abdul. "Once they had our steeds they did us no harm."

I shrank back into my chair and started praying again. *Please, God, don't let him ask me anything. Let Abdul do all the talking.* Then as an afterthought, *I'm sorry we're telling lies, but there's no way round it.*

"Well, perhaps that is so," smiled Grimwold, putting his beaker on the table. "Forgive me. One becomes distrustful in these strange times. But I should like to return to the subject of the wise-woman, this...Ertha." He looked at Abdul. "You are not going to deny that you went to visit her, are you? So perhaps you would like to tell me what you found out."

I couldn't tell anything from Abdul's expression. How was he going to get out of this?

He took a breath and began, "I found out very little. No more, I should think, than your men who had been there before me. They *were* your men, were they not? Ertha is a strong woman, and not that friendly to me. She kept her counsel."

Grimwold leaned forward and gripped his beaker tightly. His nostrils flared and there was not even a pretence of a smile on his face. I gripped the seat of my chair just as tightly and held my breath.

"We are playing games again," said Grimwold softly. "I want to know why you went there."

Abdul paused and sighed, then placed his hands on the table, palms up. "I will be honest with you," he said. "A friend of mine received a visit from two men who wanted him to be involved in some scheme of theirs. He was not interested, but he learned from them of this woman, that she had a valuable object. He asked me to investigate and she told me that she had given it to her son when he went to battle. She had not seen him since."

I stared at Abdul. What was he saying?

"I went to the victory feast at Lord Aelred's hall," he went on, "but the boy was not there. I believe he had been killed in the battle. So the object, whatever it is, is lost."

I allowed myself to breathe again.

Grimwold's eyes narrowed. "And do you know what this object is?"

"Some sort of talisman, something to do with your ancient legends, like your tapestry over there. I know nothing of such things. I was merely making enquiries for my friend."

"And why could your friend not make these enquiries for himself?" asked Grimwold.

"Because he is sick," replied Abdul. "He was struck down by a mysterious ailment just after refusing to cooperate with these men. *Your* men, I believe. Is that not a coincidence?"

Grimwold leaned back in his chair and drummed his fingers on the table. Then he smiled, though I thought, once again, that the smile did not reach his eyes. Pushing Abdul's plate closer to him, he said, "Come my friend, eat. You mistrust me unnecessarily. Those men who visited your friend, and the ones who went to see Ertha before you, they were nothing to do with me."

Oh, no? I thought.

"I *did* send men to Aelfric's estate to find this woman," continued Grimwold, "but *after* you had been there. That is how I knew what you looked like. I fear that many people may be looking for this…talisman, as you call it, and not all of them loyal to the king."

He turned to me. "Eat, little maid, and then rest. Later we will see about the horses."

I broke off a piece of cheese and forced myself to eat, though every nerve in my body was taut as a harpstring. The cheese was tasty, though, and so creamy that I could swallow it easily. And it was good to eat fresh bread after the stale old loaf from Abdul's bag. Grimwold seemed to have the best of everything.

"I am sorry I have no more news for you," said Abdul, tearing off a hunk of bread.

Grimwold shrugged. "So the boy is dead. A pity. That makes things more difficult. I suppose we must visit the battleground. But so many corpses to search, if they are not already burned or buried."

If you really want this thing, I thought, *why aren't you more upset?* With a chill, I realized that he didn't believe Abdul's story. I sat in silence for the rest of the meal, while Grimwold and Abdul made small talk. When the servants had cleared everything away, Grimwold turned to me.

"Come with me," he smiled. "You need a rest after your ordeal of being robbed."

Pulling aside a curtain, he led us both to an area behind the high table, where there were several solid-looking doors. Opening one, he ushered me inside. I looked worriedly at Abdul, who nodded slightly. This didn't reassure me much, but I seemed to have no choice, so I went in. I found myself in a small bower with a wooden framed bed, big enough for two people. Cushions were piled high on it and the walls were covered with woollen hangings of a deep red. One tiny window up high let in the only light, though a large unlit candle stood on a wooden chest. There was no other furniture.

"Rest now," said Grimwold. He turned to Abdul. "You too, my friend. I will show you to your room."

He shut the door and I tried the bed. It was the grandest bed I'd ever lain on, as good as Lady Rhiannon's, but the last thing I felt like doing was resting. Perhaps if I waited a while I'd be able to sneak out and find Abdul. Their voices moved away, and I heard another door open and shut. But then footsteps returned and a sound which could only be one thing.

A key turning in my lock.

CHAPTER FIFTEEN

WULF

I strained helplessly at my bindings. No good. They looked like spider's web, but they were really strong.

"What do you mean, we won't be seeing them again?" I choked out.

Pooka stood looking at us, head on one side. Then he turned to the other elves.

"Ah, he do care," he sniggered. "The human do care about his little friends!"

At this, the elves who were laughing lost the use of their legs and joined Beetle rolling on the ground.

"Of course we care!" shouted Oz, red in the face. "Don't you care about each other? What are you, some kind of demons?"

The laughter calmed down a bit.

"Ooh, that ain't nice," said Dandelion, winding her greeny-brown hair round her fingers. "I told you I didn't like 'em."

"What be demons?" asked Nettle.

"I dunno *ezackly*," said Dandelion, "but it ain't very nice."

Chickweed shot the two girls a look of withering scorn. "Demons," she said, "be evil bein's what do evil things, as I'd have thought even you two would know."

"Look," I begged. "Never mind that. Just tell us what you mean. Why won't we see them again?"

All the elves except Pooka were sitting on the ground, quieter now, but still grinning their heads off. Pooka carried on strutting around, eyeing us up and down, very much in control of the situation.

"Tell ' em, Spider," he said. "Tell 'em why they won't be seein' their little friends any more."

"Because," said Spider, "that's what do happen if you go visitin' Grimwold and you ain't on his side. You gets your throat cut. We finds the bodies sometimes. They got big slits in their throats and all blood down their clothes. That's what he do, Grimwold."

I felt icy cold and Oz had turned white and looked as if he was going to be sick.

"You've got to let us go!" I said hoarsely. "We've got to try and rescue them!"

This started another bout of hysterical laughing. Spider, Beetle, Chickweed, Nettle and Dandelion all began rolling around again. But not Pooka or Mugwort, who just smiled at the others…and not Toadstool, who was staring into the distance.

Oz's face turned from white back to red.

"Shut up!" he yelled. "Shut up, the lot of you!"

Pooka suddenly clicked his fingers and said softly, "Be quiet."

There was instant hush. He stood looking at us for what seemed a long time, narrowing his slanted eyes, and with a smile playing at the edges of his wide mouth. The others grinned expectantly. All except Toadstool, who seemed to be in a world of his own.

"This could be fun," said Pooka at last. "If we lets you go, what d'yous think you'd do?"

Me and Oz looked at each other.

"We'd…well, we'd…" stuttered Oz.

"We'd try and rescue them," I said, knowing how ridiculous it sounded.

The elves started to snigger again, but with an eye on Pooka. When he held a hand up, they fell quiet straight away.

"And how would yous do that?" said Pooka.

"We'd…we'd creep in there," I said, "in the middle of the night, and try and find them."

"And overpower their guards and cut them loose," said Oz.

Even as we were saying it I could hear how lame it sounded, and I could tell by Oz's embarrassed expression that he felt the same. This time Pooka didn't stop the laughter; in fact he joined in. But looking at him, I felt that he never lost control. Toadstool was gazing into the trees, as if he were somewhere else.

"And tell me, my friends," chuckled Pooka at last. "Tell me what secret weapons yous got. What amazin' magic swords an' things have yous got, to defeat grown men?"

"We've got our knives," said Oz.

This time Pooka hushed the laughter as soon as it started.

"You *has* got somethin' magic though, ain't you?" he said to me. "That rune thing round your neck."

I looked at him, startled. Of course! It had never occurred to me! Could the rune-stone be used as a weapon? But how?

As if he was reading my thoughts, Pooka nodded and said, "But you ain't got a clue how to use it, have you?"

I sank back into misery and cursed myself. All the times I could have learnt about the runes and hadn't wanted to. I'd almost taken a sort of pride in knowing nothing about them. I couldn't look at Oz. If he'd had *my* chances, he'd have known how to use it.

Pooka nodded again.

"Spider!" he said. "This friend o' theirn that you saw goin' into Grimwold's place. Did he have weapons?"

"He had a great big sword," said Spider importantly. "A great big sword an' a massive great bow over his shoulder. This big it were," he said, holding his arms wide apart.

Pooka nodded. "Now do you reckon that a man wi' a great big sword an' a massive great bow would be able to fight off lots an' lots of soldiers? 'Cos he've got lots an' lots of soldiers, ol' Grimwold. He don't do all the dirty work hisself."

"He'd have a good go," said Oz. "He's an expert fighter."

Pooka nodded. "He'd probably take a few with him," he agreed. "But they'd get him in the end. There be too many of 'em."

I thought of Bronwen and went cold again.

"Now do yous reckon that two little boys wi' their knives," said Pooka, "be havin' much of a chance in there?"

"We'd have surprise on our side!" Oz burst out. "And the dark!"

"Oh, you got cats' eyes?" said Pooka. "Yous see in the dark, like us?"

The other elves were sitting, grinning, looking from Pooka to me and Oz and back again.

I closed my eyes. I felt numb and hopeless. Pooka was right. We had no chance. For all Abdul's cleverness and fighting skills, he had done something really stupid. And he'd led Bronwen with him. Together they'd strolled to certain death, and there was nothing we could do about it... Unless...

A tiny hope started to stir in my mind. It wasn't much of a hope, but it was better than nothing. I opened my eyes and looked straight at Pooka.

"No, you're right," I said quietly. "We wouldn't have a chance."

Oz whipped round, astonished. "You giving up?" he shouted. "You just gonna leave them to get killed?"

I ignored him and carried on looking steadily at Pooka.

"We wouldn't have a chance," I said, "unless you help us."

There was a moment's silence, followed by whoops of laughter, slaps on the back, and heels drumming on the ground. In the middle of the uproar, Toadstool got up and walked over to us. Pooka narrowed his eyes and looked at him, and the others quietened down to see what he was going to do.

Toadstool gazed around at them all, still with that far-away expression on his face. Then he turned to me and Oz. At last he spoke.

"I be helpin' you," said Toadstool. "For Thistle."

CHAPTER SIXTEEN

BRONWEN

I leapt up and tried to lift the iron latch. Stiff as it was I could move it with both hands, but the door wouldn't budge. I was locked in.

My hands slipped off the latch and I realized that they were wet. My whole body was wringing with sweat. I looked frantically round the room. The window! But it was so high up! The wooden chest was more or less underneath it, so I carefully lifted off the candle and placed it on the floor, then climbed up. I could still barely reach the window, and now that I was close to it I saw just how small it was.

Not only that – it was covered with vellum to keep out the draughts. I stretched up and tried to prise the vellum away from the bottom of the window frame, but it was stuck fast. If I had something sharp I could cut through it, but what? I didn't have knife and there was nothing suitable in the room. Anyway…could I wriggle through that tiny space? It was unlikely, and there must be quite a drop on the other side.

I leaned my forehead against the wall beneath the window and closed my eyes. The wall felt cool. It was the only place, apart from the door, not covered by the red woollen hangings. My panic was ebbing away now and being replaced by despair. Hot tears trickled down my cheeks. Now would be a good time to pray, but no words would come. Slowly I clambered down off the chest and curled up on the bed, sobbing quietly. Would I ever see Rhiannon again? Worse, would I ever see dear Nain again, or my beloved Wales? At last I lay still, but however much I tried to find a way out of this mess, one thought kept repeating itself. *Abdul, you're going to have to do something, because I can't.*

Suddenly there were footsteps. They stopped outside my door and paused. I tensed. I brushed the tears off my cheeks and tried to look normal. The footsteps went away again, but they'd broken my mood. I sat up and swung my legs over the side of the bed.

What would Nain do? Well, she'd study her surroundings very carefully. But I'd already done that. There was nothing much to see. Just a chest, a candlestick and a load of wall-hangings. I heard Nain's voice clearly in my head. *And what's behind the wall-hangings, Bronwen? Haven't I told you to look at what you can't see, as well as what you can?*

I slipped off the bed and ran over to the door. There I crouched down and began to feel behind the hangings, working my way all round the room. I was beginning to think this was a dead end when, on one side of the bed, my hand felt wood. Lifting aside the heavy hanging I saw...a second door.

Oh, thank you Nain! I breathed. It must lead to another room. Anyone could be on the other side – I'd have to take great care. I put my ear to the door and listened as hard as I could. Nothing.

Carefully, carefully, I started to turn the handle. *Creak.* Immediately a voice spoke from the other side.

"Who's there?"

Abdul!

"Abdul, it's me, Bronwen!" I whispered. "Where are you?"

"I'm in a bedchamber, supposed to be resting, like you. But how can I hear you so clearly?"

"Lift the wall-hanging. There's a door in the wall."

I heard the swish of the heavy material being moved.

"Why, yes," said Abdul. "How clever of you to find it."

For a brief moment I glowed with the praise. Then I remembered our situation. I felt the handle turn, but the door didn't open.

"It must be locked," whispered Abdul.

"Like the door to my room," I whispered back. "Are you locked in too?"

"Indeed, no." Abdul sounded surprised. "At least, I do not believe so."

"Well, come and get me then!" I had to struggle to keep my voice low. "We've got to get out of here!"

"I agree," whispered Abdul. "But the best way to do it is to carry on pretending. If we try to run it will be obvious we have something to hide."

"But why have they locked me in?" I asked. What was the matter with him? We couldn't just sit around pretending everything was all right!

"I agree, that is worrying," said Abdul. "But stay calm. I still think… Hush! Someone is coming!"

I heard the wall-hanging swish back in place, but found I could also hear the creak of a door, footsteps and then Grimwold's voice.

"I trust you are rested?"

Was it my imagination, or did he sound less friendly? I pressed my ear to the door.

"Yes, thank you, quite rested. In fact, I believe it is time for us to thank you for your hospitality and take our leave."

"Not so fast, my friend," said the cold voice of Grimwold. "I would have left you longer, but two of my messengers have just ridden in with some very interesting news."

"Really?" said Abdul.

I could imagine his raised eyebrows as he spoke, one arched slightly higher than the other.

"Yes," Grimwold continued. "I have spies and messengers all over the place. It is very useful."

"Spies?" said Abdul. "And why would you need spies?"

I held my breath. How did he manage to stay so cool?

Grimwold ignored Abdul's question and went on, "My men have visited the estate of one Aelred, where the victory feast was held." He paused. "It appears that this Wulfstan, son of Ertha, was not after all killed in the battle, as you said."

"I am pleased that I was misinformed," said Abdul. "It would be sad for one so young to die."

"It appears also that he left with a friend, and that in the party was a young Welsh girl by the name of Bronwen."

This time even Abdul's quick mind couldn't come up with an answer. Leaning against the door, I stifled a sob.

"It appears, in fact, that you have been lying to me. I suspected as much. You *do* know the whereabouts of the object I want!"

But Abdul seemed to have gathered his wits.

"That is a grave accusation to make to a man of honour," he said. "Bronwen is a name not uncommon in Wales, I believe. Why do you assume that my ward is the same person? Did your men not follow the party and find this Wulfstan?"

"They did follow the party," said Grimwold, his voice rising. "My most trusted servant sent three men on after them while he stayed making further investigations. But those men have vanished!"

There was a sound like a fist thumping a table.

"But now I have the girl," he went on more calmly, "so it should be easy to find the boy and the object that I seek."

"How so?" said Abdul. "Even if she were the same girl?"

I knew what Grimwold was going to say, even before he said it. It didn't make it any easier to hear.

"Because, my friend, you will tell me." Grimwold's voice sounded smoother now, almost gloating. "You will tell me because you will not want to watch her die."

CHAPTER SEVENTEEN

WULF

There was a stunned silence and then, "Help humans?!" exploded Chickweed.

"For Thistle," repeated Toadstool.

"Thank you," I whispered.

Oz gaped at Toadstool. "Er, who's Thistle?" he asked.

Pooka put up a hand, motioning everyone to be quiet. He started strutting round again, circling the little clearing by the stream, eyeing each of them in turn, before going to stand beside Toadstool. Hands on hips he opened his mouth to speak, but he was interrupted by a gentle whinny from over the water. Noor! I kept forgetting about her. I'd cursed her for leading us into this, but now it seemed it might have been a good thing. Or how would we have known about the danger to Abdul and Bron?

Pooka laughed. "The horse do want to have her say. Perhaps she be thinkin' we should go and rescue her master."

This was too much for Chickweed. She leapt up and planted her feet in front of Pooka. Leaning forward, eyes blazing, she spat, "You ain't seriously thinkin' o' puttin' people's lives at risk to rescue *humans?*"

"We're people too," said Oz.

Chickweed gave him one of her withering stares. "You ain't people," she sneered. "You be just humans. That there be a horse," she pointed at Noor, and then up at a branch where a bright-eyed bird sat with its head cocked on one side. "That there be a throssel." She peered at the ground, where little black specks were scurrying around. "Them there be emmets...And *you* be humans. *We* be people," she announced, and folded her arms as if to say that was the end of the matter.

Toadstool stood motionless throughout all this, gazing straight ahead.

"The rest o' yous doesn't have to help me," he said slowly. "I knows how you feels about humans, especially after what they done to Thistle... but I bin thinkin'. It seems to me that not all humans be the same. These two don't seem that bad...But that ain't my main reason for wantin' to help 'em."

There was another long silence. Oz looked at me and opened his mouth to speak, but I shook my head. We mustn't say anything to interrupt Toadstool's train of thought.

Chickweed wasn't worried about that.

"And your main reason be...?" she asked impatiently.

Toadstool looked at her. "Revenge," he said simply.

A slow smile spread across Chickweed's brown face. "*Now* you be talkin'!" she said.

"Just think on it this way," Toadstool went on. "We ain't doin' it so much to help these two, nor their friends, as to hurt...*him*...that, that..." He shook his head in frustration.

"Demon?" put in Dandelion brightly.

Me and Oz looked at each other. Events seemed to have been taken out of our hands. Although we were still tied up and it wasn't at all clear what was going to happen, I felt a surge of relief. With a bit of luck, things should be going our way. Then I remembered Bron and Abdul. They could be dead already, and even if they weren't, the rescue would be very dangerous. But at least we'd be doing something, not just sitting tied to oak trees while our friends were killed.

"Yeah," said Toadstool slowly. "Demon...that be a good word for him. Demon. 'Cause it do seem to me we ain't done enough to get our revenge, after what he done to Thistle."

"We soured his milk," said Nettle.

"We put a blight on his harvest," said Mugwort. "All them fields he've got, and he had to buy a load of his grain from someone else last year."

"We let his best horse escape," said Spider.

94

Beetle guffawed. "Yeah, that were good! Me an' Spider rode him all the ways over the hills, didn't we, Spider? This farmer found him. Couldn't believe his luck, gettin' a horse like that."

Toadstool waved a hand impatiently. "That be nothin'!" he said. "That be petty little things…Pooka?"

Pooka put a hand on his shoulder. "What, my friend?"

"Pooka, you talked about doin' somethin' big," said Toadstool. Pooka nodded. "Well, I reckons," Toadstool went on. "I reckons *now's* the time. I reckons we could cause havoc, if we puts our minds to it."

He looked around at all the others. I thought I was beginning to be able to read elf expressions and that Toadstool's was pleading, almost beseeching.

"An' if their human friends escape in all that havoc," he gestured towards me and Oz. "Well, what be the harm in that? They ain't done nothin' to us."

"Havoc!" shouted Chickweed. "Yeah, let's cause some havoc!" She stopped and looked venomously at me and Oz. "But I don't see why we has to help humans at the same time. Their friends could get killed in the havoc for all I cares."

"Hm," said Pooka, narrowing his slanted eyes. "Seems to me we need to discuss this a bit more. Gather round!"

And we were left tied to our trees while the elves sat in a circle talking excitedly in low voices, continually turning round and pointing at us. Everyone seemed to have something to say except Beetle, who sat picking his nose and grinning inanely, though he nodded like mad whenever Spider spoke. At last they were all nodding and laughing, except Chickweed, who was wagging her finger at Pooka and looking extremely annoyed. Finally she shrugged resignedly, and I knew that Toadstool had won. I would have punched the air, but my arms were still firmly tied to the tree.

Pooka clapped his hands. "Untie 'em!" he ordered, and we found ourselves suddenly free.

Pooka paced around while we rubbed our arms and legs.

"We can't do nothin' till it's dark," he announced, "an' anyways, we got to have a war council."

"I thought that's what you just had," I said.

"No, that weren't a war council," said Mugwort. "That were just decidin' we was gonna do it."

"An' we got to have somethin' to eat, an' all," said Beetle.

Oz looked at him gratefully.

"Er, what d'you want us to do?" I asked.

"Jus' don't get in the ways," said Pooka.

In two ticks, Mugwort had produced a blazing fire – how, we couldn't see. Then he stuck a branch on either side. Nettle pulled half a dozen dead squirrels out of a leather bag and Mugwort placed a hand on each in turn.

"We be sorry, squirrels," he said matter-of-factly, "but you had a good life and a quick death. We's all gotta go sometime. Go to your squirrel home and be born again in the spring."

Dandelion and Nettle skinned the squirrels with little flint knives and stuck twigs through them, which they attached to the branches, making a spit. Toadstool sat wrapping mushrooms in leaves and placing them round the edge of the fire, while Spider and Beetle pushed a variety of nuts a little way into the blaze.

Me and Oz watched all this in fascination.

"I was never sure I believed in elves," whispered Oz.

"You believe in the runes," replied Wulf.

"Yeah," said Oz, "but this is something else."

Mugwort beckoned us over.

"Come and have a nut," he said, pushing a few blackened bits our way.

Oz reached to touch one, burnt his fingers and blew on them.

Mugwort glanced around at the other elves and whispered, "Can I have a quick look at that there rune-stone?"

I held it up and Mugwort's eyes narrowed as he watched it swinging in the firelight.

"Mm, interestin'," he nodded, deftly flicking a nut into his mouth. "What d'you know about it?"

"Nothing," I said sulkily. "My mum gave it to me for good luck, that's all. Look, who's this Thistle?"

"Ah, Thistle," sighed Mugwort. "She were a special little thing. Especially special to Toadstool, as I reckons you've gathered. Always adventurous, she were. Always explorin'. Chickweed often used to go with her, but one day she didn't go along. Her little sister went instead. And that were the day she explored too far."

There was a long pause. At last Oz asked, "And what happened?"

"She got caught, didn' she. She were pokin' around Grimwold's place, jus' curious, an' her little sister taggin' along. Little Bramble. Bramble never got caught, but she hid an' she watched. She seen everythin' that happened. She got away afterwards and told us about it. A right state she were in, cryin' an' screamin'."

We waited, but Mugwort stared into the fire and didn't say any more.

I remembered about the bodies found in the woods with their throats cut, and thought I could guess how Thistle had met her death.

"How did she get caught?" I asked, "If you don't mind talking about it. I mean, you elves have got magic, haven't you?"

Mugwort nodded. "But so have he, that Grimwold. He cast a spell she weren't expectin'."

Both of us sat up with a jolt. "Magic?" gasped Oz. "He's got magic?"

I groaned. How were we ever going to rescue Bron and Abdul if our enemy worked magic?

"Not ordinary magic, like us," Mugwort went on. "He can't jus' *do* things. He has to say a load o' fancy spells an' stuff, an' use them rune things like you got round your neck. 'Cos he do worship ol' One-eye. It be Woden's magic he uses."

I sat stunned. For the first time, it really came home to me that my rune could be used for evil.

Dandelion came over and offered us pieces of squirrel on sticks. I accepted numbly, and she smiled and fluttered her eyelashes at me. Then Nettle appeared with a little pile of mushrooms. She simpered at Oz as he took some.

"Seems like we're back in favour," he said, and I nodded absently.

Although it wasn't yet dark, a thin crescent moon appeared between the branches of the trees overhead. In the dimming light we saw Pooka talking quietly to Spider and Beetle, and heard him say, "Stick close to Spider, now."

"I always does," nodded Beetle happily.

Then there was that shift in the air that we'd first seen when Pooka had called the other elves to him, and where Spider and Beetle had been standing was an empty space.

"I 'spect he's sent them on a lookout," said Mugwort, licking his fingers. "They won't be long. Then we can make a proper plan."

"About time," I said. "It'll be dark soon. Anything could be happening."

"So where's Thistle's sister?" said Oz suddenly. "You said she escaped, but she's not here."

"Ah, poor little Bramble," nodded Mugwort. "It were too much for her. She moped around and in the end she said she couldn't stick around here. It reminded her too much. And she jus' wandered off. You can understand it. Seein' her sister hanging there, her little legs danglin' an' kickin'."

"What?" we said together.

"She took a long time to die, did Thistle," continued Mugwort. "She didn't weigh hardly nothin', you see, an' you got to be a good weight for a quick death, when you're hangin'."

"They hanged her?" I said, appalled.

"I thought you said he cut people's throats?" said Oz.

"He do," nodded Mugwort. "Even sometimes when it's one of his special ceremonies. But when it's somethin' extra special, he do hang 'em."

"The gallows god," whispered Oz.

I looked at him. All these bits of information were leading to one conclusion, but I didn't want to believe it.

"The gallows god," repeated Oz. "Woden."

So my rune-stone, the good luck charm given me by my mum, belonged to a god who wanted people hanged! I felt like ripping it off and throwing it into the fire. But I didn't. The stone grew warm against my skin, as it sometimes did, and it didn't *feel* evil. There must be more to this than I understood. If only I'd learned more from my mum. More? If only I'd learned *anything* from my mum!

A little breeze blew, the air shifted again, and there were Spider and Beetle, wide-eyed and panting, obviously bursting to tell their news. Spider looked around to see if he had everyone's attention, unnecessarily, as all eyes were on him.

"We bin there," he said. "We bin to that courtyard next to Grimwold's hall…They be buildin' a gallows!"

CHAPTER EIGHTEEN

BRONWEN

Oh God, I don't want to die!

A long wooden beam was lifted into place.

Oh God, don't let it hurt, let it be quick!

There was a shorter beam across the top.

The gallows.

"Oh, God, let me see Nain again! Let me go home to Wales, to my village, to the mountains. Let me see Nain!"

I was tied to a post, couldn't move, couldn't run, in Grimwold's courtyard. It was getting dark. I looked wildly around. The great hall loomed up on one side. Straight ahead was a platform, with…my eyes skittered past, across to the stables. I didn't want to look at the platform, but in the end I was drawn to it, to the thing I couldn't escape, that thing, that nightmare.

For there was no escape.

And with that acceptance came calm. Suddenly I was past screaming, past crying, almost past praying. I turned my head to look at Abdul. Watching his lips move silently, I knew that *he* was praying. He was tied to another post a few yards away. His face was badly bruised on one side and his forehead was caked with dried blood. The soldiers had wound rope underneath his armpits to keep him upright, and then over his arms and legs to stop him moving when he came to. A beaker of cold water in his face had brought him round, and when he had gasped, "Water! Water to drink!" the men had laughed. But Grimwold had ordered a soldier to give him some.

"I need him to be able to talk," he had said, in his cold voice.

He'd left us then, but now he was coming back. He stopped in front of Abdul.

"You will not escape hanging, now that you have killed two of my men," he leered. "So you will not need all this round your neck." With the point of his sword, Grimwold loosened the black cloth around Abdul's neck, and with the other hand he unwound it, slowly, mockingly, until his head was bare.

My eyes filled with tears. It was the first time I'd seen Abdul's curly black hair and it made him seem younger, more defenceless.

"But you could still save the girl," Grimwold went on, "if you tell me what I want to know."

"Believe me," Abdul croaked. "I do not know where they are. They could be anywhere in these forests."

"I have men out looking," said Grimwold. "We have until midnight. Then she hangs."

He strode off.

I'd been through terror and rage and grief, and now there seemed to be nothing left inside me. Better that way. Better to be numb than for the terror to return. Then I looked at Abdul's moving lips. He was right to pray to his god. Was it the same as my God? But he was right, anyway, and I should do the same.

"Lord Jesus, forgive me my sins" I prayed silently. "For eating meat today, and for losing my temper, and for…" My mind went blank. "For all the other things I've done. You know what they are. Please accept my soul. And make it not hurt too much. Let me die straight away." Tears welled up in my eyes again. "I don't want to die, Lord. Couldn't you work some miracle? But if not, *please* let me die quickly." The tears trickled down my cheeks. "And please look after Nain. Let us see each other in Heaven, Lord. And Lord, couldn't you accept Abdul's soul, too? I know he's a heathen, but he's a good man."

"Bronwen," rasped Abdul. I opened my eyes and looked at him.

"Forgive me," he whispered.

"What for?"

"I was stupid and arrogant. I should never have led you into this."

"No, you didn't know," I said. "You tried to look after me. There's nothing to forgive."

A loud banging started up again. I looked up at the darkening sky – anywhere but at the hideous shape in front of me – and a sliver of new moon sailed into view. *The last moon I shall ever see*, I thought, but instead of deepening my despair, the moon was strangely comforting. For a timeless moment I was up there, with the crescent moon and the few little stars beginning to peek through.

Then a loud crash brought me back into my body. The gallows was in place. And my terror returned. I heard a low moan, and realized that it came from my own mouth.

"Bronwen!" rasped Abdul. "Don't look at it. Don't think about it."

Grimwold marched over.

"What are you talking about? Is there something you haven't told me?"

Abdul looked at me.

"I will tell you exactly where we left them," he muttered. "Then you must let the girl go. I can do no more than that."

A tiny hope rose in my breast. Could I be saved? But what would Grimwold do to Wulf and Oz? Then I knew. This was a trick. He wouldn't let me go and he would kill them too.

"No!" I cried, but Abdul ignored me.

"About three-quarters of a mile away, on the road going south, a little way into the forest," he said. "But there is no need to hurt the boys. Just take what you want and let them go."

"I already have men looking around there," said Grimwold coldly. "We shall see if they find anything."

"Now I have told you, you must release the girl!" said Abdul, straining at his bindings.

"Oh, I must, must I?" sneered Grimwold. "As I said, we shall see if they find anything."

He turned on his heels and swept off, his cloak swirling behind him.

"Have you no honour?" cried Abdul hoarsely, then sagged despairingly, head down, only the ropes under his arms holding him up.

"You shouldn't have done that!" I sobbed.

Abdul turned his head to look at me and seemed to find strength from somewhere.

"I knew they must already be looking there," he said in a low voice. "It was worth a try to have you released. And if those boys have any sense they will have mounted Noor and fled at the first sign of trouble." He closed his eyes and his head drooped again. Then his chin lifted and he looked ahead, but he wasn't seeing the gallows, for a small smile played around his lips. "She flies like the wind," he went on. "None of their horses can match her. She can easily carry both of them."

"I hope so," I sniffed.

"Fire!" came a shout. "There's fire in the stables!"

CHAPTER NINETEEN

BRONWEN

The dusk was suddenly lit by an orange glow at the far end of the stables. In a second, Abdul and I were left alone, as everyone ran to the other end of the courtyard. Soldiers were dashing about, bumping into each other and cursing; buckets of water appeared from nowhere and were thrown over the roof. But they didn't seem to be doing much good. The fire blossomed and crackled its way along the thatch, laughing at the men's efforts to stop it.

Abdul and I could only watch as a great dark cloud of smoke billowed up, covering the moon.

"The horses!" yelled Grimwold. "Let the horses out!"

Then a frightened voice called, "They're gone, sir! The horses are gone!"

"What?" roared Grimwold, and vanished round the other side of the stables.

Now, I thought. *Now's our chance! Oh, thank you, God! If only these ropes weren't so tight!*

I wriggled my arms up and down, but all I was doing was hurting my wrists. Then I felt the cool blade of a knife against my skin, slicing through the ropes, and at the same moment Abdul fell forward on to the ground.

"Quick! This way!" hissed the voice – the wonderful, familiar voice – of *Wulf*. Then my hand was in his and I was being pulled into the shadows.

"But Abdul…" I gasped, looking back over my shoulder.

Oz was crouching beside him, whispering something and Abdul was nodding and Oz got behind him, put his hands under his armpits and heaved him upright. Was I dreaming? I watched in wonder as Abdul staggered and grabbed at the post, then, with Oz's arm around him, managed to limp the few yards to join me and Wulf. This couldn't be happening, could it?

"Are you all right now, mate?" said Oz.

"Yes, yes, thank you, Osric. I will be fine."

My head swam for a moment. An overwhelming wave of relief flooded through me. *Oh, thank you, Lord – the miracle!* I prayed silently.

And then my practical side took over. *Well, Bronwen,* I thought, *this is all very well, but what on earth are we going to do now?*

We were standing by a wooden fence, about a man's height. Abdul leaned against this, looked at the boys and bowed slightly.

"How you got here is…" He shook his head. "I can only pledge my undying…"

"Yeah, yeah," said Oz, "Never mind that. D'you reckon you can climb this fence, if we give you a hand up?"

"They really beat him up," I whispered. "He was unconscious."

"Ordinarily, yes," said Abdul in a slurred voice, "but I am feeling a little dizzy."

"Well, it's how we got in," said Wulf, "and I don't know another way out."

He looked worriedly back into the courtyard. A gust of smoke blew our way and set us all coughing.

"You can do it, Abdul," I spluttered. "You go over first, Osric, and help him down the other side, and you make a stirrup with your hands, Wulf, so he can put his foot on it."

"Well, *you're* back to normal, at any rate," grinned Oz.

"And hurry up," I said. "I want to get away from that gallows."

"What about you?" said Wulf, but I was already tying up my skirts.

"I think I can climb a fence," I said. The cheek of him!

"Not so fast!" came a shout, and a shape loomed up out of the smoke. One of Grimwold's soldiers stood, sword in hand, leering at us.

I shrank back. Of course, it was too good to be true. I'd never escape death that easily. Now all four of us would hang. Wulf and Oz's little daggers looked puny compared to that great broadsword, and surely other soldiers would be behind him.

What happened next was unbelievable.

"Leave them!" said Grimwold's icy voice. "Get back to the fire. I do not need them any more."

"Er...yes, sir. If you say so."

The soldier backed away into the smoke-filled courtyard, bewilderment all over his face.

I peered around, looking for Grimwold. The courtyard was now too full of smoke to see anything clearly and the bitter taste was burning my throat. What was Grimwold playing at? I couldn't believe he was going to let us go. This was some cruel trick. Then I saw Wulf and Oz's ear-splitting grins.

"It's Pooka!" cackled Oz. "He does these amazing impressions of people. He sounds just like them."

"It's *who*?" I said.

"Pooka," grinned Wulf. "And he throws his voice as well. Makes it sound as if it's coming from somewhere completely different."

Abdul, leaning against the fence, put a hand to his forehead.

"I think I may be delirious," he said.

"No, it's all right, Abdul." I placed a hand on his arm. "I don't know what's going on either, but we'd better move."

The roar of the fire grew suddenly louder. Looking back I saw that the flames had somehow leapt across the courtyard and were attacking the great hall.

"Come on, Abdul," said Wulf. "Put your foot in this."

He crouched down and held his hands out, fingers interlocked, while Oz scrambled over the fence. Abdul visibly pulled himself together and put one foot in the stirrup, while I steadied him. He clutched at the top of the fence trying to drag himself up, and Wulf strained every sinew to heave him over.

"And where do you think you are going?" came that cold voice again.

"All right, Pooka," muttered Wulf. "You've had your little joke."

"Pooka!" growled the voice. Then louder, "I might have known!" And louder still, "I should have guessed those creatures were behind this!"

Abdul collapsed on to the ground, as the real Grimwold, nostrils flaring, teeth gritted, grabbed Wulf and pinned him to the fence. He ripped the top of Wulf's shirt, then delicately lifted up the rune-stone with the tip of his sword.

No-one moved, as Grimwold's expression gradually changed to one of gloating delight.

"At last," he breathed.

CHAPTER TWENTY

BRONWEN

I dropped to the ground and eased a hand under Abdul's head.

"I am all right," he whispered. "Take care of yourself."

I looked up at Grimwold, but he seemed to have eyes for nothing but the rune-stone. The roar of the fire and shouts of the soldiers sounded muffled now, and far away. I watched as the stone swung and clicked against the metal of the sword and Grimwold's eyes followed it greedily.

"Take it then," said Wulf softly. "Why don't you take it if you want it so much?"

"All in good time, my friend," whispered Grimwold. "All in good time."

"It feels good, if you hold it in your hand," murmured Wulf. "It feels warm. Try it."

A memory of the kidnapper flashed into my mind, going mad after he'd touched the stone, backing away with an agonised expression on his face. I almost smiled. Wulf wasn't stupid.

Grimwold's free hand slowly reached toward the rune-stone. I held my breath. Was it going to work? Then abruptly he stopped. The hand hovered for a moment before he looked up into Wulf's face and burst out laughing. The spell was broken.

"What kind of a fool do you think I am?"

He moved the tip of the sword until it was against Wulf's neck.

"A nice try, little man, but I do have some knowledge of these things."

The sword pierced Wulf's skin and a tiny trickle of blood ran down over his collarbone. I saw him wince, but he didn't make a sound.

"I will hold it," said Grimwold, "when you have given it to me freely."

"You'll have to kill me first," said Wulf.

"Not first," said Grimwold, "though probably afterwards." He grinned. "I am sure you know as well as I that I cannot take it by force."

"Well, how are you gonna get it then?" asked Wulf, apparently puzzled.

But I already knew. It seemed to be my fate to be used as a hostage, to force my friends to do what they knew they shouldn't. I shifted myself so that I could cradle Abdul's head in my lap. It was useless to run. All I could do was sit, with dread in the pit of my stomach, and wait.

"Where is your other friend?" asked Grimwold almost conversationally. *On the other side of the fence*, I thought, *too scared to move.*

"Run away, has he," continued Grimwold, "and left you to your fate?"

"What other friend?" said Wulf.

At this, Grimwold threw back his head and roared with laughter.

"Well, it is of no importance," he smirked. "I am not exactly afraid that he will lead an attack against me...and the girl will do just as well. Perhaps better."

The knot in my stomach tightened. Never taking his eyes off Wulf, Grimwold reached down and grabbed my arm. Suddenly there was a thud, as he fell heavily, tripped by Abdul's foot, and then Abdul was on top of him, struggling to get the sword out of his hand. Wulf darted forward and tried to plunge his dagger into Grimwold's side, but the brute jerked upwards and the knife-thrust was turned aside by his chain mail. Then Grimwold was kneeling on Abdul's chest, Wulf was somehow on the ground, Abdul was gasping for air and I was once more in the iron grip of my enemy.

"Soon I shall call my soldiers," said Grimwold through gritted teeth. "But not yet. First I want the rune-stone. And *you*..." he dug his knee further into Abdul, who groaned and rolled his eyes. "*You* are only still alive because I have further plans for you. The gibbet is waiting. This night will see a magnificent sacrifice."

He stood up and kicked Abdul, then, holding me so tight that I felt my ribs were being crushed, he dragged me the yard or so to where Wulf was lying.

"Now, my little friend," he said to Wulf. "She is pretty, is she not?"

Wulf lay and looked helplessly up at me, but didn't say anything. I could feel Grimwold's hot breath on the top of my head and the rise and fall of his chest. Getting no answer, he kicked Wulf as well. Wulf grunted.

"Answer me, you churl!"

"Yes," muttered Wulf. "She is pretty."

Then I felt a cold edge of metal against my ear.

"But I wonder how pretty she will be if I cut off little bits of her. We won't be too drastic at first. If we start with her ear she could cover it up, and my soldiers might not mind having fun with a girl with one ear. Though they might turn up their noses at a girl who didn't have one." He laughed. "Didn't have a nose, I mean."

I felt sick, and Wulf's face started to dance in front of my eyes. *Let me just die, Lord,* I prayed. *I don't mind, just let it be quick.*

"Don't touch her!" gasped Wulf, sitting up painfully. "I'll give you the stone!"

He struggled to get the leather thong over his head. I knew I should protest, but I didn't. Someone protested for me, though.

"You leave that rune-thing be!" said a voice.

And then I knew I had passed out and was in a dream.

Over the fence leapt three, four...I gave up counting.....*creatures.* Little men with slanted eyes and snub noses, all carrying bows, with arrows at the ready. The sword point was now at my throat.

"Pooka!" spat Grimwold. "Come closer and I will kill her!"

"Oh, we don't need to come no closer," grinned one of the creatures.

Grimwold gave a cry and let me go, as an arrow thudded into his hand.

"Leave him!" cried another one, stepping forward with blazing eyes. "I claim the right! He be mine!"

"Watch out!" cried the first speaker. "He's doin' a spell!"

I looked in horror at Grimwold's moving lips. This dream, this nightmare, was no better than the waking reality of a few seconds ago. His voice grew in intensity, speaking a language I had never heard. It seemed that his mouth filled my vision, lips pulled back in a snarl, spitting the strange words out between clenched teeth. Then everything went black.

CHAPTER TWENTY-ONE

WULF

The rune-stone throbbed in my hand. I'd stopped trying to pull it over my head when the elves had arrived, and now I was crouched, still holding it, paralysed, as Grimwold growled his spell. Everyone seemed frozen in time, except for Grimwold. And then…and then…out of what depths I couldn't tell, a memory rose in my mind.

I was tiny, being held by someone…a man…and my mum was there. There was shouting, and then my mum…she held something up…she said some words and the man dropped me and fled out of the door. He *fell* out of the door. And my mum had said…

I held up the rune-stone, now almost burning the palm of my hand, and a voice…it was *my* voice…said, "By the power of Thorn, I command you to stop!"

And then everyone else came to life and Grimwold froze. And then an arrow struck Grimwold in the throat and he fell…he fell like a great tree crashing to the ground. And then one of the elves…it was Toadstool… was on top of Grimwold, hacking frenziedly at his neck with a flint axe. There was blood…blood spurting everywhere, black in the dim light, all over Toadstool. And then Toadstool was holding the head up in both hands. Its mouth gaped and its sightless eyes glared. And the other elves were cheering, but the fire was roaring so loudly that no-one would hear them, and Toadstool said, "Well, it don't bring her back, but it do make me feel a bit better."

And the stone still throbbed in my hand, and then a few more elves climbed over the fence. They were all there now, and Bron was waking up and Abdul was trying to sit up, and then Oz's head popped over the fence. Oz looked at Toadstool, holding up Grimwold's bloody head. His jaw dropped and his eyes grew as big as plates.

"Blimey!" he said. "Looks like I've missed something."

I started to laugh. *Oz, I love you*, I thought, but I didn't say it. I let go of the rune-stone and it flopped back against my chest. Then I couldn't stop laughing, but I was crying as well. The sheer, total relief of it overwhelmed me and I rolled on the ground in hysterics.

"It wasn't *that* funny," said Oz, jumping down off the fence.

Bronwen crawled over and put a hand on my shoulder. "Are you all right, Wulfstan?" she asked. I carried on laughing. "Stop it, Wulf, stop it!" she said.

I stopped and smiled stupidly at her. "You've never called me Wulf before."

Two small brown hands grabbed my shoulders and turned me round.

"I reckon you've forgot," said Pooka, "but the rest of us ain't, that there's a great big crowd o' soldiers likely to come down on us any time now."

I shook my head. "No, I'm sorry. You're right."

"What be the point of us gettin' them four horses," Pooka went on, "an' saddles an' bridles an' all, if you're gonna sit there, laughin' your silly head off, waitin' to be run through with a sword. Or worse."

I staggered to my feet. "I'm sorry," I said again. "Horses? Where are they?"

"Over the fence," said Oz, "and one of them's Noor."

"Noor! My beauty!" whispered Abdul and tried to scale the fence, but fell back down on the ground.

"Looks like you need a bit o' help," said Pooka. "Toadstool, put that thing down an' come here. Spider, Beetle, Mugwort, give him a hand over the fence."

Toadstool put the head on Grimwold's chest, stood back to admire it, thought better of it and carefully placed it between the dead sprawled legs. Apparently satisfied, he leapt over the fence with Mugwort, while Spider and Beetle each took one of Abdul's feet and heaved him over.

"Oh, be careful!" cried Bronwen.

But the elves had obviously caught Abdul, for he called out, "I am all right."

I shook my head. I'd got to pull myself together! Forget the rune-stone, forget everything, and just get out of there. The fire roared even louder. I looked back. Another part of the Great Hall was alight. The blaze was now so bright that I could clearly see countless black figures running around with useless buckets. Pooka looked back with me and chuckled.

"They won't put that out," he grinned. "That be elf-fire, that be. Come on."

He turned and leapt over the fence. Oz was helping Bronwen over and suddenly I didn't love him quite so much. That should have been *me* with my arm round her waist. Oh well, it was my own fault. I'd *got* to pull myself together! I ran at the fence and scaled it.

About twenty yards away, on the other side of the fence, was a path. Abdul was standing with his face buried in Noor's and she was whickering softly. There were three other horses, beautiful beasts, one grey and two darker, whose colour I couldn't see clearly in this light. Bron stood by one of them and looked around at all the elves.

"I thought I was dreaming," she said. "I don't know who or what you are, but you've saved Abdul and myself from a horrible death. I thank you with all my heart. If ever we meet again, perhaps I may be able to do you a favour, although nothing so great as you have shown to me."

There was a burst of laughter, and I recognized Chickweed, with her wild bush of curly hair.

"I shouldn't think there's anythin' as you could do for us!" she said mockingly.

"Watch your tongue, Chickweed!" said Pooka. "I've got a bit fond o' these humans."

"Oooh!" replied Chickweed, and turned her back.

Then it was Abdul's turn. "And may I also add that I shall be forever in your debt." He bowed, a little unsteadily.

"Yeah, thanks a lot," said Oz. "We'd better be off."

"Afore you go," said Pooka, "can I just have another look at that there rune-thing? Seems like they can be useful in a tight place."

He walked up to me and put his hand out.

"No, don't!" called one of the girls. I thought it was Dandelion. "It do hurt you!"

Pooka paused, then lifted up the rune-stone with a smile on his face. I gasped.

"You can touch it!"

"But don't it hurt, Pooka?" asked Dandelion. "It hurt me."

"Interestin'," said Pooka, "but I ain't surprised, after what Mugwort told me."

"Well, I am," I said.

Pooka nodded knowingly. "It hurt Dandelion when we was keepin' you prisoner, but now you reckons we be your friends, and the stone do know it. Ain't that right, Mugwort?"

"'Tis that," said Mugwort.

"Wow," said Oz. "It *knows* things!"

Pooka nodded. "So you best be careful who you reckon to be your friend."

While he was speaking, Mugwort had been walking among the horses, gently stroking their legs and muttering something inaudible. They snuffled softly in reply. Now he turned to us.

"This one be Chestnut, this one be Sorrel, this one be Cloud, and, o'course, you knows this beauty," he said, giving Noor an extra stroke. "Be good to them an' they'll be good to you."

Pooka looked around at all the elves. "Come on lads, and lasses too. *These* four humans might be all right, but there be too many of the other sort around."

Once again I saw that shift in the air, and then we were alone. Four humans, four horses, but no elves. And I hadn't even thanked them. Still, the others had, and that would have to do.

Abdul put a foot in the stirrup and, clinging tightly to Noor, managed to pull himself into position on the saddle. She stood patiently, seeming to adjust the way she was standing to help him. We all mounted our horses, Bronwen looking slightly nervous. I remembered her little pony, now lost, and far smaller than this magnificent creature. I took a deep breath.

"We'd better get moving," I said.

"But where to?" asked Bronwen.

There was an ear-splitting yell from the other side of the fence. The body had been found.

I gripped the reins and dug my knees into my horse's flanks.

"Anywhere away from here!"

CHAPTER TWENTY-TWO

WULF

The horses galloped along the path into the dark, leaving the glow of the burning buildings behind. What Mugwort had said to them I didn't know, but they ran steadily and safely, keeping together. When the path narrowed and entered a wood, they slowed to a canter, and then a gentle trot, arranging themselves one behind the other with no direction from us.

I found myself in front without a clue where we were heading, but feeling surprisingly calm about it. The rhythmic movement almost lulled me to sleep, and to keep myself awake I looked behind. It was nearly pitch black now we were in the forest, but I could just about see Abdul, next in line, his head resting on Noor's neck. It looked as if he'd given in to the rhythm and fallen asleep. I hoped he wouldn't fall off. I couldn't see past Abdul till the road curved, and then I glimpsed Bronwen's face staring straight ahead, and behind her Oz, who kept glancing into the forest on either side. Not that he'd be able to see much. Oz and Bronwen's pale faces showed clearly in the darkness and I could make out the shape of Oz's grey horse, Cloud. That was all.

I had no idea where we were. Heading roughly north I supposed. Even though a lot of of the trees had lost their leaves, the branches were so thickly tangled together that I could only see the odd star peeking through. The forest must have a name, but I didn't know it. *Jog, jog* went my body on the horse's back. There seemed to be a lot of forest in England. I'd never thought about it before. Never really been anywhere until the march down south to the battle. I should be nervous, surrounded on all sides by the trunks of trees behind which any danger could lurk. *Clip, clop* went my horse's hooves. But somehow I wasn't scared. And I knew why.

The rune-stone jiggled comfortingly against my skin as I rode. My mum had given it to me to protect me, and it had *worked*. It would work again. *Thank you, mum,* I whispered.

Of course, there was the uncomfortable fact that I'd had the words put into my mouth by some deeply buried memory. I'd never have known them. Would the same thing happen again? But I knew them now, didn't I? I'd just have to say the same words...What were they?

"By the power of...*something*...I command you to stop!"

I panicked. The power of what? Suddenly the darkness seemed more menacing. Mum! I'd got to remember her voice, her face as she held up the rune-stone! Then I heard it.

"By the power of *Thorn!*"

Of course! Idiot! I'd known its name for a long time, ever since Father Wiglaf taught me to read – Thorn was the only rune still used in ordinary writing. I remembered when I learned it in school. I'd thought it looked like one of my mum's runes and it had struck me as funny that a priest of the church was teaching me something from the old religion. How could I forget that? But I *had* almost forgotten it. In the chill of the night I found that I was sweating.

Without warning, all four horses slowed to a halt.

"Why have we stopped?" came Oz's voice from behind.

"I don't know," I said. "Nothing to do with me."

I pressed his knees into Chestnut's flanks.

"Come on boy," I urged. "Let's get a move on."

The horse didn't budge.

"What is it, Noor?" I heard Abdul murmuring.

Then, just as suddenly as he had stopped, Chestnut veered to the right and started to walk into the trees.

"Whoa!" I called. "Stick to the path, boy!"

The horse took no notice, but carried on calmly walking into the forest, followed by the other three. I pulled at the reins and cried, "Stop! What are you doing?" but Chestnut just shook his head, making me loosen my grip, and walked on.

But only a few more paces. Then he stopped abruptly, whinnied to the others, who snorted and whickered in reply, and waited.

"What's going on?" said Oz.

"It's a clearing," said Bronwen. "They've brought us to a clearing, to have a rest."

She was right. We were in a small dell surrounded by trees. No-one would be able to see us from the path.

Abdul laughed. "I always said some horses had more sense than humans."

"Especially horses that have had a bit of help from elves," said Oz. "Did you see old Mugwort, going round stroking them and muttering to them? I wonder what he said."

I felt a bit uneasy about this. I wasn't an experienced rider, but it still felt wrong for the horse to be the one making the decisions. I dismounted to have a look, or rather a feel, round the clearing. Chestnut immediately rubbed me with his long nose, and snuffled gently into my ear. I smiled.

"All right, boy," I murmured. "I trust you."

And I was dog tired, weary to my bones. It would be such a relief to lie down and go to sleep. The others were dismounting now, and I heard a few yawns.

"It's cold," said Bronwen. "Could we light a fire?"

"That'd take forever," said Oz.

"And it might not be safe," I added. "The great thing about this place is that no-one can see us."

"But I'm freezing," said Bronwen. "Surely a very little fire would be safe? I don't mind trying to light it."

"It's too much bother," said Oz. "Forget it."

"And there is no need," came Abdul's voice, "with a big, warm creature beside you. Just lie as close as you can to your horse. It will help, as well, if we lie in a circle with the horses on the outside."

Why hadn't I thought of that? Abdul's long experience as a horseman was showing.

"Yeah, but how d'you get your horse to lie down?" said Oz.

"*Do* they lie down?" asked Bronwen. "I thought they slept standing up…usually…don't they?"

"They can do either," said Abdul, and, as if to demonstrate, Noor folded her legs underneath her and laid her head on the ground, while Abdul slowly tried to position himself next to her. Suddenly he gasped and jerked his head back.

"Oh, you're hurt!" cried Bronwen, rushing to his side. "We were forgetting."

"No, it is all right," he muttered. "I will be fine. I just need to rest. Thank you, just go to sleep."

Oz looked at his horse.

"Right then," he said. "Lie down."

The horse stood there. Despite my tiredness, I couldn't help grinning.

"Ask him nicely," said Bronwen. "Use his name."

Oz sighed. "This is stupid. It's only a horse."

"Oh, you're hopeless," tutted Bronwen. She stroked the nose of her mare and murmured, "Lie down now, Sorrel. Let's go to sleep."

Sorrel placidly bent her legs and arranged herself on her side, while Bronwen snuggled into her.

That looks easy, I thought, and stroked my horse just like Bronwen.

"Come on, Chestnut," I said in an encouraging voice. "Good boy. Let's get some sleep."

And Chestnut joined the other two on the ground.

"Right," said Oz. "Trust me to get the awkward one."

The horse pushed him, none too gently, with his nose.

"All right, all right, I'm sorry," said Oz hurriedly. "Let's be friends and get a bit of sleep, eh?" Nothing happened. "Oh, come on…er…what's your name?"

"Cloud. His name's Cloud," said Bronwen sleepily.

"Right, come on, Cloud," said Oz, patting the horse's flank. "How about having a lie down…? Please?"

At last Cloud buckled his front legs, then the back ones, and arranged himself on the cold, damp ground. Within a minute I could hear Oz's gentle snoring, mixed with the whiffling of several horses.

But sleep refused to come. I waited and waited, but still I was awake. The ground was very hard, and cold seemed to rise from it and creep into my bones. The others were all asleep and I was so tired. What was the matter with me? Even with my cloak over me and a horse's warm body next to me, I couldn't get comfortable. The cloak was thin and worn – it'd be no good for winter weather. We'd have to get some warmer clothes, and some decent weapons too. Abdul must have lost his. That beautiful bow, that took a year to make. What a shame. Still, we were lucky to be alive. The horse shifted in its sleep and made a little snuffly sound. Perhaps it was dreaming. What did horses dream about? Fields of lush green grass? Food. We'd need some food tomorrow, and it would have to be Oz and me, hunting with our little knives. Yes, we definitely needed some good weapons. At least we had horses now. You could travel a lot faster on horseback. But where were we going? And why couldn't I get to sleep?

I stared into the darkness and gradually felt myself drifting off. There was one star peeking down between the branches. And another one over there. My eyelids drooped. But that one was too low to be a star…And it was moving.

I sat up, wide awake. There was a gleam of light in the distance, bobbing about. And it wasn't on the path we'd left, but in the other direction, deep in the forest. I stared at it. It seemed to be getting bigger. It was coming towards us!

I crawled over and shook Oz.

"Wha…what," mumbled Oz.

"Sh!" I hissed. "Don't wake the others!"

But it was too late. The others were awake.

"What is it?" whispered Abdul.

"I think we've got a visitor," I whispered back.

The other three followed my gaze to the light bobbing and weaving in the distance, sometimes disappearing, but always reappearing, and definitely coming towards us.

"That's not human," gasped Oz. "It's a ghost light!"

We all sat motionless, as the ghost light flickered and wavered and danced its way toward us.

CHAPTER TWENTY-THREE

WULF

I slipped my dagger out of its sheath, and saw Oz do the same. It was pointless to try and run. By the time we'd got ourselves up on our horses, the light would have reached us. Besides, it could be a friend, though I didn't feel inclined to trust anyone after what we'd been through.

As if she was aware of my thoughts, Bronwen spoke. "It's all right," she said in a dreamy voice. "It's not an enemy."

"How d'you know that?" hissed Oz.

"I just know it," said Bronwen simply. "I just have a really strong feeling."

"Yeah," replied Oz. "Like that really strong feeling you had that Abdul was some evil monster."

"Oh, you're never going to let me forget that, are you?" snapped Bronwen.

"Be quiet, you two!" I said in a low voice, just about controlling my temper. "This is not the time!"

The glimmer of light was bigger now, more of a glow, still swaying around.

"We must just wait quietly," murmured Abdul. "Be alert, and do not do or say anything stupid."

"Amen to that," I muttered.

By this time the light had grown, from the original pinprick that I'd thought was a star, to what was obviously a lantern. I strained to see who was holding it, but it vanished behind a tree. Then it reappeared and came towards us, quite high up, then bobbing down to avoid branches. I held my breath. Was the lantern-holder a giant? No, now we could all see that the lamp was dangling from a tall staff. And holding the staff was an old, old man. He stepped into the dell and looked around at us all.

If anyone could be described as ancient, it was the figure standing before us. His wispy hair and untidy beard were long and white, and in this chilly night he had no cloak on, just a ragged tunic and sandals.

"Greetings, father," said Abdul. "Can we help you?"

The old man smiled and looked at Abdul through narrowed eyes.

"Assalamu alaikum," he said, bowing his head slightly.

Abdul's eyes widened in surprise. Then he too bowed his head.

"Wa alaikum assalaam," he replied.

"Thank you," wheezed the old man, "but, no, you cannot help me. I was under the impression, rather, that I might be able to help you."

"I am not sure how," said Abdul.

"Do you not need food and rest?" asked the man. "Is not one of you injured?"

"How did you know that?" gasped Oz.

"God tells me these things sometimes," croaked the old man. "I have learned to listen."

"I told you!" said Bronwen triumphantly.

The man stepped over to her. She was kneeling, and he hardly had to bend his head to look into her face. He said nothing for a while, just studied Bronwen, who looked steadily back.

"I think God talks to you sometimes, as well," he said at last.

"Not with words," said Bronwen.

"There are many ways of speaking," said the old man. "But come. Bring your horses and follow me."

"Hold on, hold on, wait a minute!" I said. This was all moving too quickly for my liking. "Where are we going? I don't want to be rude, but we don't know your name, or anything about you."

"Oh, how can you not trust him?" asked Bronwen indignantly.

"No, he is wise," said the old man. "My name is Walter and, as you can see, I am not capable of harming you." He looked intently at me, in the same way that he had looked at Bronwen. Then he smiled. "You have a lot of worries on your mind for one so young. You fear that I may be leading you into a trap, but I promise you, that is not so."

A trap – that was exactly what I'd been worrying about. This old man seemed to be a mind-reader. Unless…suppose it really was a trap and he was saying that to give us a false sense of security? A sort of double bluff. I realised that the other three were all looking at me, waiting for a sign about what they should do. Oz looked as if he was glad it wasn't him who had to make a decision, while Bronwen's face was glowing with hope. But I was so tired! Why were they all depending on me? Then Abdul shifted his position and a spasm of pain crossed his face. For a moment, I thought I knew what to do. Why shouldn't we trust the old man? He was probably some sort of hermit with a few extra powers, like Bron's…But suppose he *had* been sent by enemies? There was no certainty anywhere. I closed my eyes in despair. I wasn't cut out to be a leader, and I wasn't the oldest or most experienced person there. I opened my eyes.

"What do you think, Abdul?" I mumbled.

"I have little faith in my own judgment at the moment," replied Abdul, "after leading Bronwen into such danger." He paused. "But, nevertheless, if you ask my opinion, I think we should go with this venerable old man."

"But of course!" declared Bronwen. "What are we waiting for?" She got up and patted her horse's neck. "Come on, Sorrel. Time for another walk."

Oz looked at me and raised his eyebrows. Noor and Chestnut followed Sorrel's lead and got themselves into a standing position. Cloud, however, remained on the ground.

"I don't *believe* this!" said Oz through gritted teeth. "I really have got the awkward one!"

I started to laugh, but forced myself to stop. I knew I could become hysterical again in the blink of an eye.

The old man, Walter, padded over to Cloud. "Come, my fine warrior," he said to the horse. "You have seen some fighting in your day, no doubt. Be a good soldier and obey your master."

He looked at Oz, who muttered, "Come on then, Cloud, up you get," and Cloud got up.

"You have to treat your horse like a friend," said Bronwen smugly, "but let him know who's in charge at the same time."

Oz took the reins with a disgruntled expression on his face. "He knows who's in charge," he said. "It's *him*."

Walter led us slowly and carefully through the trees, away from the road and deeper into the forest. I stayed behind Abdul, who was leaning on Noor rather than leading her. We walked for what seemed like an age, and all the while my nerves were on edge. There wasn't much to see as the only light came from the lantern, but my other senses seemed sharper than usual. Every rustle, every night cry of the creatures of the forest set me turning my head this way and that, to see if it spelt danger. There was a damp woody smell everywhere, mixed with the comforting horsy scent of Chestnut, then the sudden whiff of fox. All these creatures belonged in the night-time. They were at home in the dark of the forest, but I wasn't. I didn't feel I had a home anywhere now. And what was waiting for us at the end of this journey?

All at once, Walter stopped and held his lantern up even higher.

"Welcome to my home," he said, and I peered ahead expecting, even hoping, to see a simple hermit's hut. And there *were* wooden walls with a thatched roof. But as Walter walked along to the door, the lantern gradually revealed, not a hut, but a long, long building, as big as a great hall in a middle-sized village. I stiffened. No! This was wrong! Who was waiting for us in there? Walter reached the door and opened it. He turned to face us all and bowed slightly.

"Please come inside," he said.

CHAPTER TWENTY-FOUR

WULF

"Our horses?" said Oz.

"Of course, how stupid of me," smiled Walter. "You can tether them round here. I think there is still some hay left, but we shall give them more in the morning."

He led us round the back of the building where, to my surprise, there was a simple shelter, just three walls and a roof, with a feeding trough and a wooden bar to which we loosely tied the horses' reins. It was all very convenient.

"The latrine is there," said Walter, pointing to an area behind the stall.

"I need that in a minute," muttered Oz.

"I imagine you all do. Why not now?" smiled Walter, who was evidently not deaf, despite his great age.

I looked at the others. Abdul nodded slightly, while Bronwen shook her head stiffly. I hoped she'd be able to get out there later, on her own. After we'd relieved ourselves Walter ushered us into the building, his shoulders suddenly racked by a spasm of coughing.

"Is that you, Brother Walter?" came a voice from inside.

I froze in the act of stepping over the threshold.

"It is, it is," coughed Walter.

"I'll wager you went without your cloak again!" continued the voice.

Walter laughed, between fits of coughing.

"You are like an old nurse, Brother Edmund," wheezed Walter. "It is I who should be caring for you, not the other way round."

Then he looked at me and indicated with his arm that I should go in. I realized that I was stupidly standing with one foot in the air, and also that I was keeping the others waiting behind me. Carefully, I put my foot down and moved into the hall, or whatever it was. The conversation didn't sound too menacing, but I just didn't know what was going on.

At first I couldn't see a thing. Then the others moved in after me, last of all Walter with his lantern, which he removed from its staff and held in his hand. At intervals along the walls were straw pallets, with covers thick enough to keep out any draught, and on the end one was the person who had spoken. He sat up.

"Found your waifs and strays I see, Brother," he said, looking at us curiously.

I stared back. The man was middle aged, short-haired and clean-shaven. His face was not the only part of his head that had seen a razor, because the lamplight shone on the bald patch in the middle of his tonsure. A monk.

"Indeed," answered Walter, whose cough had quietened down. He turned to us. "Please choose a bed and make yourselves comfortable. And you, my dear," this was to Bronwen, "would you like to sleep down the other end?"

"A girl!" exclaimed Brother Edmund.

"She stays with us!" I said, putting my hand on my dagger, then taking it off again and hoping no-one had noticed. Although it wouldn't hurt if they saw I meant business.

"I believe I was asking the young lady," said Walter mildly.

"Oh," said Bronwen. "Um…thank you, but we've sort of got used to all sleeping together…for safety, you know."

"As you wish," said Walter, "but no-one will harm you here."

"This is most irregular!" spluttered Brother Edmund. "If the abbot learns I have been sleeping in the same chamber as a woman!"

Bronwen drew herself up to her full height.

"I'm not infectious, you know," she said haughtily.

"Hush, child," said Walter gently. "Brother Edmund *was* infectious, but is so no longer, or I should not have brought you here. Do not fret yourself, Brother," he went on in the same mild tone. "Our guests shall sleep at the other end and I will contrive some kind of partition to safeguard your honour. You shall return to the abbey with your reputation untarnished."

Oz snorted and was obviously having difficulty keeping a straight face. Walter led us down the other end of the hall with a little smile on his lips. As well as the straw pallets there was a table, and the old man started to try to shift it sideways.

"Will you help me?" he asked us and me and Oz each grabbed one end. It was heavy, but we managed to drag it round.

"Thank you," puffed Walter. "I am not as strong as I was. Now, see, if I put these bedcovers over it, you cannot see underneath. There, Brother Edmund, you have a wall between you and the maid! And this space at the end is the doorway for our guests to go in and out."

Me and Oz grinned at him. My fears were melting away. Walter was just so likeable. But Brother Edmund was not so easily satisfied. He got out of bed and stood at the table, glaring.

"But I can see *over* the table!" he declared. "This is no wall!"

"Oh, tush, Brother Edmund," said Walter wearily. "Go back to bed. You will see nothing when you are lying down. Imagine this upper space to be a great window in the wall, as in the abbey, but sideways on. You will see nothing through it, I promise you."

Brother Edmund harrumphed, glared at us all one more time, and went back to his pallet.

"We are indebted to you for your trouble," came Abdul's voice from behind. "I still am not sure how you found us, but we can talk in the morning."

"Indeed we can," said Walter, "and in the morning I shall examine your injuries. Now sleep, all of you. I wish you a good night, watched over by our Lord."

He turned and left via the 'door' space between the table and the wall, and we all eased ourselves down on to the pallets and underneath the woollen covers. Soon the lamp was put out and we were wrapped in a darkness which somehow managed to be comforting instead of threatening.

I couldn't quite believe I was lying on a thick mattress under a blanket which was actually keeping me warm. I could smell the straw through the sacking, just like at home. Perhaps our luck really had changed. I yawned. So many questions. We were safe for now, but what next? Grimwold was dead, but other people were still looking for us, desperate to get their hands on my rune-stone. And now I knew why. It did seem to be a thing of great power. But where should we go? We couldn't stay here for long.

And then my mind drifted back to the long buried memory that had saved all our lives. Who *was* that person? The man who'd been holding me when my mum had said those words...those words...I jolted awake again. What were they?..."By the power of *Thorn* I command you to stop!" It was all right, I remembered them...Mustn't forget them...It was important. I drifted off. But who *was* that man? That was important too...I thought I knew him. He was somehow familiar...He'd been going to take me away, but my mum had stopped him...Must try and remember...I was finally asleep.

CHAPTER TWENTY-FIVE

WULF

I woke up to the homely smell of bread baking and couldn't think where I was. I knew I wasn't at home, but the last few days had been so confusing that everything was jumbled up in my mind. I was warm, though, under my woollen cover, and I felt safe. I half opened my eyes and saw Oz, still dead to the world. By the opposite wall, Abdul was smiling at me. But no Bronwen. I sat up in panic. Bronwen's bed cover was neatly pulled back. I stared at it.

"Do not worry," said Abdul. "She has not been abducted. She got up some time ago to help our host. I would have joined her, but I have been ordered to stay in bed."

"Need the latrine," I mumbled and pushed my cover off, not nearly so neatly as Bronwen's.

Stumbling past the table that formed the make-believe wall of our bedchamber, I noted that Brother Edmund was also up and about. Outside, in the weak late autumn sunshine, I found them. Squatting on the ground with her sleeves rolled up, Bronwen had her hands deep in a bowl of dough, while Brother Edmund was helping Walter shift an upside-down cooking pot. They'd cleared away the surrounding charcoal and were now, with cloths thickly wound round their hands, carefully lifting the pot itself. It was from under this old lump of iron that the heavenly smells of baking bread were wafting.

"Ah, I shall miss your help, Brother Edmund," said Walter, as he took a steaming round loaf out of the makeshift oven.

"But the abbot sends you supplies, does he not?" asked Brother Edmund, putting the pot back to keep the heat in.

"Oh, yes, Brother. I want for nothing," said Walter. "But I cannot manage this heavy pot now on my own, and there is nothing so good as fresh-baked bread."

"Ah," nodded Brother Edmund. "I wonder if we cannot build an oven easier for you to use."

"Good morning, Wulfstan," came Bronwen's clear voice. "You've finally decided to grace us with you presence, then."

"Er, yeah, good morning everybody," I muttered, and hurried on round to the latrine at the back. It was really just a smelly pit, and I thought about Bronwen as I stood over it. I couldn't imagine that a girl would be happy to use this. She probably went further off, into the trees. But was that safe? I frowned. As soon as you woke up there was another problem to think about.

When I got back, Bronwen was moulding the dough into another flat round loaf on a wooden board, and Brother Edmund was stoking up the fire. I found Walter inside, examining Abdul, with Oz stretching and yawning in his bed.

"Come on, lazybones," I said, as if I'd been up for hours. I pulled Oz's cover off. "I think they can do without us around here."

Walter smiled. "I shall not be long, and then we can all break our fast."

True to his word, Walter soon hobbled out with Abdul's arm round his shoulder, though who was supporting who it was hard to say.

"What a beautiful morning," said Walter, beaming round at them. "We may not have another like this. Winter is long enough, when we eat in the dark indoors. Shall we break our fast out here?"

The sun was gathering strength and there was a general murmur of agreement.

"Good," nodded Walter. "May I ask our two strong young lads to bring out the table?"

Oz's jaw dropped, and I knew why. We'd just about managed to shift the heavy oak table round last night. Carrying it out here would be beyond us.

Walter laughed. "There is a small one inside the door. We do not need to disturb our bedchamber wall." He glanced mischievously at Brother Edmund. "Oh, and we shall need two benches as well."

By the time the benches were outside, the table was set. There were six trenchers of stale coarse bread with a knife on each, six cups, two jugs and two little pots, all of earthenware, and the new loaf.

"Do you boys want to wash before you eat?" asked Abdul.

Oz looked at him in disbelief, and I examined my grubby hands. "It's all right," I muttered. "I'm clean enough."

Abdul rolled his eyes and shook his head.

"Please sit down," said Walter, "and I shall ask Brother Edmund to bless our food."

Brother Edmund stood and looked round at us importantly, as if to make sure we were paying attention. Then he put his hands together, closed his eyes and chanted a prayer in Latin. I was ravenous by this time and thought he'd never stop. I half opened my eyes to look at Oz, who wasn't even pretending to pray, but was just staring at the crusty loaf. When the prayer was finally ended, Walter said, "Thank you Brother Edmund, and thank you Lord for this good food. May it give us strength to do your will." Which I thought was all that needed to be said in the first place.

Then Walter broke off pieces of the loaf – it was large enough for six, with plenty over – and gave one to each of us. Oz took an enormous bite out of his, broke the rest in two and reached out to dunk half in one of the pots. I had a feeling that wasn't what you were supposed to do. Each pot had a spoon by it, and then there were the knives. I was just as starving as Oz, but I held back.

"May I suggest, Osric," said Walter mildly, "that you try the curd cheese first, like so," and he put a spoonful of soft cheese on his trencher, then used his knife to spread a little on his bread. "Then, when you have tired of the cheese, you can try some honey butter."

"Er, thanks," said Oz, looking slightly pink.

As I gratefully took my turn with the curd cheese, I noticed Bronwen smiling at me in a kindly, but knowing way. I sometimes felt she knew everything that was going through my mind. And of course, she'd know all about what to do with knives and spoons. She'd seen Lady Rhiannon dining often enough, even if she didn't sit at table herself. But at the first bite of the warm bread and the slightly melting cheese, I forgot about everything else. It was truly delicious. There wasn't much conversation for a while, as everyone was too busy eating.

Then Walter started to pour a dark red liquid into each cup, topping it up with water. Wine? At breakfast? Where was the ale? I hardly ever drank wine. It was for very special occasions. Surely Walter didn't drink it every morning? Abdul put up a hand to refuse the red liquid, but Walter poured it anyway.

"In honour of our friend from Cordoba, who does not touch strong drink," said Walter.

Abdul looked puzzled, then his face cleared. "It is the juice of some berry," he said with a broad smile.

"Indeed, indeed," laughed Walter. "I had some mulberries, which I had pulped, ready to ferment into wine. But now we may drink it unfermented, with a little water from our stream, and everyone is happy."

He clapped his hands together, obviously pleased with himself, and I grinned at him.

But Brother Edmund looked at Abdul disapprovingly.

"Our Lord turned water into wine at the wedding in Cana," he sniffed, "so I fail to see why our guest should object to drinking it."

"Hush, now, Brother Edmund," said Walter, before Abdul could say anything. "Let us remember the laws of hospitality. There are none more hospitable than the people of Andalusia, as I remember from years ago, when I myself was in Cordoba."

Abdul's face was a picture of astonishment. "You have been in Cordoba?" he gasped. Then, as Walter nodded happily, Abdul went on, "But of course. I should have realized by the way you greeted me. You have studied medicine in Andalusia, have you not?"

Walter continued to nod and beam around at them all.

"I knew there was something in the way you examined me," said Abdul. "You knew what you were doing, more than…I do not mean to be rude, but more than some doctors I have observed in this country."

"Ah, we have much to learn from you people," said Walter. "I have never been in such a place as Cordoba."

By this time, Brother Edmund's eyes were practically popping out of his head. I found it hard not to laugh as I watched him struggling to obey the laws of hospitality.

"You young people would not believe it," said Walter. "The streets are paved and lit at night, so you may go about without fear. And I have been in houses where they have running water."

"Running water?" said Oz. "What, like a river running through your house?"

"No, a fountain," laughed Abdul. "We have a small fountain in my house at home. And public baths everywhere. It is so difficult to keep clean in this country."

"And the great mosque," sighed Walter. "So beautiful, with its endless red and white columns."

"What is a mosque?" asked Bronwen, whose eyes were shining in wonder.

"It is where we worship God," explained Abdul. "A sort of church, if you like."

Brother Edmund couldn't contain himself any longer. "Then if we are so inferior," he blurted out, "I suggest that you return to Andalusia and worship your heathen god in your heathen temple."

There was an awkward silence, before Walter said softly, "I believe you are still not quite well, Brother Edmund, or you would not have spoken to our guest in that way."

Brother Edmund looked at the table. "I apologize," he muttered. "Perhaps I had better go and lie down."

"No," said Abdul. "It is our fault. It is something I always try not to do, to make unfavourable comparisons. But it is so good to talk to someone who has visited my city."

Brother Edmund nodded sheepishly.

"And indeed," Abdul went on. "I do plan to return soon. But I would like to tell you, Brother Edmund, that we worship the same God, you and I."

"But you do not know the saving power of Christ," said Brother Edmund.

"The saving power of Jesus, peace be upon him," said Abdul, "is God. My God and your God."

"And when do you plan to return?" said Walter quickly, with the definite air of someone trying to change the subject.

"As soon as I have helped these children solve their mystery," said Abdul.

"Mystery?" said Walter.

"Yes," said Abdul. "It is a real mystery. Wulfstan has something, an ancient stone, which seems to be very powerful, and which a number of people, not very nice people, are trying to take from him. We need to find out exactly what they want with it, and what we should best do with it. Show them, Wulfstan."

Everyone looked at me, and a bit reluctantly I drew the rune-stone out from under my shirt. The effect was instant. Walter drew back, startled, but Brother Edmund gave a loud cry, turned white and fell off the bench, where he lay sprawled, moaning and gabbling in Latin.

CHAPTER TWENTY-SIX

WULF

Walter rushed to Brother Edmund's side and tried to hush him, but the monk would not be hushed.

"Quickly!" said Walter. "Fetch something to drink!"

I looked around wildly and grabbed the jug of water on the table. I handed it to Walter, who poured a bit into Brother Edmund's mouth and splashed some on his face. The monk blinked and coughed and Walter helped him to sit up, but as soon as he got his breath back he started to gabble again, though at least this time it was in English.

"Lord protect us!" gasped Brother Edmund. "It is evil! It is evil! Lord keep the plague away from us! Drive the devils away! Lord protect us!" all the time crossing himself.

"Calm down, Brother Edmund, calm down," said Walter in a soothing voice. Then to me, "Put it away!"

I slipped the rune-stone back inside my shirt and, because the shirt was ripped, I stood holding the torn pieces together. Brother Edmund's breathing gradually became more even, though he was still muttering under his breath.

"Now sit yourself on the bench and take a drink," said Walter. "I think ale would do you more good than juice. Osric, there is a flagon of ale inside, if you would be so kind."

Oz leapt to his feet and I went with him. We searched around and soon found the ale.

"What d'you reckon that was all about?" I whispered.

"He's nuts," said Oz. "He's one of those churchmen who sees the devil in everything. A bit like our priest at home, old Wiglaf."

"I dunno," I said. "I think there's more to it than that. Wiglaf doesn't throw fits and fall on the ground. I thought he was going to peg out on us."

"No," said Oz thoughtfully. "I suppose he doesn't. But the way he looks at your mum sometimes...he really hates her."

The light became even dimmer as a figure darkened the doorway.

"Are you *brewing* the ale," said Bronwen, "or are you just too dozy to find it?"

"Nope, got it," said Oz. "If your ladyship would care to get out the way, I'll take it out to them."

I gave Bronwen a half-smile and followed Oz. I wished those two would stop bickering.

"Ah, thank you, Osric," said Walter. He poured the juice from Brother Edmund's cup into his own and replaced it with ale. Then he waved a hand over the table. "We may as well continue eating while our brother recovers himself."

Me and Oz didn't need to be told twice. We each reached over to break off another piece of bread, and as I did so my arm brushed against Brother Edmund's shoulder.

"No, no!" he shrieked. "Keep away from me!"

I jumped back. I was beginning to feel like a leper.

"Perhaps you could sit on the other side of the table," said Walter gently. "He means no harm, but he is not quite himself. Now calm down, Brother Edmund. I am just going to ask Wulfstan if I may have a proper look at his stone, but I do not want you to get agitated."

He hobbled round and reached out a bony hand. "May I?"

"All right," I said, "but be careful. It might hurt you."

The rune-stone was tingling against my skin. Walter looked nervous but didn't flinch as he lifted it closer to his rheumy eyes.

"No, put it down, Brother!" gasped Brother Edmund, flapping his hands. "It is evil!"

Walter said nothing at first, just weighed the stone in the palm of his hand, turning it over to examine both sides. Brother Edmund's breathing grew more rapid, and Abdul put a hand on his arm to comfort him.

136

"It is not evil," said Walter at last, "but it is a thing of great power. I think it could be used for either good or ill."

"But those men," sobbed Brother Edmund. "Those men were evil!"

"Exactly!" said Walter, letting go of the rune-stone. "The men were evil, so they made evil use of the stone."

"Hang on!" I said. "What men? What stone?"

Walter ignored me and continued talking to Brother Edmund.

"I need you to look at this, Brother, but look at it calmly. Tell me if it is the same type of stone that the men were carrying."

"Yes, yes! I can see that it is!" Brother Edmund put his head in his hands. "I do not have to look at it any more closely."

By now, Abdul, Bronwen, Oz and me were all leaning forward, agog for some kind of explanation. Walter took my arm and guided me back round the table to stand in front of Brother Edmund.

"Look at it, Brother!" he said firmly. "Is it the same?"

Walter grasped the stone, again without flinching, and held it in front of Brother Edmund's face. The monk peered between his fingers.

"It is the same! It is the same!" he moaned. "Except...the shape carved on it may be different. I cannot remember that. But the general appearance is exactly the same. Now take it away!"

Walter nodded. "Sit down again, Wulfstan, and finish your meal," he said kindly.

"Would somebody like to tell us what's going on?" said Oz. "If it's not too much trouble."

"There is no need to be rude, Osric," said Abdul, "but we would be very grateful for an explanation."

Walter lifted Brother Edmund's cup and made him drink some of the ale.

"A few weeks ago," the old man began, "our abbey had two visitors, late in the evening. It was Brother Edmund's turn to be gate-keeper. The men wanted to see the abbot immediately, but Brother Edmund said he would be at prayer. Am I telling it right, Brother? Would you like to tell it yourself?"

Brother Edmund slowly nodded his head. "Yes…I think I could do that." He took another sip of ale. "I offered them the hospitality of the abbey, but they insisted I take a message to the abbot. They said they believed we had something their lord needed and that it was in the casket containing the bones of our blessed St Winfrith."

I had to hide a smile at that – I had a fleeting vision of our old cow Winfrith, at home, and the cow's bones, horns and all, on the high altar.

"I told them that on no account could I disturb the abbot and that it must wait till morning, but one of them put his hand on his sword in a very threatening way." Brother Edmund shuddered and took another sip. "The other man held up a stone, just like the one…the one the boy has. He said…he said that another such stone was in St Winfrith's casket. I said that was impossible, but the first man started to draw his sword. So of course, I went to the abbot." Brother Edmund looked around at them helplessly. "I am a monk, not a warrior," he said.

"Of course," said Abdul and patted his shoulder.

"No-one would expect you to resist two armed men," nodded Walter.

Brother Edmund looked at them both gratefully and continued his tale.

"As I expected, Abbot Deorlaf said that he would see them in the morning, but on no account would he allow the bones of our blessed saint to be disturbed." He paused again and shook his head. "I am not a brave man," he murmured, and for the first time I found myself liking him. "I was afraid to return with this message, and would have been even more afraid if I had known what was to happen, but I prayed to our Lord to protect me and went back to the men.

"They were very angry at the message and one of them held up the stone and cried out something in some heathen tongue. I fell down, and remember no more except dark dreams, until I woke one day and found Brother Walter tending me in this place."

Walter nodded. "Our abbot quickly realised that he should not have sent Brother Edmund on his own. He roused another brother and they arrived just after Brother Edmund had been cursed. The two men forced Abbot Deorlaf to lead them to the holy remains. They threatened to kill the other young monk, and he had no choice but to show them. They smashed the casket and scattered our beloved saint's bones, but they obviously found what they were looking for. Apparently they held something aloft – a small stone like this one – with a cry of triumph, and then they fled the abbey."

"So there are at least two more of these things," said Bronwen.

"There are," said Walter, "and they are dangerous. Brother Edmund was brought here with a high fever. We feared he was infectious, but no-one else has caught this illness. Fortunately, because I do not think I could have nursed a whole abbeyful. I feared for his life, and it was only with constant care that he has pulled through."

I'd been clutching my rune-stone all the way through the story, and now I gripped it so tightly that my nails dug into my palm. What was this thing my mum had given me? I looked around at them all, hoping for an answer in somebody's face, but when I came to Abdul I stopped. He'd gone pale and was looking horror-struck.

"But this is exactly what happened to my friend Godwin," he gasped. "It is exactly the same! He would not co-operate and they cursed him. He became very ill, but he was lucid enough to talk to me. He sent me to warn the wise-woman Ertha on Lord Aelfric's estate. They had mentioned her name and Godwin wanted me to warn her. When I found her she said she had given the stone to her son, Wulfstan, and this is how I came to be with him. But I must get back to Godwin! He could be dying!"

"Where does your friend live?" asked Walter.

"At Wendham, near Hereford," said Abdul. "And I had decided we should go there next, asking for his help. We need weapons and warm clothes for the winter. And advice. He is a wise and a good man. But now I must return immediately, to see if he is all right."

"Godwin of Wendham," said Walter softly. "A good man, indeed. and a generous giver to the church. Our abbot knows him. Or...I am afraid I should say, *knew* him."

"Knew him?" repeated Abdul, though it was obvious from his face that he knew what Walter was going to say.

"I fear you will receive little help from him now," said Walter sadly. "Your friend is dead."

"As you all will be, if you do not give me the rune-stone," said a voice from the trees.

CHAPTER TWENTY-SEVEN

WULF

I froze for a second, then grabbed my rune-stone. But who was it? I heard a moan from Brother Edmund, as out of the forest stepped two mail-clad figures. One of them, a tall, golden bearded man, took his helmet off and smiled round at us all. The morning sun, which had glinted on his polished helmet, was now shining on his shoulder-length fair hair.

And I knew him. This was the man who had watched from the shadows, as Guthrum had been given the letter and the purse full of money.

"A merry gathering of heroes!" he mocked. His smile vanished. "You sit here, feasting, while my lord lies headless, awaiting the funeral rites. Though doubtless his soul is also feasting, in Woden's hall."

Grimwold's men! We'd been tracked here, and how many were behind these two? My stomach turned to water. What would happen if I said the words now? *I command you to stop*, the spell said, but the man wasn't actually doing anything yet. I didn't want to waste my only powerful weapon, but I didn't want to miss my chance. Oz was giving me agonized looks, obviously willing me to use the stone.

"Your lord would still be alive if he had not planned murder," said Abdul coldly.

"I scarcely call it murder," said the golden-haired man, his mocking tone back again. "More like the slaughter of two pigs."

Bronwen gasped and jumped up, but was shoved back down again by Oz.

The golden-haired man started to walk up and down, slowly and deliberately.

"Hm…" he said, as if weighing up his options. "What shall we do with them, Leofric? Who shall live and who shall die?"

The other man's mouth twisted into a smirk. It was the only part of his face visible behind the noseguard of his helmet.

"And how shall they die, Leofric? We must think of something amusing."

With an almighty thud, Brother Edmund fell backwards off the bench for the second time that morning, this time in a dead faint. Walter leapt up to look after him, but was knocked flying by Leofric, who'd moved amazingly quickly for a big man.

"Leave him!" he grunted, then went and stood once again behind his captain – it was clear that the golden-haired man was in charge.

It had happened so fast that I didn't have time to think. Maybe I should just act now? I might not have the time when I really needed to. Walter was staggering to his feet and Bronwen looked as if she was about to explode.

"You brute!" she burst out. "He's only an old man. I suppose you think you're brave!"

Both men roared with laughter.

"You can have her, if you like," chuckled the golden-haired man to Leofric, "in a little while." He drew his sword and stared round at us all.

I clutched the rune-stone. Now! Now was the time! What was the matter with me?

"Leave us, we beseech you," came Walter's feeble voice. "You have desecrated our abbey, and the bones of our beloved saint. Is that not enough? Leave us in peace!"

"Your wits are wandering, old man," said the golden-haired man contemptuously. "I know nothing of your abbey, or your precious saint. I am Arnulf, formerly in the service of Lord Grimwold. I believe that one of you boys possesses a rune-stone, and I believe it is *you*," pointing the sword at me, "by the way you are hanging on to something round your neck."

Oh, stupid, stupid, I thought, to make it so obvious. Just say the words! Brother Edmund moaned, and Walter gave up the struggle to get to his feet.

"I have no quarrel with you boys," said Arnulf in a more friendly tone. "I can see that you are Englishmen, though you keep strange company. A Moor, a Welsh trollop and two churchmen." He glared at the brothers, one flat on his back and one crouched on the ground, and spat in their direction. "The church has ruined this country, but some of us still worship the old gods, even after all these years. Perhaps you follow the true gods?" He looked enquiringly at me. "I believe your mother does, and that she gave you the stone."

My mouth was dry. How did he know so much about me?

Arnulf rested the tip of his sword against the table, and the morning sun, rising above the treetops, flashed on the blade. He stood there, shifting the blade slightly from side to side, and the light glinted rhythmically into my eyes. Now on...now off...now there...now gone. I stared at it, fascinated.

"Your mother gave it to you to protect you," said Arnulf softly. "You were going into battle, and she wanted to keep her son safe, so she gave you this precious treasure."

That was true. How did he know? And the light continued to dance on the blade of the sword.

"But you do not need it now," murmured Arnulf. "The battle is won. All your troubles will cease if you give it to me. No-one will chase after you. You will be free."

It *was* tempting. Why should I carry this burden? Just give it up. It would make life so much easier. He knew so much, this man. And the light flickered from side to side.

"You could even join us, if you like," said Arnulf gently, "in our great work."

"Oh, yeah!" Oz broke in. "As if you're gonna let your lord's death go unavenged! Don't listen to him, Wulf."

Oh, thank you, Oz! I shook off the spell of Arnulf's voice and saw his expression harden. Then Arnulf reached inside his mailshirt and I moved. Or something moved for me, more quickly than I could normally move myself. I heard my own voice say the words, just a fraction before Arnulf's voice also called out.

"By the power of Thorn," said my voice, "I command you to stop!"

143

And, "By the power of…" cried Arnulf, but he got no further before he crashed to the ground.

"My Lord!" gasped Leofric, falling to his knees beside Arnulf. But almost before he was there, Abdul leapt from the table and jumped on him. Abdul had the advantage of surprise, but Leofric was fit, a trained housecarl. He gripped Abdul in a bear-hug as they rolled on the ground, his helmet falling off, and he struggled to draw his seax, his short stabbing sword, out of its sheath.

I stood paralysed, still shaken by the power of the spell. Then I saw Oz jump up, his eyes fixed on Arnulf's long sword, which had fallen by his side. I shook myself and made a dive for the sword, reaching it just before Oz. But it felt heavy and clumsy in my hand and it was hard to attack Leofric without hurting Abdul.

Oz made a second dive, at Arnulf's body, and slid his seax out of its sheath. Abdul was on top of Leofric now, but still gripped in a fierce bear-hug. Then they rolled over, with Leofric on top, and Oz rammed the sword into his back. It didn't pierce the mail-coat, but Leofric yelled and slackened his grip, and in that instant Abdul pulled Leofric's seax out of its sheath and plunged it deep into his midriff.

Time seemed to slow. Leofric looked down in amazement to see his own seax sticking out of his mail-coat. Eyes wide, he watched the coat turn red around the sword. Crimson liquid started to bubble out of his mouth. He tried to say something, but he could only gurgle blood. Then he collapsed backwards and stared up into the sky, still with that amazed expression on his face.

I heard a sob and turned to see Bronwen with her hands over her face. She looked over her fingers.

"Is he dead?" she whispered.

Oz looked at her as if she was mad.

"Oh, I think so, Bron," he nodded. "Lying there with a dirty great seax sticking out of his belly, and blood all over him, I reckon he's dead, don't you?"

"But this one isn't," said Abdul, crawling over to Arnulf's body. "Your spell stuns, Wulfstan, perhaps for a long time, but it does not kill. So what are we to do with him?"

"Well, obviously," said Oz. "We'll have to kill him."

CHAPTER TWENTY-EIGHT

WULF

"No!" came Walter's voice. "There has been enough killing!"

Bronwen ran to help him up. She led him to a bench, but he wouldn't sit down.

"Tie him up," said Walter, tottering over to Arnulf. "Do what you like, but no more killing."

"Whaaat?" said Oz. "Are you mad? After what he was going to do to us?"

"But he did not," said Walter, "and I do not want to sink to his level."

Abdul sat up, wincing. "I also have a horror of killing in cold blood," he said, "but we must think of the practicalities. If we leave him he will follow us, perhaps bringing more men with him."

I looked uneasily into the surrounding trees, which grew thickly all around except for the narrow path we'd travelled on. Was that only the night before? I seemed to be losing all sense of time. We had to hurry, and I was still feeling shaky from the after-effects of the spell. I couldn't quite believe that Arnulf and Leofric had been on their own, but so far no other soldiers had appeared.

Bronwen finally managed to guide Walter to the bench and make him sit down.

"I know him," I said, looking at Arnulf lying motionless on the ground. "I saw him after the feast. He was watching when that other bloke gave Guthrum the letter. I bet it was him who arranged our kidnap."

"And I recognize *him*," said Bronwen, pointing at the dead Leofric. "He was the one who first arrested us and took us to Lord Grimwold."

"Yes," said Abdul, "I remember his face when his master welcomed us in, instead of treating us like prisoners."

146

"Right, while you lot are wandering down memory lane," said Oz, "we've got a decision to make, and it's clear as daylight what we've got to do."

"Is it?" I said, finally finding my voice. "I wish I was as certain as you."

"Oh, not you as well!" said Oz in exasperation.

"Well, *I'm* not going to kill him," I muttered. This was all happening too quickly. How was I supposed to know what to do? But I had a gut feeling about it. "I'm beginning to trust my rune-stone," I said to Oz. " It's not evil, despite what Brother Edmund said."

As if on cue, the monk started to moan on the other side of the table.

"If it stuns to protect us," I went on, "but it doesn't kill, that's good enough for me."

Oz marched over and stood in front of me, still brandishing Arnulf's seax. His eyes were narrowed and he looked as if he wanted to attack me.

"Perhaps you should have made that little speech to old Toadstool," he said through gritted teeth, "before he hacked off Grimwold's head."

"Where am I?...What...oh, my head," moaned Brother Edmund, and Bronwen flew round to comfort him.

"Calm down, Osric!" said Abdul, staggering to his feet. "Whatever we do, we must do quickly, and be gone from here. I also am not happy about leaving him alive, but nor do I want to kill him in cold blood." He looked down at Arnulf who, like Leofric, was lying open-eyed, apparently staring up at the sky. "We fought in Grimwold's hall, and if I could have killed him then, I would have. But I only had my knife. There were too many of them, though I killed one of his companions. But now...I cannot bring myself to do it."

"Well, I'll do it!" said Oz. "You're all mad!"

"Oh, be quiet, Osric," said Bronwen, standing up and putting her hands on her hips. "One against the rest of us – you lose!"

Oz gaped at her in astonishment and I felt a rush of affection for her.

"We'll tie him up really tight," she went on. "You must have some rope, Walter." Walter nodded, with a half-smile on his face. "If he dies, he dies. If not, we're in God's hands and we'll be long gone."

Walter was now grinning broadly and I couldn't help doing the same.

"Now," said Bronwen, "There's an old horse and a donkey tethered with ours. Will you be able to ride them to your abbey? When Brother Edmund recovers, that is, which he'd better do pretty quickly."

"I don't believe this!" said Oz, still gaping at her.

"Then you must stay at the abbey, Walter," Bronwen went on, "at least for now. You mustn't be here on your own."

"She is right," said Abdul. "And I think *we* should still go to the hall of my friend Godwin." Abdul passed his hand over his eyes. "Godwin...I cannot believe he is dead...I should not have left him...But he begged me to. He insisted that I find the wise-woman – Wulf's mother – and warn her." He bowed his head. "I cannot think about this now."

"Can we still get warm clothes there," asked Bronwen, "and weapons?"

"Yes, I know the steward well. But we have *some* weapons."

Abdul bent over Leofric's body and grasped the seax with which he had killed him. He put his foot on the blood-soaked torso and heaved. The seax came away with a squelch and an ooze of dark red. Then he unbuckled Leofric's sword-belt, with its two scabbards, and buckled it on to himself. After cleaning the bloody seax on the grass, he sheathed it, so that he now had a weapon on either side.

"I prefer my own swords to these English ones," he said, "but that cannot be helped."

"Looks like you and me have got a weapon each," Oz said to me, "and the way things are going, I reckon we should take them. But there's only one belt."

I looked down and realised I was still holding Arnulf's sword. I shook my head, still feeling as if I wasn't quite there.

"It's no good," I said. "This is too heavy for me. You take it." I held it out to Oz.

"We'll hang it from a saddle," said Oz, unbuckling Arnulf's belt and dragging it off his stunned body. "This'll do me nicely." He put on the belt, drawing it as tight as he could, kissed the seax and slid it into its sheath.

148

All this while Bronwen had been seeing to the two monks, helping Brother Edmund on to a bench and pouring them both ale.

"Thank you, my dear," said Walter. "What a blessing to have you here. Now, please, all of you listen to me."

We all turned and looked at him.

"There is another sort of weapon here, which must on no account be left on the man called Arnulf."

"A rune-stone!" I cried, jolting out of my daze for the first time. "He was reaching for it and I just beat him to it with mine!"

Abdul bent down and felt inside Arnulf's mail coat. Carefully, he drew out the stone, at first glance exactly like mine, but on a silver chain. He tried to lift Arnulf's head, but the body was rigid, and Oz had to help him hold the shoulders up so that the chain could be slipped over the golden hair.

Abdul held it up and the stone dangled, turning this way and that. I felt that it was drawing me towards it. Such a little, insignificant-looking thing, but so powerful. My hand automatically reached for my own stone, which throbbed against my skin as if it was alive. Then I shuddered.

"I don't want it!" I said. "One's enough. Someone else'll have to look after it."

"Let me look at it first," came Walter's quavery voice.

Without touching the stone itself, Abdul held the chain over Walter's hands and the old man cradled it, as if he was holding a baby bird.

"It is not evil," he murmured. "It is men who are evil." He looked up at Abdul. "But you must be very careful with it."

He let his hands drop and the stone dangled once more.

"I'll take it," said Oz suddenly. "I don't know how to use it, but if it's not evil, it can't hurt me."

He marched over to Abdul, took the chain and put it over his head. I stared at him. Was it my imagination, or had a subtle change come over him?

"And there's something else," said Oz. "We never finished our little conversation about what to do with *him*."

149

He strode across to Arnulf and drew his seax. Then he stood looking down into the blank face before turning to face the rest of us.

"I know you all think I'm a blood-thirsty git, but I don't think you've thought this through." He paused. "If we tie him up and leave him, and he wakes up too weak to untie himself, he'll die of thirst, or some creature of the forest'll get him. So it'd be murder, as much as if we kill him now."

I listened, fascinated. This did not sound like Oz. Walter was nodding and everyone was silent.

"He's got no weapons and we've got the rune-stone. When we find their horses, we can drive them away, or take them to the abbey – whatever you want. It'll take him forever to find us. Let's just leave him and go."

Oz suddenly grinned round at them all.

"You didn't expect me to say that, did you?"

Even more suddenly, he yelled, as Arnulf lunged at him and grabbed the seax.

CHAPTER TWENTY-NINE

WULF

With one arm tight round Oz's neck and the other waving the seax, Arnulf glared around wildly. But we hardly had time to take it in before Abdul was there. In one fluid movement his sword was out of its scabbard and had struck deep into Arnulf's armpit. As the man gave an unearthly cry and released his grip, Oz grabbed his sword back, spun round and thrust it with all his might into his enemy's midriff. And this time he managed to pierce the mail and the leather beneath as, with gritted teeth, he used both hands to force the sword in.

Arnulf staggered back, his eyes glazing over, and crashed to the ground beside Leofric. Oz turned, red-faced and panting, to Bronwen.

"I think *he's* dead now, as well," he said.

Abdul smiled and gave a half-bow to Oz.

"Well done, Osric," he said. "Between us we have solved the problem. And I am glad we did not have to kill him in cold blood. Now we should retrieve our weapons and clean them."

I watched them uneasily. Was I losing the will to fight? I had the rune-stone, but what about ordinary swordplay? Me and Oz had trained together since we were small, and Guthrum had occasionally hinted that, if we were good enough, we might not only be part of the fyrd, but maybe even become housecarls. And Oz would be good enough – I could see that. But where had my own fighting spirit gone? I walked over and looked down at Arnulf.

"Well, at least we know how long the spell lasts," I said.

"Not very long," said Bronwen, coming to stand beside me. "So if this happens again, we've either got to get away quickly or..."

"Kill them," nodded Abdul. "Next time I will not be so squeamish. Come, we must fetch our steeds and ride to the abbey."

Now that the immediate danger was past, I became aware of an acrid smell which had been in my nostrils for a while, but which I'd been ignoring.

"Something's burning," I said.

"My bread!" cried Walter, flying to the upturned iron pot. He grabbed a cloth and heaved at the pot, while Bronwen, with the aid of another thick cloth, removed the blackening loaf.

"That's the one I made," she said, looking down at it mournfully.

"It's probably all right in the middle," said Oz, giving it a poke.

Walter nodded. "I shall cut off the burnt parts, and we must fill some bags with such food as I have here."

"And quickly," said Abdul.

"But are you all right, my friend?" asked Walter, laying a hand on Oz's arm.

"Yeah," said Oz. "I've never seen anyone move so quickly. And... er...I didn't really thank you for saving me."

"My pleasure," bowed Abdul. "And *I* must thank Brother Walter for his care, and the good food and mulberry juice. I am sore, but feel much better."

Walter beamed at him. "Be careful, though, my friend. You still need some rest."

I suspected that the recovery was partly due to Abdul's years of experience kicking in. He'd reacted to the threat by instinct. *I've got a lot to learn from him*, I thought.

Walter fetched three large leather bags, and he and Bronwen stuffed them with food. All this while, Brother Edmund sat and looked around as if he didn't know what was happening.

"Should we call *you* Brother, as well, Walter?" asked Bronwen. "Abdul just did, but that's not how you introduced yourself."

"Tush," smiled Walter. "I am only a lay brother, not an ordained monk. I do not concern myself with titles."

"Come on," I said to Oz. "Let's get the horses."

Oz's face fell. "This'll be fun," he said. "I wonder if old Cloud'll be in a better mood today."

But when we got to the stall round the back of the building, the big grey horse walked up to Oz and whinnied softly in greeting.

"Hello, boy," said Oz, looking puzzled. "How are you, then?"

Cloud nodded his head and nudged Oz, all the while whiffling softly. Then he rubbed his nose against Oz's shirt, just where the rune-stone was tucked away.

"He wants to see your stone," I grinned.

The horse nudged harder and Oz laughed. "All right, all right, I'll show you."

He pulled it out and Cloud rubbed it with his nose. Then he threw back his head and gave a loud whinny.

By now I was laughing too. "What's all that about?" I said.

"I dunno," said Oz, holding up the stone and looking at it. Then his expression changed as light dawned. "Hang on, I *do* know," he said. "This is *Eh*, the horse rune. Cloud knows it."

"Never mind Cloud," I said, irritated. "How do *you* know it?"

"I told you," said Oz. "I'm interested in that stuff. I don't know much, but I'm sure I'm right on that one."

"So how was Arnulf going to use a *horse* rune to curse us?" I said. "It doesn't make sense."

"Perhaps he was going to turn us into horses," grinned Oz.

"No, seriously," I said. "It doesn't make sense."

Oz shrugged. "I think they have more than one meaning. There must be lots of different ways of using them."

"All right, then, clever boots," I said Wulf. "If *Eh* is a horse, what's *Thorn?*"

Oz thought, "Just a thorn, I suppose. I think it's something to do with protection."

I frowned as I started to undo the reins. "My mum definitely should have had you for a son, instead of me."

We untethered the four horses in silence, and led them round to the others. Then I went back to fetch the old nag and the donkey for Walter and Brother Edmund. I felt as if a black cloud had descended on me, and I couldn't push my way out of it. Not only was Oz becoming a good fighter but he also knew some rune-lore, while I, a wise-woman's son, didn't know the first thing about it. Except for that memory...the man, and my mum calling out those words...*By the power of Thorn, I command you to stop...* And who was that man? I knew him, I was sure of it, but from where?

The black cloud hovered round my head all the while we were getting ready to go, all through the banter about Oz having made friends with his horse, all through helping the complaining Brother Edmund on to his donkey, and all through the slow ride along the forest path. We followed Walter, whose old mare looked almost as ancient as he did.

Walter said that the abbey was not far away, and he was right. We came out of the trees and in front of us loomed a huge grey stone church with outer buildings, behind a high wall.

Walter got off his mare and approached the gate, with its massive iron knocker. He lifted it and knocked firmly, three times. We waited, but nothing happened.

"It is I, Brother Walter, seeking entry with Brother Edmund and four travellers," came his reedy voice.

We waited again. There was no reply.

CHAPTER THIRTY

WULF

"This is very strange," muttered Walter. "There is always someone at the gate."

"They are all murdered!" wailed Brother Edmund. "And we shall be, too. It is a trap, a trap!"

"Well, it's not a very clever trap, Brother Edmund," said Bronwen waspishly. "They're not exactly inviting us in, are they?"

Oz sniggered, and even I managed a little smile. My senses were starting to waken again, and I thought I felt the black cloud lift a bit. Why now? Because there was a mystery, and I needed to be alert. I was an idiot to mope around feeling sorry for myself, when I had good friends and a job to do, though I still wasn't sure what the job was.

Well, we needed to get Walter and that idiot monk inside to safety, whatever else happened. I rode up to the gate and leaned across to the knocker. Then I banged it three times with all my might.

"Hey!" I shouted. "Is anybody in there?"

We listened.

"I heard something," muttered Oz.

"Me too," I said. I stood up in my stirrups and tried to see over the wall, but found I'd need to stand on the saddle itself to climb over. Precariously, I put one foot on the saddle and took a breath. The horse didn't seem any happier about this than me, however. He shifted around, making little protesting noises and nearly sending me flying.

"All right, Chestnut, keep still will you," I gasped, grabbing the horse's neck.

"I've seen people do that trick," said Oz, "but they've had years of practice."

And while I was righting myself, Oz and Abdul dismounted. Abdul bent down to let Oz climb on to his shoulders, then carefully stood up. Oz grabbed the top of the wall, heaved himself up and disappeared over the other side.

There was a scuffling noise, then "No, no!" squeaked a voice.

"Well, it's not very nice," came Oz's voice, "to keep your visitors waiting, is it? Where's your famous hospitality?"

I grinned, suppressing my irritation that Oz had once again taken the initiative.

"No, no!" came the first voice. "I am not allowed to open the gate. Not until the abbot comes."

"And how long will that be?" I called.

"Brother Oslac has gone to fetch him," whimpered the voice.

"That's what we heard, then, Wulf," called Oz. "A little mouse scurrying away."

"Brother Egbert?" said Walter. "Is that you? Did you not recognize my voice?"

"Oh, Brother Walter!" sobbed Egbert. "It really is you! Such terrible things have been abroad. And creatures that mimic other people's voices." I immediately thought of Pooka, but didn't say anything. "We had thought you were lost," Brother Egbert went on, "and we do not know who to trust any more!"

"Well, I am not lost," said Walter, "but I am rather tired of waiting out here."

"Come on, give us the keys," said Oz. There was a jangling sound. "You do it, I don't know which one's which."

The gate creaked open and a small and terrified-looking monk peered out at us.

"Brother Edmund!" he cried, and the two monks fell sobbing into each other's arms, or arm, in Brother Egbert's case, as Oz was still tightly holding on to him.

Oz looked at them with distaste and then at Walter.

"I can see why you'd rather live on your own than with this lot," he said.

"Do not judge them too harshly," smiled Walter. "They have been in the abbey since boyhood, and the outside world is a strange and frightening place to them."

"Brother Egbert! Brother Egbert!" came a panicky voice. "You have opened the gate!"

A scrawny red-haired monk skidded to a halt some yards away and stood wild-eyed and panting.

"Oh, Oslac, they made me," sobbed Egbert, "but see, it is our brothers, Walter and Edmund. I am sorry, Holy Father, but they made me."

This last remark was clearly not addressed to Brother Oslac, but to an imposing middle-aged man striding towards us. Tall, grey-haired and with an unmistakable air of authority about him, he looked quite unworried by the open gate.

Taking in what had happened at one glance – Oz was still hanging on to Egbert's arm – the abbot bowed slightly.

"If you had waited a very short time," he said, "I should have opened the gate myself. I am unwilling to expose the brothers to any more danger. And," this bit was to Oz, "I think you might let go of Brother Egbert's arm now and allow him to close the gate. Once you have all come inside, of course."

Oz reddened slightly and let go, while we all dismounted and led the horses, with Brother Edmund's donkey, into the abbey grounds. Then Egbert pushed the heavy gate to. Once the key had turned in the lock, the abbot smiled and held out his hand, palm down.

"Brothers Walter and Edmund, how good to see you again. We were worried about you."

Brother Edmund knelt and kissed the abbot's enormous ring, and when Walter did the same, the abbot took him by the shoulders and helped him up.

"We have much to discuss, old friend," he said to Walter. "But please, introduce me to the rest of your company."

Walter said nothing but stretched out a hand, nodding at Abdul, obviously inviting us to introduce ourselves.

Abdul swept a low bow. "I am Abdul Mutazz ibn Haroun of Cordoba," he said, "friend of Godwin of Wendham."

The abbot raised his eyebrows. "Friend of...but have you heard?"

Walter stepped forward. "I have told him of Godwin's death, my lord."

To my surprise the abbot bowed almost as low as Abdul.

"You are most welcome, Abdul of Cordoba. And these?"

His eyes swept over me, Oz and Bronwen. I felt embarrassed and out of place, and Oz looked as if he wished the ground would swallow him. All trace of his former cockiness was gone. But Bronwen swept a deep curtsey.

"I am Bronwen of Powys, in the service of the Lady Rhiannon, wife to Lord Aelfric. And this is Wulfstan and this is Osric, both in the service of Lord Aelfric, and lately returned from fighting Duke William of Normandy."

I held my head a little higher, then remembered that I was supposed to bow, which both me and Oz did rather awkwardly. Really, Bronwen was a surprising person and at the moment I felt I owed her a debt of gratitude. All she'd done was introduce us, but it was that *'returned from fighting Duke William'* bit that made all the difference.

The Abbot bowed again. "I am Abbot Deorlaf, and I welcome you to our abbey. I am afraid the guest quarters are a little crowded at the moment, but I am sure we can find room for you in the monks' quarters, if that is what you wish."

Brother Edmund's eyes nearly popped out of his head. "But Holy Father, what about the girl?"

"We have many womenfolk inside our walls at the moment, Brother Edmund. I am sure she can be made comfortable."

This conversation was raising more questions than it was answering in my mind, and I could see I wasn't alone in this. Walter's puzzled expression was outdone only by Brother Edmund's comical amazement.

"Women?" he mouthed, scarcely able to get the word out.

"Yes, Brother," smiled the Abbot, "you remember, the other half of the human race."

He turned and spoke, but who to? "Please feel free to show yourselves. Our guests are not dangerous."

And from behind buildings, out of doorways, round corners and even down from the branches of a great yew tree crept a silent, wide-eyed crowd of people. Old men, children and, as the abbot had said, women, dressed in plain, patched garments. Villagers, like Wulf and Oz. But no young men, no fathers of families.

I stared at them all and they stared back.

"But Holy Father," said Walter. "What has happened?"

"'Tis too dangerous out there for the likes of us," said an old man. "The able-bodied men are guardin' the animals and the buildin's, an' the Holy Father is lettin' the rest of us stay here."

"And my Edward is out there," said a young woman with a child clinging to her skirt. "And I wanted to stay with him, but…but it's the children." Her voice wobbled and she put a hand up to her face.

"But what are you afraid of?" I burst out.

A young boy stepped forward. "Monsters," he said solemnly. "Like in the old stories. Black things in the night that freeze your blood."

CHAPTER THIRTY-ONE

WULF

Black things in the night that freeze your blood! My own blood felt frozen as I stood trying to take it in. I clutched my rune-stone and it tingled in my hand, spreading warmth slowly up my arm. It didn't feel evil, it couldn't have anything to do with all this, but things were happening too fast. I couldn't make sense of it. But worst of all, if it was true, how could my little stone protect us against monsters from the old stories? It worked against humans, but...supernatural creatures?

"But is this really true?" said Abdul. "Was it not some little thing that happened, spreading panic, so that tales grew and became exaggerated?"

"You think as I thought at first," said the abbot. "But I am afraid it is true. We have lost several folk from the village, and many of the livestock that they depend on."

"How is this possible?" gasped Walter, but the abbot held up his hand.

"We will not talk here. Come into the refectory, all of you. Let us exchange news over some refreshment."

"But Holy Father..." began Brother Edmund, looking at Bronwen.

"Yes, the maid too," interrupted the abbot. "I have the authority to make exceptions to rules."

"I do not doubt that, my lord," said Brother Edmund, hanging his head.

"Brother Oslac," the abbot continued, "find someone to help you with the horses."

And he led us through the staring villagers, past the magnificent abbey, into a lower stone building behind. We found ourselves in a hall with long tables and benches on either side. At one end was the high table, and the abbot invited us to sit round it. I felt slightly out of place and

160

Oz looked awkward, but Bronwen seemed to be getting used to all this. When we each had bread and ale in front of us, or water in Abdul's case, the abbot began.

"It started in the village almost a week ago, when a scream was heard in the night. It was so blood-curdling, apparently, that it woke everyone up. Several of the men ran to investigate and found the shepherd flat on his back, stone dead, with an expression of terror on his face. About half of the sheep were dead as well – it is only a small flock – but there was something strange about their corpses. They seemed to have had their insides sucked out in some way, leaving only an outer skin and bones."

My stomach turned over.

"And the shepherd was stiff, as if frozen," the abbot continued, "though he could only just have died."

"So he did not die in the same way as the sheep?" said Abdul. "His insides had not been removed?"

"They had not," replied the abbot. "The village priest buried the poor shepherd, and instead of coming straight to me, he himself kept watch the following night." The abbot sighed. "Father Beocca was a brave man, but foolhardy I fear."

Walter rose from his bench, his hands gripping his beaker of ale.

"Do not tell me that Beocca is dead," he whispered. "I knew him well."

"I am afraid so, Brother Walter," said the abbot. "Sit down friend, and take some ale."

Bronwen put a hand on Walter's arm, and the old man nodded and slowly sat down again.

"It was exactly the same as the night before," the abbot continued, "but Father Beocca had at least been persuaded to have a companion, who lived to tell the tale. Garwulf, one of our bravest young men, kept watch with him."

The abbot paused for a sip of ale, but the suspense was too much for Oz.

"So what did he see?" he gasped.

"Osric," murmured Abdul holding up his hand, warning him to stop.

Abbot Deorlaf smiled. "No, I am sure you are all eager to know, but the truth is that he did not see much. In the dead of night they both suddenly felt colder, with an unearthly chill. Then a shadow appeared, on the other side of the sheep pen. Father Beocca stood and held up his cross."

As he said this, the abbot stood and held up an imaginary cross.

"'In the name of Christ be gone!' he cried out, and then Garwulf heard a low hiss. The shadow seemed to retreat a little, although it did not disappear. Father Beocca must have taken courage at his partial success, for he strode towards the shadow, still holding up the cross. But then he gave a strangled cry and suddenly, Garwulf did not see how, the priest was flat on his back, dead, with his eyes open, and the shadow was stooping over the limp body of a sheep, before departing into the darkness."

I clutched my rune-stone yet again and prayed (but who to?) that the stone would prove more powerful than the Christian cross.

The abbot sat down again.

"And this Garwulf," said Abdul. "He came to no harm?"

"He is severely shaken," said the abbot. "And worse, he blames himself for cowardice, which is not true. He says that his blood seemed to freeze and his limbs become immobile, but he feels that is a poor excuse, as Father Beocca had the courage to confront the demon. I am certain, however, that if he had, he would now be dead. I told him this, but it seemed to be little comfort. 'Better a dead hero than a living coward,' he said."

There was a knock on the door of the refectory.

"Enter," called the abbot.

A brown-haired monk came in and knelt before him. He looked up at the abbot and I leaned forward, my brain working overtime.

I knew that face. But from where? Where had I seen it before? Then I felt the hall spin round.

It was the man!

The man from my memory, who had tried to take me from my mum The man I remembered hadn't worn a monk's tonsure and habit, but he had the same grey eyes, though the lines round them were deeper now. And the face was exactly the same, just a bit older.

I took a deep breath. All right, I knew where I'd seen him before. *But who was he?*

"Forgive my intrusion, Holy Father," said the monk.

"What is it, Brother Beorn?"

"My lord, I have just learned that you have in this hall a boy, a young man, Wulfstan, of the estate of Lord Aelfric."

His eyes searched around the group and stopped when they came to me.

And suddenly…suddenly…I knew exactly who he was. I clutched the table for support.

"You may stand, Brother Beorn," said the abbot. "What is it that you want with him?"

The monk got to his feet. "A word, my lord Abbot. A private word with him."

The abbot nodded. "Do not go out of our sight, or take too long."

I stood up, my heart thudding against my ribs, and followed the monk to the other end of the refectory.

"You will be surprised at what I have to tell you," said the monk.

"No, I won't," I said. "I know who you are."

"But you were so young," said the monk. "Surely you cannot remember."

"No, I do," I breathed. "I remember you." I paused, fighting for breath, struggling to get the words out. Finally I gasped, "You're my father."

CHAPTER THIRTY-TWO

WULF

Once again, the monk knelt down. Not this time to the abbot, but to me. He reached out and clasped my hands.

Then he whispered, "I have come to beg your forgiveness."

I pulled my hands away. "For leaving, you mean? Or is there some other terrible thing you've done?"

"No, I have tried to live a holy life since that day," said the monk. "But I have been tormented with worries about you, my only son."

"Not as tormented as all that," I said bitterly. "Otherwise you'd have come back to find out how I was getting on."

"You don't understand!" said the monk, grabbing one of my hands back.

"Look…get up, will you?" I said, looking at the other end of the hall. Oz was staring at us with his mouth open and the others kept glancing in our direction and then back at the abbot, who'd carried on talking. "Let's sit down and look normal."

Brother Beorn nodded and we sat at one end of a long table. I still felt as if I was struggling to breathe. Why did I feel so angry? Shouldn't I be pleased to find my long-lost father?

"Do you remember when I left?" asked Beorn.

I nodded. "It's about the only thing I do remember," I said. "I can't have been more than two or three."

Beorn leaned forward. "Tell me exactly what you remember," he said intensely.

"Why?" I said. "What's so important about it?"

Beorn paused and looked into my eyes. "I see you are a strong character, like your mother," he smiled. "All this questioning would not do in a monastery."

"Lucky I don't want to be a monk then, isn't it?" I said.

"Did Father Wiglaf not teach you to respect your elders?" asked Beorn, raising his eyebrows.

"Oh, we're coming on heavy now, are we?" I scowled. "A minute ago you were begging my forgiveness."

Beorn sighed and shook his head. "I am sorry," he said. "This conversation is not going at all the way I intended. I simply wanted you to understand why I left. And that will be easier if you tell me what you remember."

I leaned forward. "Why don't *you* just tell *me* what happened? You were the grown up, after all. I was just a helpless little kid."

That was it. That was why I was so angry. How could you do that to your child – just go away and never see him any more? Then I looked into my father's eyes. They were swimming with tears. The anger started to drain away.

I shrugged. "We were in our cottage and you picked me up and went to go out the door, but my mum stopped you."

He paused.

"But how did she stop me?" asked Beorn urgently.

"She said...*By the power of Thorn I command you to stop!* and she held up...this."

I dived into the front of my torn shirt and brandished the rune-stone at him.

The colour drained from his face and he stood and backed away from me.

At the other end of the hall the abbot also stood up.

"Is something wrong, Brother Beorn?" he called. "I believe your interview has gone on long enough."

Beorn took a deep breath and bowed. "No, I beg you, my lord, a few moments more."

The abbot looked at me, and I nodded. Beorn returned to his place and spoke quickly in a low voice.

"It is as I feared. Your mother has been bringing you up as a heathen. Did Father..."

165

"She hasn't!" I interrupted. "She told me the old stories, but everyone knows them. I don't know anything about the runes." I didn't say that was because I didn't want to learn. My mum would have loved to teach me if I'd been interested, but this monk didn't need to know that.

"And did Father Wiglaf teach you the true religion?" asked Beorn. "He promised me he would, and that he would teach you to read."

"Oh, *that's* what it was all about!" I smiled as light dawned. "I wondered why he was so fussy about me going to school. Church I could understand – he used to round everybody up – but he never bothered about most of the kids learning to read if they didn't want to come."

"So you can read?"

"Yeah, I can. English, that is. I'm not much good at Latin."

"And did your mother not mind?"

I shook my head. "She was quite pleased. She said all knowledge is a good thing and most boys didn't go to priest school unless they were going into the church, but old Wiglaf..."

"*Father* Wiglaf!" corrected Beorn.

"*Father* Wiglaf knew I wasn't going to do that, but he still taught me."

Beorn sighed. "That is good. He is a good man."

We sat in silence for a few moments. I didn't know what to say. I felt there were things hanging in the air, waiting to be said, but I was floundering, struggling to come to terms with my feelings about this man, my father. I was relieved when Beorn started talking again.

"I am sorry I reacted like that when you held up that...thing," he began, "but it reminded me of..."

He shook his head.

"I knew your mother had certain healing powers when we were married, and that she was interested in what she called 'the old ways'. But we were young, I loved her, it did not seem important. But then she spent more and more time with her runes, and she had one special old stone, the one you have there. She changed, and I began to believe I should take you away from her influence." He paused. "You remember what happened."

I nodded.

166

"She cursed me with that stone and I entered hell…Or so it seemed. I was in a place of darkness and evil, with shadowy figures mocking me, and no way of escape. If that is what hell is like you must do anything, *anything* to avoid going there. I was in terror and despair for what seemed like years, but was really less than an hour. When I came to I was outside the cottage door, and she had taken you away.

"I should have searched for you…forgive me…but I could not shake off the horror of that place…the place the rune-stone had sent me to. Father Wiglaf said he would keep an eye on you and that I needed spiritual healing. I found my way here, where I have found peace, and I have been here ever since."

"So you just left me," I said. "Didn't you think she might do something bad to me?"

"No, she loved you," said Beorn, putting his head in his hands. "And I trusted Father Wiglaf. But I can see that you think I am a coward, and you are right."

I didn't say anything.

"But how did you come to have the stone?" asked Beorn. "Is your mother dead?"

"No, she's alive," I said. "She gave it to me to keep me safe. I've been in battle, and it was the best she could do to protect me."

"You see, she loves you. I was right. It must have taken a lot for her to part with that."

We looked at each other awkwardly.

"I must be about my duties," said Beorn, rising from the bench. "Perhaps we could meet again before you leave? If you would like, that is."

"Perhaps," I said, and watched my father bow to the abbot and leave the hall.

I felt numb as I walked back to the high table. It was getting late and the afternoon sun was too low to reach the high windows, so a monk was lighting candles on the table. They cast a pool of light around the abbot and my friends but seemed to plunge the surroundings into a deeper blackness. I stared at them all on what seemed like an endless walk. Was it only this morning we'd had breakfast outside Walter's sanctuary? So much had happened. The killing of Arnulf and Leofric, the journey here, the news of these blood-freezing monsters and now…meeting my father. Time seemed to be playing tricks on me, but at last I reached the high table.

Abbot Deorlaf smiled. "If you need my advice in private, I should be happy to give it. Meanwhile we have a choice to make." He looked around at everyone, then back at me. "It has been decided to confront these evil creatures again, using both the power of the church and possibly some other power which Brother Walter feels may be wielded for either good or evil. I believe you have an ancient rune-stone, which we may be able to use. I would not, however, wish to put your young life at risk. Perhaps you would allow us to borrow it, and teach someone the correct form of words?"

"I told them I've got one too," said Oz, "but it was Arnulf's, and I don't know how to use it. I mean, I don't know what words to say or anything."

I looked at the abbot in astonishment. Give my stone to someone else? But it was *mine* to bear, *my* fate to use it. That's what my mum would say, that my fate was somehow bound up with the stone.

But did I have the guts to confront these shadow creatures, that sucked the insides out of animals and froze men to death in an instant? My father had said I was strong, like my mum. Not a coward like him. Yes, my own father had called himself a coward.

I took a deep breath.

"I'm not a coward," I said. "The stone is mine and no-one else's to use. Tell me what you want me to do and I'll do it."

CHAPTER THIRTY-THREE

WULF

"But how did you know he was my father?" I asked Bronwen. "Was it your second sight?"

We were sitting in a corner of the abbey's enormous kitchen, on two wooden settles facing each other across a board table. One of the monks had given us an early supper of bean soup and rye bread and, as usual, Oz was too busy eating to bother with conversation.

"I didn't need second sight to see that," said Bronwen. "First sight was enough."

"First sight?" Oz slurped. "What's that?"

"A pair of eyes," said Bronwen. "He looks just like Wulf." She sighed. "I bet the abbot won't let me go with you. It's not fair – just because I'm a girl!"

"You don't actually want to be there, do you?" I asked. "I don't, but it's got to be done."

"I'm proud of you, mate," said Oz, tearing off a hunk of bread. "I knew you'd say that. I just wish I knew how to use Arnulf's stone. Anyway, I'm still coming."

"I mean, what use would you be, Bron?" I said. "You'd be putting other people in danger as well as yourself."

"Oh, and Osric's going to be really useful, isn't he?" Bronwen splashed her spoon down in her bowl. "He's just admitted he doesn't know how to use his rune-stone."

"I've got a sword now, haven't I?" said Oz indignantly. "You seem to forget it's not long since we were in a battle! I mean a proper battle, fighting alongside the king!"

"And I suppose you were in his personal bodyguard?" said Bronwen. "Oh no, weren't you stuck on top of a hill shooting arrows, and then throwing stones when the arrows ran out?"

"That is hardly fair, Bronwen," came Abdul's voice from behind. "Do not underestimate the brave part they played in that decisive battle. They did their duty courageously, and helped England to remain a free country."

Bronwen went pink.

"Thank you, Abdul," said Oz, smirking at Bronwen. "And where've you been?"

"I have been talking to Walter and Abbot Deorlaf, who is a very intelligent man," said Abdul. "We have agreed that I should come with you, Wulfstan, but we are not yet sure which of the monks should carry the abbey's great cross. The abbot wishes to come himself, but Walter feels he should not put himself in such danger when he is needed here."

"And can I come – please?" implored Bronwen.

"Why no, that would not be…"

"You see, everybody but me!" she interrupted him.

"But Osric also is staying here," said Abdul. "Do not be so…"

"Hang on, wait a minute!" said Oz, rising to his feet. "Who says I'm staying here?"

"Abbot Deorlaf," said Abdul, "if I may be permitted to finish a sentence, and I must say I agree with him. Although I do understand your wish to come."

"Where is he?" said Oz. "I want a word with him!"

Abdul put an arm round Oz's angrily squared shoulders.

"Osric, Osric," he said soothingly, "you will gain nothing if you go to him in this mood. And remember, he is an important man. His word is law in the abbey."

Oz stood fuming for a minute and I caught sight of Bronwen's amused expression. I wished they'd get on better – my best friend and a girl who…well, a girl who I liked a lot. But more importantly, now, did I want Oz with me? I didn't want to put Oz in danger, but the answer was, yes, I did want him to come.

"Sit down, Oz," I said. "Let's all calm down and finish our soup. Then I'll go with you to see the abbot."

"You will?" said Oz.

"Yeah, I'll explain that we've always done everything together and that it'd be a big help to me if you were there."

Oz nodded and sat down. "Cheers, mate," he said, frowning into his soup-bowl.

Abdul sat on the settle next to me.

"I am not sure if this is a good idea," he said gently, but he was interrupted by a gasp from Bronwen.

"No, don't!" she sobbed. "Osric mustn't go!"

"What's the matter, Bron?" I said.

"He mustn't go! He mustn't go!" Her voice was rising hysterically and the kitchen monks turned round to look. "Something terrible will happen if he goes!"

Oz leaned forward with narrowed eyes. "You're making this up," he hissed. "You don't want me to go, so you're having one of your visions. But I don't believe you."

Bronwen burst into tears and I turned on him.

"Can't you see it's real?" I yelled. "She wouldn't make this up!"

"So *you* don't want me to come either!" Oz yelled back.

"Be quiet, both of you!"

Abdul didn't raise his voice, but we both fell silent. He moved across to sit beside Bronwen and put his arm round her.

"Now calm down and tell us what happened."

Bronwen gave a few shuddering gasps and wiped her eyes with her sleeve.

"It was the clearest vision I've ever had," she sniffed. "Usually it's just feelings."

"So what did you see?" I asked.

"Well, I was looking over at the oven and then it wasn't there. And there was this dark place near a village, and I realized it must be where you're going tonight." She sniffed and wiped her nose with a bit of her skirt.

"And?" I said urgently.

"And you were all there, and a few of the monks – not the abbot – and then it got even darker around Osric, and then he wasn't there. Then I was back in the kitchen and when I looked at you, Osric, there was a darkness around you, and it felt evil…evil."

Oz leaned back, his eyes still narrowed. "I don't believe all this."

"You think she'd make it up?" I exploded.

"So you're not coming to the abbot with me now?" said Oz bitterly.

"Be quiet, Osric," said Abdul. "There is no question that Bronwen experienced this. The question is, did she understand what she saw?"

"But it was clearly evil," said Bronwen.

"Just like you thought Abdul was evil," said Oz.

"Oh, you…you…" Bronwen couldn't find any more words. She shook her head, fighting back what now looked like tears of anger.

"No, he's right, Bron," I said gently, putting my hand on her arm. "You *were* wrong about Abdul."

"But I was right about Walter!"

"That is true," said Abdul. "I was wavering, but this vision of Bronwen's has confirmed my original feeling, that Osric should stay here."

"And how long did this…*vision* take?" said Oz.

"I don't know," said Bronwen. "It's like you're out of time."

"Only it seemed pretty quick to me," said Oz.

Bronwen banged her fist on the table. "I hate you, Osric, and I don't care if you don't believe me! Go, then, and get yourself killed!"

She got up and ran out of the kitchen.

But Abbot Deorlaf would not be moved.

"The maid's vision has nothing to do with my decision, although in itself it is very interesting," he said. "Even if our friend Abdul had not told me of it, I would not have allowed you to go."

"Thanks Abdul," muttered Oz under his breath.

The abbot raised his eyebrows.

"I am very unhappy about letting Wulfstan go," he continued, "but the rune-stone belongs to him, and I respect his wish."

So after a few hours lying down, in which I'd been completely unable to sleep, I found myself outside the abbey's great gate with Abdul and three monks. The abbot had blessed us all, and one of the monks was carrying the great jewelled cross of St Winfrith. The other monks held smaller crosses. Oz had offered to lend me the short sword he had taken from Arnulf's body, as the long sword was heavy for me to wield in a fight. But I'd decided to go without any weapons except my knife and the rune-stone.

"If the stone can't protect me," I said, "then nothing can."

Abdul was the only one with battle weapons, although they were Leofric's two English swords and not his own, which he had lost at Grimwold's hall. The others were trusting to God or to…*What am I trusting to?* I thought. *Who controls the rune-stone? Is it Woden, or just… Fate?*

It had been raining hard and there was still a light drizzle, so the path to the village was squelchy with mud. The monk in the lead held a lantern on a pole, but even so I slipped a couple of times and my shoe leather was soaked by the time we reached the sheep pen. There were no animals in it.

"What's happened to the sheep?" I asked the monks.

"They are in the cottages with the men," said Father Edwin, the monk carrying St Winfrith's cross. "The villagers cannot afford to lose any more."

"That is brave of them," said Abdul. "If this thing can smell it will sniff them out."

"But we think it will come here first," said Father Edwin. "The animals have always been here before, and that is what it will expect."

I stood and shivered, despite the warm cloak I'd been given. Why on earth hadn't I let someone else have the stone? I could have been safe in bed. I'd been trying to prove that I wasn't a coward. Well, I didn't feel very brave now.

The monk with the lantern stuck the pole into the wet ground and Father Edwin stood behind it with his great cross. On either side were the other monks holding aloft their own crosses. The sky was heavy with clouds, so the only light came from the lantern.

"What do we do now?" I muttered to Abdul.

"We wait," said Abdul, "and remember, do nothing until I tell you."

I stared ahead, trying to make out any denser patches of blackness. Both my hands were wrapped around the rune-stone. Was it my imagination, or was it even warmer than usual – hot, even? I was glad of that on this cold night, though I was also worried that the stone might have sensed danger. My feet were freezing. For a second I wondered what would happen if I took the rune-stone off and put it in a shoe. *Stupid, concentrate,* I told myself.

Suddenly there was a squelching sound behind us. Me and Abdul whipped round, Abdul with his sword drawn and me holding up the rune-stone.

In the dark on the path stood two figures, cloaked and hooded.

CHAPTER THIRTY-FOUR

WULF

"Declare yourselves!" cried Abdul.

Every muscle in my body tensed, as I ran through the words in my mind. *By the power of Thorn*...that was it.

The shorter of the two figures started forward and Abdul stepped to meet him, sword at the ready. Then the figure pushed back its hood.

It was Oz, hair plastered to his forehead in the rain.

"Hold on, hold on!" he said. "It's only us."

I let out a huff of relief and saw Abdul's shoulders slump, as he relaxed.

"I suggest you declare yourselves earlier when approaching friends," said Abdul, "if you do not wish to be run through by a friendly sword. And who, might I ask, is 'us'?"

Oz turned to look at the taller figure with him, who was carrying a long staff.

"Come on. Show yourself," he said, and the figure threw back his hood.

It was my father.

"Brother Beorn!" gasped Father Edwin, and I realized that all three of the monks were staring at the newcomers and that no-one was watching for monsters.

"You lot!" I said, "keep the look-out!"

I was sure that wasn't the proper way to talk to monks, but I didn't care.

"He helped me escape," said Oz. "He knew this secret door in the wall. I'd never have got here without him."

"There will be consequences for this act of disobedience, Brother," said Father Edwin.

Beorn walked up and stood beside the priest.

"I have a higher duty than obedience, Father," he said. "I have neglected my son for all these years and the boy Osric put me to shame. He was desperate to come and face danger with his friend and I thought… perhaps…that I might make amends a little if I came also to help protect him."

"Your son?" gasped Father Edwin.

"Yeah, never mind that. How are you gonna protect me?" I said, conscious all the time that we weren't concentrating on what we'd come for. Luckily Abdul was back on duty, scanning the dark and directing the other two monks to do the same.

"We will speak of this later," said Father Edwin. "While you are here you may as well keep watch with us."

"I *said*, how are you gonna protect me?" I repeated angrily.

Brother Beorn shook his head. "You must learn to let go of your anger, my son. I shall protect you with my prayers and with my staff and, if necessary, with my body."

"And I've got my sword," said Oz with a flourish, "so bring 'em on."

I couldn't help smiling. How did Oz do it – manage a joke in the middle of a dark, wet night, when we were waiting for a demon to appear?

"Hush!" whispered Abdul, and there was instant silence.

But not quite silence. From the other side of the sheep-pen came a slithering sound. I strained my eyes but there was nothing but blackness to be seen. The noise stopped. Then from a different direction, another slither. It sounded like a giant worm crawling on its belly. Then from somewhere else, a third noise, a sucking, slurping sound, coming slowly towards us.

Panic rose in my throat. The rune-stone was practically burning my fingers now, as I held it up, ready to speak the words. Which direction should I face? There, straight ahead. Was that something in the darkness? A patch of black, deeper than the surrounding blackness? Only…those little red glimmers…were those *eyes?*

I stepped forward and startled to gabble, "By the power of –", but Father Edwin had beaten me to it.

"In the name of the Father, the Son and the Holy Spirit, I banish you, foul fiend!" his voice rang out. "Go back to Hell, and trouble us no more!"

There was a hiss, and the two little points of red vanished and then reappeared, slightly further away. Father Edwin stepped forward, holding St Winfrith's cross straight out in front of him. It must be heavy, I thought. *Oh concentrate! Stop thinking about stupid things!*

"Careful!" warned Abdul. "Remember what happened to the first priest!"

Father Edwin ignored him.

"Return to your master in Hell and never trouble us again!" he cried.

There was a slithering sound to my left and I spun round, keeping the rune-stone high up in front of my face.

"By the power of Thorn," I gasped, "I command you to..." *To what?* I always said *to stop*, but Father Edwin had told the thing to *go*. Should I say *stop* or *go?*

A shadow reached a black arm towards me. It was cold...so cold. What was I supposed to say? I was in a freezing mist. There was nothing to say, I thought dully, nothing to do. There were shouts, but so far away. I was falling...falling into blackness. Then someone grabbed me, stopped me falling. I was thrown backwards. Someone was between me and that freezing shadow. I heard a voice, nearer than those other shouts had been.

"Leave him in God's name! Leave him and..." The voice rose to a shriek which filled my head and wouldn't go away. It wouldn't go away! *Please, make it stop!*

And then it did go away and I was flat on my back on the muddy ground, staring up at a sliver of moon that had just broken through the clouds. How long had I been there? Then Abdul's face covered the moon, staring down with an agonized expression, which softened into relief as I blinked up at him.

"He's alive!" he called, helping me into a sitting position.

I stared around. My hand still clutched the rune-stone, now only warm. Three monks were bending over someone, Father Edwin giving the last rites to the figure lying stiffly on the ground. I looked at the dead man's face. My father.

He had done what he said he would. He'd protected me with his prayers and with his own body, and he'd died doing it. And all I'd done was snarl angrily at him. Not one single word of kindness or forgiveness had I given him. Tears welled up in my eyes as I watched Father Edwin make the sign of the cross on his forehead. And I hadn't even said the spell properly. If I hadn't dithered I could have protected myself and my father would still have been alive.

"We've all survived, then," I said in a slurred voice, "apart from him."

"Wulfstan," murmured Abdul, "prepare yourself."

I pulled myself away from Abdul's supporting arm and looked around wildly.

"Oz! Where's Oz?"

"Wulfstan, be strong!" said Abdul. "We have searched the area and we cannot find him."

CHAPTER THIRTY-FIVE

BRONWEN

I pushed back the coverlet and put my feet on the cold floor of the outhouse. I'd got to find the abbot! Quietly I felt around for my shoes, trying not to wake the other women and children. It was lucky my pallet was near the door, because I was in almost pitch blackness and had to feel my way. Stretched out in front, my hand met a heavy iron ring. The handle was stiff – I had to use both hands – and the door creaked.

"Who's that?" said a woman's voice.

"Only me, Bronwen," I whispered. "Call of nature."

"Use the straw in the corner, like the rest of us," muttered the woman.

I didn't answer. I closed the door behind me, pulled my cloak tighter and stepped out into the cold, wet night. How was I going to find my way in this dark? And if I reached the abbot, what would he say? Outside the building I was not much better off. But then the clouds parted, revealing a thin crescent moon for a few moments before covering it again. Now, although once again in total darkness, I had seen enough to know where to go. Treading carefully on the muddy ground and holding up the hem of my skirts, I soon found my way to the great abbey, squatting black and solid in the night. I wasn't even sure where the abbot's quarters were, but once round the corner that problem was solved. A group of monks was standing by the great gate holding lanterns, and in the middle, taller than the rest, was Abbot Deorlaf.

I walked over to him as quickly as the squelchy ground would let me. He turned and looked at me in surprise.

"Holy Father," I began, making a little curtsey. "I had to find you."

"Why?" he asked. "What has got you out of bed on a night like this?"

"I had a dream, my lord," I said. "At first I couldn't sleep, and then I found I was dreaming. At least," I hesitated, "I *think* it was a dream. It might have been another vision. But anyway, it's the same thing really."

"And what was this dream, my child?"

"I dreamt that my vision – that I had earlier, in the kitchen – I dreamt that it came true. I think that Osric went to find Wulfstan, and that something terrible has happened!" My voice started to rise. "Someone has been killed and I think that Osric has gone, and, oh, Holy Father, we need to go and help them!"

"Send the child back to bed," said one of the monks. "There are enough of them out there. Besides Father Edwin, there are Brother Sigeric and Brother Oswold – and the Moor, of course."

"And Wulfstan," I put in, slightly indignant that he was being overlooked.

"Oh, yes," replied the monk. "The boy."

"But it is only a nightmare," said another monk, more kindly. "Understandable that the child should be having bad dreams."

I shook my head. How could I explain to these men that I could tell the difference between a normal dream and one that meant something? The abbot was looking at me with penetrating eyes.

"I am not sure," he said, and my spirits lifted a little. It didn't help with whatever danger the others were in, but it was good to be believed.

Abbot Deorlaf turned to the monk who had spoken kindly.

"Check the boy's quarters," he said. "I put our guests in the furthest dormitory. If he is there we shall know that Bronwen has only been dreaming."

The monk scurried off and the abbot turned back to Bronwen.

"I am sorry that we had to put you in an outhouse. I thought it best that you should be with other women and children, but if you stay here longer we may find something better for you."

"That's all right," I replied, liking the abbot more and more, "only it would be good to be a little nearer my friends."

180

"They're coming back!" shouted a monk standing at the great gate, and I realized that he'd been looking through a spyhole. I ran over and almost pushed him out of the way.

"Oh, let me see!" I begged. "Is Osric there? Are they all right?"

The monk looked at me haughtily. "If you would be so good as to move out of the way, I could open the gate and we can all see."

"Sorry," I said, but the wait, while the monk unbarred the gate and turned the enormous key, was almost unbearable.

Then the gates swung open. First came Father Edwin with St Winfrith's cross, followed by another two monks carrying the body of a fourth. Was he dead, or just unconscious? Then came Abdul with his arm around Wulf, who was struggling to walk.

There was no Oz.

As soon as they were in the abbey grounds, the gatekeeper once again barred the entrance. I ran to my friends, but before I could say anything, Father Edwin began speaking.

"Holy Father," he said, bowing. "Bad news and good news. We were followed by Brother Beorn and the other boy."

"I told you!" I gasped.

"The demons appeared," Father Edwin went on. "There seemed to be more than one of them, and in the struggle Brother Beorn was killed. But we prevailed, with the help of St Winfrith's holy cross. We banished them! We left the other crosses there to keep them away."

"But where's Osric?" I cried.

Wulf raised his head. Even in the lamplight, I could see that he was deadly pale and he had a look of such anguish on his face that I wanted to fling my arms round him.

"I've probably killed him," said Wulf, "like I killed my father."

"What?" said several voices together.

"The boy exaggerates," said Father Edwin severely. "He is over-dramatizing."

Abdul stood up straight and glared at the priest.

"And so might you," he said, "if you had been through what he has."

Abbot Deorlaf turned to Abdul.

181

"May I ask *you*, my friend, to tell us what happened?"

I thought that Father Edwin looked distinctly put out as Abdul began his story. It seemed they had seen very little clearly, but they had all heard and felt the evil presence of probably three of these creatures. Then Wulf had begun to be wreathed in some kind of mist. Mist? I hadn't seen any mist in my dream. Then Brother Beorn had dragged Wulf away, but had himself been wrapped in this strange misty substance. I hadn't seen any of that, either – just a body, lying still. No-one saw what had happened to Oz. At the end of the confusion he simply wasn't there.

"So the rune-stone didn't work this time?" I said in a small voice.

"I messed up, didn't I?" sobbed Wulf. "It would have worked, only I got confused when Father Edwin shouted his stuff out, and I sort of forgot what to say…

"It's my fault – I killed them!"

"What do you mean?" asked the abbot. "Did you not use your rune-stone first, before Father Edwin spoke?"

"I didn't get the chance, but it's still my fault," whispered Wulf, and then collapsed on to the muddy ground.

"Come inside, all of you," said the abbot. "What am I thinking of, keeping you out in this weather? And we must send for Brother Walter."

Inside the abbot's quarters, with both Walter and me fussing round him and giving him wine to drink, Wulf looked slightly less pale but just as anguished.

"Did you not understand my instructions, Father Edwin?" asked the abbot. "I told you to let Wulfstan speak first and only then to use the prayer of exorcism."

I listened.

"Forgive me, Holy Father," said the priest stiffly. "In the presence of these demons, I reacted instinctively." He paused. "And besides…"

The abbot waited. "Besides what, Father Edwin?"

"This evil, heathen thing!" burst out the priest. "It did not seem right!"

"It is not evil," said Walter mildly. "Not everything is evil that was here before Our Lord and Holy Mother Church. It can be used for either good *or* evil."

"And...forgive me, Holy Father," continued Father Edwin. He looked beseechingly at the abbot. "I could not understand *why* you gave those instructions. I know this is the sin of disobedience, and I am ready for whatever penance you see fit to impose."

The abbot sighed and shook his head.

"I also have a confession." He looked down at his hands and then back at the priest. "I was curious," he said simply. "Father Beocca had been killed, and he had been carrying a cross. I wondered...if something else might have power over these demons."

I looked at Father Edwin to see how he would react to this, and then suddenly he wasn't there. The candlelit room vanished and I was on a dark moor. I clutched the arm of Wulf's chair. I could feel it, but I couldn't see it, and I couldn't hear voices, only the wind. What was happening? There were three figures on the moorland, two dragging a smaller one in the middle. Then I did hear a voice.

"Come on! Use yer legs, you lump! We ain't gonna carry you any more."

The figure in the middle lifted his head. It was Oz.

CHAPTER THIRTY-SIX

OZ

My head felt as if there was a hammer inside it, rhythmically trying to crack my skull open. And my legs wouldn't do what I wanted them to. I felt a sharp tug under both armpits.

"Get a move on!" said a rough voice.

"I'm trying," I gasped.

I didn't want to do anything to put their backs up, whoever they were.

"Try harder!" said the rough voice, and I tried to force a little more strength into my jelly-like legs. Then I stumbled against the man on my left. He staggered, cursed and let go of me, and the ground came up to meet me. Thud. I thought I was going to be sick.

"This is no good," said a different voice. "We was better off when he was out cold. We're nearly there anyway. I'll sling him over me shoulder."

I felt myself lifted and thrown roughly over the man's shoulder before everything went black once more.

When I came to I was in a long room, lit only by a feeble little fire in the middle. It didn't feel like a cottage, more like the great hall of a very small village. The hammer in my skull was still trying to split it open. *Shit*...Bron had been right! Why hadn't I listened to her? I should have stayed behind in the abbey. And who were these people? And, most important, when were Abdul and Wulf going to come and rescue me?

I felt as helpless as a baby. I put a hand to my pounding head and realized with surprise that I wasn't tied up. Even my feet had been left free. But of course, it'd be useless to try and run for it, even if I had the strength: because there were my captors, a few feet away from me.

The two men were sitting by the fire cradling mugs of ale in their beefy hands and next to them crouched an old woman, poking at the embers of ashy logs. I shifted my head and the room swam. Best to lie still.

"When d'you reckon he'll get here?" said one of the men.

"Any time," said the other. "You know him. Turns up when you least expect it. We've done our bit. All we can do now is wait."

"I reckon he'll be pleased with us," said the first man. "Got him what he wanted."

He turned to look at me, and I quickly closed my eyes.

"What's so important about *him?*" said the old woman in a high, cracked voice. "He's just a kid."

"It ain't what he is, it's what he's got round his neck," said the second man. "We should have had him before now. He was supposed to be delivering a letter to the boss, but he never turned up."

My eyes opened again in surprise. So their boss was the person the letter was addressed to! What was his name? I struggled to remember.

"The boss reckons somebody warned him," said the first man.

The letter had turned out to be a death sentence. My head was still thumping, but I had to try and remember what it said. Closing my eyes tight, I pictured Abdul sitting by our campfire. I heard his deep, foreign voice translating it from Latin. It had said something about a treasure – the rune-stone – on Wulf's body, and when whoever it was – I still couldn't remember his name – had got it, our bodies – mine and Wulf's bodies – could be disposed of.

I felt even sicker. It wasn't looking good. These men thought their boss would be pleased because of what was round *my* neck…my own horse-rune that I'd taken from Arnulf. It sounded as though they thought I was Wulf. Or was my rune-stone just as valuable as Wulf's? Or maybe they didn't know the difference. They didn't seem that bright. I gave up.

The old woman started speaking again.

"You sure you don't want any more of my stew?"

She had a funny accent. It reminded me of someone.

"No thanks, Morwen, that was good."

The other man muttered his agreement.

185

Morwen. That was a bit like Bronwen. *That was it.* Though her voice was as different as could be from Bron's, her accent was Welsh.

"D'you reckon *he* wants any?" said the old woman.

Both the men laughed. "What's the point?" said one. "We don't wanna waste it on him."

"Oh, don't be so heartless," mocked the other. "Don't they give a condemned man his last meal before they top him?"

There were guffaws of laughter from all three of them and I went icy cold from head to toes. I heard the old woman shuffle over to me and smelt the ale on her breath. She poked my leg.

"Wake up!" she cackled. "Don't sleep the rest of your life away. You haven't got much of it left."

More laughter. I kept my eyes shut, but the old woman poked me harder.

"Ow!" I said, and found myself looking at a wrinkled, gummy face, leering into mine.

"D'you want some of my stew?"

I didn't answer. Would the stew make me feel less sick, or even sicker than I already felt? Perhaps I'd throw up all over her. That'd be good.

"Not very polite, is he?" she said to the others.

Couldn't she leave me in peace to think? There must be some way out of this, if only I could *think.*

"I just wanna sleep," I muttered.

"Oh, you'll get plenty of sleep soon enough," she cackled. "For ever and ever."

"But why?" I couldn't help saying. "I haven't done anything wrong."

They seemed to find this the funniest thing yet.

"You go back to sleep, dearie," chortled the old woman, "if that's what you want. There's a nice little hole in the ground out back for you to sleep in."

One of the men grinned at me and did an imitation of a throat being cut.

"How d'you reckon he'll do it, Morwen?" he gloated. "Likes a bit of fun, does the boss."

I thought I really was going to be sick now, but I had no choice but to listen.

"Well, he's got lots of methods," nodded the old woman. "Sometimes he just ties 'em up and chucks 'em in the pit."

What?

The old woman ran a finger over her whiskery chin. "After all…it's no fun burying somebody if they're already dead."

CHAPTER THIRTY-SEVEN

WULF

"Osric!" cried Bronwen, her hands clenched into fists. "Osric, where are you?"

I jerked myself upright in my chair.

"He's alive!" I rasped. "You've seen him! Tell me he's alive!"

"Yes, I've seen him," gasped Bronwen. "He's alive."

Abdul caught hold of her as she swayed and almost fell.

"A chair for the maid!" he ordered.

Suddenly I came to life.

"She can have this one," I said, jumping up. "I'm all right now."

And I *was* all right now. I had a purpose again. My father had died. That was sad, but he'd died doing what he'd promised, trying to protect me. And I hadn't really known him. But if Oz was alive, my best friend from when I was born, then we had to leave straight away. We had to find him!

Now it was Bronwen's turn to be cosseted and have a wine flagon put to her lips. But she shook her head and pushed it away.

"I'm sorry," she said. "It was the shock of being back here so suddenly, after seeing Osric on the moor."

I knelt by her and gripped one of her hands.

"Tell us what you saw!" I urged.

"He was with two big men, one on either side. They were dragging him along, trying to get him to walk faster. And they were on this moorland." Bronwen shook her head. "But I don't know where it was."

"I could make a guess," said the abbot. "If he was taken only a short while ago, and if they are not on horseback, it could well be Wentworth Moor."

"But my lord," protested Father Edwin. "Surely you are not giving credence to this child's fantasies."

"I am indeed, Father," said the abbot coldly. "This child had a 'fantasy', as you put it, that one of your party was killed, and that the boy Osric had vanished. At the time she told me, we did not even know that Osric had gone with them, and neither did she, but when you returned, we found that it was so."

Father Edwin's eyes widened.

"Devil's work!" he hissed.

Abbot Deorlaf sighed and closed his eyes, but before he could answer, Walter stepped up to the priest.

"Some might think that you are obsessed with the devil, Father," he said. "But were there not prophesying dreams in the bible? Didn't our Lord's father – His human father I mean – the blessed Joseph, didn't he dream that they should go to Egypt, to escape the wrath of Herod? Was that devil's work?"

"Surely you are not comparing..." began the priest, but he was interrupted.

"Well said, Brother Walter," smiled the abbot, ignoring Father Edwin. "Remind me why you have never become a priest."

"Because I'm happy as I am," replied Walter.

This was all too much for me. Standing around discussing the devil and whether Walter should be a priest, when Oz was in urgent need of rescue!

"Excuse me, Holy Father," I said, "but I think we ought to be going. Now if you'd just like to point us in the direction of this moor."

Abdul smiled. "And if you could provide us with a very few provisions?" he asked the abbot. "You have already been so kind, and I do not like to ask, but it may be some time before we can stop to hunt, and build a fire."

"But of course, my friend," said Abbot Deorlaf. "But the two of you on your own? Should I not send someone who knows the country around here?"

189

"Excuse me," said Bronwen, sitting up very straight. "Don't you mean the *three* of us?"

"My child," said the abbot, "I could not dream of letting a young maid go on such an adventure."

"But Osric is my friend!" she protested.

I raised my eyebrows and laughed at this.

"Well, we might have had a few arguments, but he's still my friend!" said Bronwen. "And besides, Holy Father, we wouldn't even know he was still alive if it weren't for my vision. I could have all sorts of other helpful visions when we're looking for him!"

She looked at the abbot triumphantly, as if to say, *find a good argument against that!*

Abbot Deorlaf smiled and shook his head.

"I see you are determined," he said. "Very well. I am sure that our friend Abdul is more than capable of looking after you both. But think carefully. This is a dangerous mission."

"I know that, sir," said Bronwen. "I'm not rushing into it thoughtlessly."

"You should all have a few hours sleep now," said the abbot.

"Excuse me, but we shouldn't!" I said. "Every second counts!"

So a short while later we said goodbye, with many thanks, to Abbot Deorlaf and Brother Walter. Bronwen flung her arms around Walter's neck.

"I'll never forget you!" she said.

Then we set off on horseback, with bags of provisions and a guide to take us just beyond the village.

The guide was a boy called Odda, and I spotted straight away that he couldn't take his eyes off Bronwen. I told myself not to be stupid. He'd be leaving us soon. All the same, I watched him like a hawk. A chilly grey dawn was breaking when we reached the village, on the path that me and Abdul had trodden earlier that night.

"Have you got any weapons?" Odda asked Bronwen. "'Cos I can see they got swords, but have you got anything?"

"No, I wish I had a bow," said Bronwen. "I'd be no use with a sword."

"You can have mine, if you like," said Odda. "My dad's just made me a new one, 'cos mine's too small for me now. It's still in good nick, though."

"Oh, thank you, thank you!" said Bronwen. "Are you sure?"

He nodded, went a bit pink and vanished inside one of the cottages. Bronwen got off her horse and looked eagerly at the cottage door, while I sat and fumed. I should be pleased that Bron was going to have a bow, but if only *I* could have found one for her. Then I caught sight of Abdul's amused expression, which showed that he knew exactly what was going on in my head. I frowned, leaned forward and started patting Chestnut.

Odda came out with a small bow of ash wood and a quiver half-full of arrows.

"I'm sorry there's not more arrows," he said.

Bronwen looked so delighted that I was afraid she was going to fling her arms round Odda's neck as well. Thankfully she didn't.

"Oh, that's brilliant," she sang. "Oh, it's just the right size for me. You're so kind!"

She looked at Odda with shining eyes and, aware of Abdul, I tried to look as uninterested as I could.

"We should dismount here as well," said Abdul. "I should like to look at that sheep pen now that we have a little light."

So when Bron had fastened the bow on her back and the quiver at her side, we led the horses to the sheep pen.

"This is where it all happened," I said, looking round at the muddy ground.

Abdul crouched down, examining footprints and flattened grass. It all looked a mess to me.

"Oz was standing here last time I saw him," I said, but Abdul ignored me.

"What are these strange marks," said Abdul, "as if some creature crawled on its belly here?"

I shuddered. "Yeah, one of them came from there, and there should be some over here and over there too. Yes, there are, look. There *were* three of them."

Odda turned pale. "You saw three of the things?" he whispered. "Weren't you scared?"

"We were here to do a job," I said airily. "There wasn't time to be scared."

Panic was rising inside me as I remembered the night before, but I wasn't going to show that to Odda.

"What are they?" said Abdul, shaking his head.

"But *this* is where I last saw Oz," I said again. "And there's none of those funny marks round here."

"No," said Bronwen, "but he was here, I can feel it. And look! Over there! Boot marks. Two sets of big boot marks, and…it looks like something being dragged away."

"Well spotted, Bronwen," said Abdul. "But the drag marks look like boots too, not like these other strange markings. This looks like someone being dragged between two others. Two men. But why did we not see them?"

"It was that mist," I said. "Don't you remember, the mist everywhere?"

Abdul shook his head. "And we didn't see these prints last night, either. Was I blind?"

"It was dark, Abdul," I said. "There was mist everywhere, my dad had just been killed and you thought I had, too. Don't beat yourself up over it."

"So all we've got to do is follow these prints," said Bronwen, "and we'll find Oz."

"You make it sound easy," said Odda admiringly.

"The tracks will not be so clear once we reach the moor," said Abdul, "so I suggest we start right away. I think we do not need your services any more, Odda. I thank you for what you have done."

"Yeah," I said. "Thanks a lot and goodbye."

"But don't you need me to show you where the moor starts?" said Odda, looking disappointed.

"It is not necessary," said Abdul. "We can follow the tracks, and I should be happier if you were back in the safety of the abbey."

"Oh, well," said Odda, downcast. "The moor's over that way."

Bronwen went up to him.

"Thank you so much for the bow and arrows," she smiled. "I'm sure we'll see you when we get back with our friend."

Odda brightened up a bit, and we got back on our horses and set off slowly, keeping our eyes on the tracks we were following. When I looked back he was still gazing after us. Bronwen turned and waved at him and he slowly waved back.

"Are we going back to the abbey, then," I asked, "once we've rescued Oz?"

"I've no idea," said Bronwen.

"Who knows where we shall end up," said Abdul grimly.

The tracks did become harder to follow once we reached the scrubby grass of the moor, and several times Abdul got down and scanned the ground for clues. At midday we stopped and ate some of the bread and cheese from our bags. Bronwen looked around her.

"This looks a bit like what I saw in my vision," she said. "Only it *was* dark, and one bit of moorland looks much like another."

Not long after our stop we climbed to the top of a hill and saw below us a small settlement. There was a hall and a cluster of other cottages, but no sign of village life. No farm animals, no people, just apparently empty buildings. There was one horse tethered outside the hall. That was all. Then a dog barked.

"Strange," said Abdul. "A deserted village, but there is *someone* there."

Suddenly a small figure appeared out of nowhere and stood in front of us. She was less than three feet tall, with a snub nose and slanting green eyes. Through her long curly hair stuck two large pointed ears. I felt a grin spread across my face.

"You mustn't go down there," she said. "It be *bad*."

CHAPTER THIRTY-EIGHT

OZ

My stomach turned to water. This might really be it. As soon as this 'boss' arrived, I was done for. I'd had as much life as I was going to get, and the ending wouldn't be pleasant. Even if Wulf and Abdul turned up, they'd probably be too late.

The old woman shuffled back to join the others by the fire.

It wasn't *fair*. I hadn't lived long enough. There were loads of things I wanted to do. But people did die young. Lots of people. My sister Elfgyfu died of the fever when she was younger than me. Though I'd swap that death for the one I was likely to suffer.

"What was that?" said one of the men.

"It's him," said the other one, and I heard a horse outside, whinnying as it was tied up.

My stomach lurched even more. Where was the battle courage an English warrior was supposed to feel? I hadn't felt like this when I was facing the Normans. But this wasn't battle. It was just murder.

Then into the hall strode a big man with a dark beard. The two men leapt up and bowed, but the old woman clapped her hands with delight and tottered over to him.

"My darling boy," she crowed. "My baby!"

I stared. Her *baby*? Surely this old crone couldn't be his mother?

The man smiled indulgently.

"Morwen," he said. "How's my old nurse, then?"

Oh...she'd been his nurse when he was a child.

"Let me take your cloak, cariad," fussed the old woman, reaching up to undo his shoulder brooch. He let her do it, laughing, and then sat in the carved wooden chair that the men pulled forward.

"No, leave my boots, my dear," he said, "but I could do with a drink, and something to eat, too."

All this while he ignored me and I tried to make myself invisible. But when the ale was poured and Morwen was heating the stew, the man finally turned a pair of piercing dark eyes on me.

"So," he said. "Let us see it, then."

"See what?" I muttered.

What did I say that for? Stupid! It'd only make him angrier.

The man smiled. "I don't think this is the time for games, do you?" he said. "We both know what I mean."

Suddenly my head cleared a bit. I had nothing to lose. My death would be pretty unpleasant whatever I said.

"First tell me why you want it."

The man's eyebrows shot up, then he burst out laughing.

"Shall we introduce ourselves?" he said. "My first name is Sigelac, son of Ordgar, but nowadays I prefer to be known by my second name, Gethin, which is the one my mother gave me."

Sigelac! That was it! And didn't the letter say something about calling him by his English name, 'to allay suspicion' — whatever that meant?

Morwen turned round from stirring the stew.

"Ah," she said. "She was a great Welsh lady, was your mother."

"Evidently the letter which you should have been delivering has been lost," smiled Gethin. "But it makes no difference now, does it? For I know who you are...Wulfstan."

"Actually, I'm not," I said quietly.

Gethin started forward in his chair and the two men looked at each other, terrified, and tried to disappear into the wall hangings.

"What!?" said Gethin, with a face like thunder.

"I'm Wulfstan's friend, Osric," I said.

Gethin sprang from his chair and turned to the men.

"You idiots!" he shouted. "Can't you get anything right?"

One of the men fell on his knees.

"Please my lord," he begged. "All we was told was to look for a boy about this age, in that place where your creatures was, and that he'd have a rune-stone round his neck."

"And he has got one!" joined in the other man, who was edging towards the door.

"Has got one what?" snarled Gethin.

"A stone round his neck," whispered the first man, looking as if he was about to pass out.

Gethin's expression cleared just as abruptly as it had darkened. He turned back to me.

"Have you?" he asked.

I nodded.

"So your friend gave it to you?"

I shook my head. Gethin strode over and ripped my tunic open. He took hold of the leather thong and dangled the stone, without touching it, in front of his eyes. At first he looked puzzled, but slowly a smile spread across his face.

"Well, well," he said. "Not what I was expecting, but not bad. Not bad at all."

He turned back to the men, who were glancing uneasily at each other, unsure whether or not they were off the hook.

"This was one of those in Grimwold's possession," he told them, before turning back to me. "So how did you get it?"

"We got it off Arnulf, one of Grimwold's men, after we killed him," I said.

"After you killed whom, Arnulf or Grimwold?"

I frowned. "Both, actually," I said.

Gethin roared with laughter.

"Quite the little English warrior, aren't we? This may turn out well, after all."

He turned once more to his two men, still hovering uncertainly.

"Ulf, Gar, you are stupid oafs. What are you?"

"Stupid oafs, my lord," they muttered.

"But this time you were lucky stupid oafs. What were you?"

196

"Lucky stupid oafs, my lord."

"Good. Sit down then and shut up. Is that stew ready, Morwen?"

"It is, my sweet."

"Good. Give him some as well. We don't want him dying of hunger just yet."

To my amazement, a table was dragged nearer the fire and two bowls of stew were placed on it.

"Come on," said Gethin. "Bring him a stool – no…a chair."

One of the men – I didn't know which was Ulf and which was Gar – rushed to fetch a chair for me, while the other stood by with a *please let me do something for you, my lord,* expression on his face. I lowered myself nervously into the grandest chair I'd ever sat in, the twin of Gethin's throne-like seat. It had curved arms, which seemed to get in the way, and a high carved back. I'd rather have sat on a stool.

"Eat, boy," said Gethin, and, unbelievably, I found that I was hungry.

"So you are Wulfstan's friend?" said Gethin as we ate.

I nodded.

"Good friends, are you?"

I wasn't sure where this was going, so I just nodded again. A wolfish smile spread across Gethin's face.

"Good," he said. "You can be my little honeypot to catch the wasp."

I stopped eating. Now I knew where it was going.

Gethin took a draught of his ale. "Have some," he said, and one of the men rushed to fill my beaker.

"You ask me why I want these things, and there is no harm in your knowing," said Gethin, leaning back in his chair. "But the true answer is a long one. The short answer will do for now. Power."

I took a sip of my ale, but realized I'd better not drink too much. It was good quality, and there was no water mixed with it. I'd better keep a clear head.

"I have found," said Gethin, "that the more of these runes I have, the more I can use them for my own ends. It is the magic of my father's people, not my mother's, but if I have enough of them I can use them to avenge my mother's people."

He paused for another drink, while I tried to make sense of this. I couldn't.

"Neat, isn't it?" Gethin continued. "To use a nation's deep, ancient magic against it."

"But – you're English, aren't you?" I said.

Gethin laughed again. "Only on one side," he said. "But I'm having such fun playing with these English things. I mix them with a little magic of my own and you wouldn't believe what I come up with…For instance…"

Gethin closed his eyes and started to murmur an incantation in a language I'd never heard. Or had I? An image of Grimwold flashed into my head, gabbling words like these. Gethin's voice grew louder, and at the other end of the hall a mist began to form.

I watched in horror as the mist grew thicker. Ulf and Gar shrank back against the opposite wall, behind the table, but Morwen nodded, smiling.

Half the hall was now full of a swirling black cloud. I froze, as in the middle of the cloud appeared one, two, then three pairs of red eyes.

Gethin turned to me.

"Have you met my pets?" he said.

CHAPTER THIRTY-NINE

OZ

The black cloud wafted towards us and I heard a hissing as the red eyes snaked around, now higher, now lower, but all the time coming towards me. I couldn't move, couldn't do anything but stare into those horrible unblinking eyes. A curl of mist reached me and started to twist around my leg, and one pair of eyes rose higher and gleamed down at me. Now I could dimly see the body behind it, a thick black serpent's body, even blacker than the cloud. I couldn't breathe. All I could do was stare into those burning eyes as they sank towards my face. And then…nothing.

I woke up. I was still alive!

Then I relaxed. God, what a nightmare. It was all getting too much for me. Perhaps I shouldn't tell the others. Where were they, anyway? What was the last thing that had happened to us? I tried to open my eyes, but they were so heavy. It was as if they were stuck. I forced them to open a slit – just enough to see a sliver of some room. I couldn't remember coming into this place. *Come on, wake yourself up.* I tried to move my head, but that was stuck too.

Then I realized I wasn't lying down, but sitting in some chair. My arms were resting on curved wooden arms, my hands cradling the rounded ends. My back could feel knobbly carvings through my thin shirt. But when I tried to shift in my seat, I couldn't. Panic rising, I tried to raise an arm, but that was stuck fast as well.

There was a glow at the other end of the room, or hall, or whatever it was. I stared at it, horror growing inside me. It reminded me of…glowing eyes…no…no…I was still in the nightmare! *Wake up!*

"Wake up, you oafs!" said a familiar cracked Welsh voice to my right.

"Leave us in peace, Morwen," said a rough voice behind him to his left. "We've had a heavy night."

Oh my God, it wasn't a dream.

I struggled with all my might to move, but it was as if my body didn't belong to me. It all came back to me, the whole nightmare, but it had been real, all of it. And the last thing I could remember was the mist curling round my legs, the red eyes bearing down on me. What had happened next? A sob rose in my throat, but no sound came out.

Though I *was* alive. I'd thought that snake thing was going to kill me. *Be pleased about that, at least*, I thought. Only...didn't that mean my horrible death was still to come? It'd all be over now if I'd been killed. *Don't think like that!* Where there's life there's hope, my dad always said. Images of home floated in front of my barely open eyes. My mum cooking over the fire, my dad chopping wood. Where there's life there's hope. I felt a hysterical laugh gurgling up, but I couldn't utter a sound. *What* had they done to me? *Think, think!* It had been night, but now there was daylight. What had happened in between?

The cracked voice started up again. "What about guarding him?"

"He don't need no guarding," said the other voice. "The boss has got 'im under a spell."

"I know that, you idiot! But you should still keep watch. What do you think he pays you for?"

"Oh, leave it off, Morwen," said a third voice from behind. "The kid's all right." He sniggered. "At least, I wouldn't exactly say he's *all right*, but he can't do nothin'."

The second voice joined in the sniggering. "He may not be all right, but he's better than he will be when the boss has finished with him."

They started guffawing, and I felt sick. Could I vomit in my paralysed state?

"Got any porridge, Morwen?" said one of them. "Since it don't seem like we're gonna get any more sleep."

"Of course I have, but you'll have to shift yourselves. Do you think I'm going to bring it over and feed you, like a couple of babies?"

"I need a piss," grunted one of them.

"Me too," said the other.

"Well, get outside then!" scolded Morwen. "A pair of animals you two are!"

I heard their heavy movements as they got to their feet and shambled off, then I felt a cold draught of air before a door banged behind them. A hunched figure shuffled into my sideview and moved where I could see her more clearly, down the other end of the hall. She stood stirring something in a pot over the glow, which must be a fire. The mist was gone, and those horrible creatures. My breathing grew faster. I could breathe, then. Well, of course I could, or I'd be dead.

The men came back and joined the old woman, sitting by the fire with bowls in their hands. I could smell the porridge. I felt even more sick.

"Funny thing that, last night," said one of them. "I never seen that before."

"What?" said the other one.

"That thing going for the kid, and then not killing him."

"Yeah, you're right. Usually they just strike 'em dead with their eyes and that's that. And then they suck 'em dry, if it's an animal. You're right. I never seen that before, neither."

"Ah," Morwen joined in. "He's got complete control over them, he has. He can make them do whatever he wants. When he wants them to stop, they obey him instantly."

I listened intently. *Calm down, calm down, you might learn something.* Then another cold draught from behind told me someone else had entered the hall. Firm footsteps sounded on the wooden floor, and Gethin strode into view.

"Stuffing your faces again, I see. You feed them too much, Morwen. You're too kind-hearted."

The old woman laughed her cackling laugh.

"It's for you, my sweet," she said. "I'm keeping them good and strong for you."

"Well, you can put those bowls down now," he ordered. "I've got a job for you."

I jolted inside, though my body didn't move. *They were going to kill me!* But why hadn't they done it last night? *They were going to torture me, find out what I knew!*

Gethin turned to look at me, then walked up and bent down, so that I could clearly see his face.

"And how's my little friend?" he sneered. "Got yourself stuck in the spider's web, have you? And, oh dear, the spider's paralysed you, so you can't escape. All you can do is wait and wonder when the spider's going to finish you off. Well…not just yet. Cheer up, I've got a nice surprise for you."

CHAPTER FORTY

WULF

The elf-girl folded her arms and stood looking each of us up and down, while I tried to remember all the elves we'd met. There'd only been three females: Nettle, Dandelion and the tomboy Chickweed. So who was this? Was she from a completely different group? She didn't seem unfriendly. It had taken Pooka and his gang quite a while to consider us as anything other than human vermin.

"Did you hear me?" she said. "I'd turn around if I was you."

"No, you wouldn't, Bramble," said another voice, one that I remembered. "Not if it was *your* friend down there, you wouldn't."

The horses gave little wickers of recognition, and now I really was grinning, despite the danger and the fears for Oz. For there stood Toadstool, right beside the elf-girl.

"Toadstool!" I cried. "What are you doing here? And how do you do that? That thing where the air goes funny and you appear out of nowhere?"

Toadstool grinned back, a lopsided grin as of one old friend to another.

"Oh, that," he replied. "That be elf-stuff, that be. You can't explain it, you just does it. But we wasn't air-flittin', was we, Bramble?"

Bramble shook her head.

"It's true, then, what they says about humans," she said. "They ain't got proper eyes to speak of."

"What do you mean?" I said.

"We was just lyin' in that grass over there," said Bramble, "and you never seen us. They never does see us, humans, unless we wants 'em to."

"Which ain't very often," said Toadstool. "But they does see other humans an' horses, so if I was you I'd go back a bit, the other side o' this here hill top, out of sight o' that there village."

203

"Good thinking," I said, and we turned the horses and retraced our steps a little way.

"But you didn't answer my first question," I said as we walked down the slope. "What are you doing here?"

"I come to find Bramble, didn't I," said Toadstool.

I felt I was supposed to know who Bramble was, and the name did seem familiar, but I didn't quite like to ask.

Abdul cleared his throat.

"Ahem…do you think some introductions are called for?"

"P'raps," said Toadstool. "Well, I knows Wulf an' he knows me, an' I met you two at Grimwold's place, though I can't say as we was ever properly interduced, but Bramble here ain't met none of you before, though she've heard about you from me."

At the mention of Grimwold's place, I thought Bramble shuddered, but now she recovered herself and spoke up.

"And that be why I be willin' to be friends," she said, "'cos you did help Toadstool kill that monster."

And suddenly I knew who she was. She was Thistle's sister. Thistle, who was Toadstool's sweetheart, and who'd been murdered, hanged, by Grimwold, while her little sister watched, terrified and grief-stricken, from the shadows. This was Bramble, who couldn't get over her grief and had gone wandering off, away from her elf-clan. I didn't think I'd ever told this story to Bron or Abdul, and now was not the time. But good old Toadstool – he'd come to find her, to bring her news of the revenge they'd taken.

Bronwen had been sitting on her horse, wide-eyed, drinking in every word, but now she got down and, to my surprise, dropped a deep curtsey.

"I am Bronwen," she said, "whom you rescued from Grimwold's gallows, and I don't feel that we gave you enough thanks for saving our lives."

"Indeed," said Abdul who, following Bronwen's lead, got down and swept an elegant bow. "Abdul Mutazz ibn Haroun, forever at your service for saving our lives."

Toadstool burst out laughing and motioned for them to get up.

"What a fuss and palaver you humans makes. 'Tweren't nothin'. We wanted him dead. But I be pleased to see you lookin' all right now. You, in pertikler," he pointed at Abdul, "wasn't lookin' too special last time I seen you. Been bashed about a bit by that thug an' his bully-boys, I reckons."

Abdul smiled. "You are right, but I am much better now."

Bramble looked at me. "So it were you, then, what had that rune-thing what stopped Grimwold in his tracks."

I nodded and, since I seemed to be the only one still on horseback, I jumped down and joined the others on the ground.

"Have you still got it?" asked Toadstool.

I nodded again.

"'Cos you're gonna need it," said Bramble, "if you're goin' after your friend."

"There's another bad'un down there," said Toadstool, "what's got your friend Oz, an' you're gonna need every weapon you got."

"So you know Oz is down there?" I said, and then realized that Toadstool had already mentioned 'your friend down there', but I'd been so surprised to see the elves that I hadn't taken in the meaning of his words.

"Have you seen him? Did he look all right?" I asked urgently.

"Calm down, Wulfstan," said Abdul. "Let us sit, and, if you would be so good, tell us everything you know."

"We don't know nothin' much," said Bramble, squatting on the rough grass. "We was jus' doin' a bit o' huntin' last night when we seen these humans draggin' another, littler one between 'em. An' then one of 'em picked him up an' slung him over his shoulder an' Toadstool says, 'I know 'im,' he says. 'That's that Oz,' he says, 'what was friends with Wulf, what helped us kill Grimwold.' 'What's he doin' here?' I says, an' he says, 'I dunno,' an' we watched 'em carry him into that buildin' down there."

Toadstool took up the story. "And then we crep' a bit closer and then this other human come ridin' up on a gurt black horse an' I says to Bramble, 'I don' like the look of him,' I says, an' she says, 'An I don' like the feel of him, neither. He do feel *bad*,' she says."

"But he don' jus' *feel* bad," put in Bramble. "I acksherly *knows* he be bad, 'cos I seen him before, 'cos I been around these parts a while."

We all leaned forward.

"What have you seen?" whispered Bronwen.

"Well…" said Bramble, then she stopped, kept quite still for a second and pounced on something in the grass. Between her small brown fingers was a beetle, which she popped into her mouth.

"D'you want one, if I sees another?" she offered, crunching her snack.

"Erm – no thank you," said Bronwen politely. "But we do want to know what you've seen."

"He've got *creatures*," nodded Bramble. "Creatures what don't belong on this earth. Horrible things, like gurt snakes with mist all round 'em. *Toadstool* do reckon they come from some other place – not from this world at all."

Toadstool nodded. "I've heard about these things, what humans that does bad magic conjures up. Not ordinary sort of magic like us, but stuff like what Grimwold did. They comes from some other world, if you can believe such a thing."

"We can believe it," said Abdul, "for Wulf and I saw them. Indeed, they attacked Wulf."

Bramble's eyes grew so big they almost filled her little face.

"And here you be, still alive," she breathed.

"I was saved by…someone," I said.

"And I think you are right, Toadstool," said Abdul. "These creatures are demons from another world."

Bramble looked admiringly at Toadstool, then back at the rest of them.

"Toadstool do know everythin'," she said proudly, and the elf put his arm around her shoulders and pulled her closer to him.

It dawned on me then that Toadstool hadn't just looked for Bramble to tell her the news about Grimwold. Or if he had, things had changed since he found her. It seemed she might be filling the gaping hole left in his life by the death of Thistle. I hoped so. I looked at Bron, but she was busy with her own thoughts. Why couldn't she be like Bramble? Why couldn't she see how much she meant to me? I felt a sudden irritation at her blindness, though I knew that wasn't fair.

"So what are we going to do?" asked Bronwen. "How on earth are we going to rescue Osric from a man with that kind of magic?"

"What about your rune-thing?" said Toadstool. "It worked before."

"True," I said, "but the trouble is, he knows I've got it."

"Do he now?" said Toadstool.

I nodded.

"I'm pretty sure he wants it for himself," I said.

We sat in silence for a while.

"We need a plan," frowned Bronwen.

I almost said, *oh really? I didn't know that*, but I bit the words back. The last thing we needed was to start bickering.

"You couldn't get Pooka and the rest of them to come and help?" I said suddenly.

"I thought o' that," said Toadstool, "but I'd rather have some idea first, o' what we're gonna do. I mean, there ain't nothin' in it for us elves this time. We got revenge before. Chickweed wouldn't come out o' the goodness of her heart."

"Nor she wouldn't," giggled Bramble.

"*She* wouldn't have to," I said, "but some of them might."

"I suppose it be worth a try," said Toadstool, grudgingly. "Pooka do like you. An' it'd be good for 'em to see Bramble again, to see she's all right an' that. Would you like that, Bramble?"

She nodded solemnly.

"Well, we'll have a little think and then we'll make a little trip, shall we?" said Toadstool.

"I doubt that will happen," boomed a deep voice, and over the crest of the hill walked three tall figures, black against the afternoon sun.

I froze.

"It was a good idea to get out of sight," said the man with the deep voice. "Not such a good idea to post no guards."

CHAPTER FORTY-ONE

WULF

Out of the corner of my eye I caught sight of Bramble's agonised expression, before the two elves vanished. I grabbed my rune-stone and yelled at the top of my voice, "By the power of Thorn, I command you to stop!"

A man who'd been lunging at me fell to the ground as if he'd been turned to stone. But that was only one man. Before I even touched the rune-stone Abdul had drawn his sword, and the hilltop was ringing with the sound of blade on blade as he fought the man with the deep voice.

I was dimly aware of the horses whinnying and galloping away. I wasn't sure what to do, it was all happening so quickly. I should finish this brute off before he came round, but...*Oh God, where was the other man?* There he was, backing away, his eyes on the rune-stone, which was still in my hand. At the same time I saw Bron running a little way back down the hill. Well, I couldn't blame her. She should get herself to safety. I kept my eyes on the bloke backing away.

"Gar!" bawled the deep-voiced man. "Come back here!"

Gar stopped, his eyes darting in terror from his master to my hand and back again. Then he too fell to the ground like a boulder, pierced by an arrow. Bronwen ran back to my side, holding her bow.

"I just needed to get a good aim," she explained, panting. Then, pointing at Abdul's opponent, "Well, go on! Use your rune-stone on *him!*"

I gaped at her, then at the man she'd so coolly done away with. He was lying on his back, his legs jerking, the arrow embedded deep in his chest. A sudden gush of blood spurted from his mouth and he lay still.

"Go on!" said Bron. "What are you waiting for?"

"Good shot," I said feebly, wondering if I really knew this girl after all.

"*Wulfstan!*" hissed Bron, and I blinked and turned to the two duellers.

Abdul was higher up the hill, gradually forcing his opponent back, seeming to have the upper hand till, with a flick of his wrist, the other man knocked the sword from Abdul's grasp. But even as it flew against the pale blue sky, Abdul leapt at it and caught it by the hilt before it reached the ground. The other man laughed.

"Well played," he called, then lunged at Abdul as he was still finding his feet.

But Abdul was quick. He sprang aside and the sword sliced the air.

"Oh, do something, Wulfstan!" begged Bron.

"I can't!" I said. "I'll get Abdul too!"

"Then we'll just have to wait for him to come round!"

I raised my rune-stone and tried to hold it so that it faced Abdul's opponent. The two men were moving so quickly that I decided I might have to risk knocking both of them out. Then my chance came. The stranger backed away, one, two, three steps and I took a deep breath.

"By the power of..." I began, but the man had raised both arms and begun a murmuring chant. My tongue froze in my mouth just as I reached the magic name. The chant grew louder and the man closed his eyes and smiled as he chanted, a smile full of malice and the knowledge of his own power.

I couldn't move a muscle, not even my tongue, as the deep voice chanted on in some unknown language. Then I saw that Bron was standing like a statue and that Abdul's sword-hand was motionless in mid-air.

Abruptly, the man stopped and stood looking at them all.

"Did you really think you could defeat Gethin ap Ordgar?" he said. "I enjoyed our swordplay, Moor. It was good practice. I always enjoy fighting your people. You are well-trained." His smile widened. "Now, what shall I do with you?" He pointed at me. "You, of course, are the one I want, but these others?"

He sauntered around them, looking them up and down, while I died inside. Why hadn't I acted sooner? Could I have caught him off guard? There was a moan from the ground. The man I'd stunned! Why hadn't I finished him off? Couldn't I do anything right?

Gethin walked up and kicked his servant.

"Get up, you oaf! This is the boy you were supposed to get last night!"

The man on the ground sat up, groaning, and rubbed his eyes.

"Now *you*, little maid," continued Gethin, circling Bronwen. "I was impressed with your bravery. You had more courage than that idiot Gar. Besides, I heard you speak. You are Welsh. I might let you go." He paused. "A pity about those elves. They were too quick, even for me."

In all the horror, I felt a tiny moment of relief. I hadn't been sure if Gethin had done something to Bramble and Toadstool or if they'd gone 'air-flitting'. Now it seemed that at least *they* were safe. But the relief didn't last long.

"But *you*, my friend, are a little too dangerous to let go." Gethin stood by Abdul, gazing into his face. I had a clear view. They were both tall, dark-haired and bearded, but there the likeness ended. Even in its frozen state, Abdul's face had a nobility completely lacking in the other man. And I prayed. *Oh God, please don't let him kill Abdul! Please, please!*

Gethin sighed. "Nevertheless, I did enjoy our fight. I think I will merely wound you and let the gods decide whether you live or die."

To my horror and disbelief, Gethin pierced Abdul's side with his sword, pulled the blade out and wiped it on the grass.

"There," he said, "you have a chance. The sword did not go too far in. But you will lose a lot of blood." He smiled again and nodded. "Yes, when the spell wears off you will start to bleed. Then only the gods, and perhaps this fair maid, will decide if you will live. But if you do, my friend, you will be in no fit state to come after me."

He turned to his man, still sitting in a daze on the ground.

"Get up, Ulf! Take that boy down to join the other one."

Gethin marched off down to the hall not even glancing at his dead servant, lying with Bronwen's arrow sticking out of him. I felt rough hands under my arms and my heels scraping the ground as my rigid body was dragged down the hill. My last view of my friends was of two statues waiting for the spell to break and Abdul to start bleeding.

CHAPTER FORTY-TWO

BRONWEN

No! I screamed, but no sound came out. *No!* I screamed again, and the sound rang round and round in my head. But on the hillside...silence. I stood like the statue I had become, useless, unable to move a muscle. And Abdul's face showed no pain, just the concentration of someone trying to land a blow on an opponent, as he had been when the spell struck – his brow slightly furrowed, his lips slightly parted.

A crow glided to earth a few yards away on the hillcrest. It cocked its head one way and looked at Abdul with its beady eyes. Then it cocked its head the other way and looked at me...and waited. After a while it strutted over to me until it was by my feet, where I couldn't see it. There was a sudden sharp pain in my leg and I screamed another silent scream. Then a wind blew up, ruffling my dress, and the crow squawked and jumped away. My skirts had protected me but my leg smarted. So you could feel pain when you were under this spell...Abdul! He must have felt it when the sword pierced his side! He must be feeling it now!

After a little while the crow walked deliberately over to Abdul, jerking its head back and forth as it went. Then it spread its wings and leapt on to his raised sword-arm, where it perched, staring into his face. It inched along until it reached his shoulder. *No!* came yet another silent scream, as I watched the long, cruel beak tap Abdul's cheek. *No, not his face! Not his eyes, oh God, not his eyes!*

Then Abdul opened his mouth wider and moved his jaw around. *He could move!* The crow shot off, landed a little way away and shook its feathers, and suddenly I felt a tiny sensation in my neck. A tingling spread into my cheeks, my whole head. I could blink. I could turn my head. The tingling reached down my arms to my fingertips. I could wriggle them.

It moved down my legs. I could move a foot...slowly, slowly...it still felt a bit numb.

There was a neighing and the horses cantered back into view. The crow cawed loudly, spread its wings and flew away. Then Abdul moaned and collapsed on the ground. I rushed to his side and knelt down by him.

"Oh, you poor, poor thing! That evil man! We've got to stop the bleeding!"

Feverishly I began tearing a strip from the bottom of my skirt, but Abdul was already unwinding his turban.

"No, use this!" he gasped.

"Oh, I don't know what to do!" I panicked, as blood seeped through his jerkin. "It's not like an arm, where you can..."

"Just plug it," said Abdul. "Cut the clothes around the wound... there's a knife in my boot."

I grabbed the dagger and gently enlarged the hole in his jerkin, but that only made the blood flow faster, so I stuffed the turban into the gap and pressed down.

"Aagh!" yelled Abdul and gritted his teeth.

"Oh, I'm sorry!" I gasped.

"No, that's right," said Abdul. "We've got to bind it round with something."

So I went back to ripping my skirt while Abdul tried to hold the plug of material in place. Between us we managed to tie the pad of cloth over his wound and slow down the bleeding.

A shadow fell across us and I looked up in alarm, but my eyes met the dark horsey eyes of Noor, nudging Abdul. He smiled through his pain as she nibbled at his face. Then Noor was joined by Chestnut and Sorrel, walking delicately up and waiting.

I looked at them in wonderment.

"I thought they'd run away," I said.

"Noor would never leave me for long, would you my beauty?" murmured Abdul. "And whatever good spell the elves put on these others has given them loyalty and courage as well."

"Well, good," I said in a firmer voice. "So now I know what to do. We've just got to get you up on Noor's back and lead you to Brother Walter in the abbey. He'll be able to save you."

I stood up. "Kneel down, Noor, and let your master on."

She obediently knelt and Abdul somehow managed to get on her back, though his face showed the agony he was in. I mounted Sorrel, then turned and spoke to Chestnut.

"We're going back to the Abbey," I told the horse, "where Cloud is waiting for us. We're going very slowly, but you just follow on. All right?"

Chestnut whinnied softly and tossed his head.

But however slowly we went, it seemed to be too much for Abdul. At last, as we were getting near the village where Odda had left us, he stopped and slid off Noor's back.

"I can't go any further," he whispered, collapsing on the ground.

"But we're nearly there!" I said, dismounting.

Then I saw that Abdul's side was drenched with blood and his face was dead white.

"Oh, Abdul, I'm sorry, I should have realized!"

He shook his head.

"Ride on. Bring Brother Walter here."

I put my arm round him and tried to lift him, but he was too heavy.

"Please, Abdul, look…just make it to that hut. We can make you comfortable and bind it tighter. Then I'll ride as fast as I can to the Abbey. Please!"

Abdul tried to get up, but fell back again. Then Noor nudged him and somehow pushed her great head under his arm. So between us we managed to help him stagger to the little shepherd's hut, where he collapsed on to a straw mattress. The sun was going down and it was dark inside, but I could see well enough to tear off some more of my skirt and add it to the pad on Abdul's wound. Then I tied it again as tightly as I could.

Abdul put his hand on mine.

"Don't go," he murmured.

"I don't want to leave you," I whispered, "but I must if we're to save you."

Abdul wearily shook his head.

"I think it may be too late. The pain is lessening. That means that Allah is calling me."

"No!" I cried. "Don't say that! Brother Walter is marvellous! He'll save you."

Tears started to trickle down my cheeks and I tried to get up, but he pulled me back.

"It's so comforting to have you here," he said. "Just stay a little while and then you can go."

I let myself be pulled back down so that I was squatting on the edge of the mattress.

"All right," I said, "but don't waste your energy in talking."

"No, the pain is much less now. I want to talk...You know," he said with a slight smile. "I've never told you, but you remind me very much of someone."

I waited, but he was silent for a while and seemed to be somewhere else in his head.

"Who do I remind you of?" I said at last.

"My wife," he whispered, "my Aisha."

"Your wife?" I said, startled. This was the first time he'd mentioned that such a person existed. "And where is she now?"

"With Allah in Paradise," said Abdul.

"Oh, I'm sorry," I said, not knowing what else to say.

"She was not so much older than you when we married, and there are some things about you that remind me of her very much – the way you hold your head, some expressions you have..." he tailed off.

"How did she die?" I asked gently.

"In childbirth," said Abdul. "Allah did not will that we should have children, and when the third one died, a son, she died with him. And so I decided to go on the Hajj, to forget, to come to terms with Allah's will, and it was on my travels that I met my friend Godwin." He paused. "He also is now in Paradise." He paused again. "But you do not forget, and I have found it hard to come to terms with Allah's will...But now I hope it is His will to let me into Paradise, to be with her."

I took his hand in both of mine.

"No, Abdul, not yet," I said through my tears. "Don't leave us yet."

He smiled. "I'll tell you a secret," he whispered. "It does not matter now that I am dying. Do you remember when we were going to the village of Grimwold? One of the most stupid things I ever did. Do you remember?"

I nodded.

"And we were talking about what story to tell, about why we were travelling together? And Osric said you were my young wife?"

"And I hit him with a branch!" I laughed through my tears.

"Well, my secret is that I thought, just for a moment, I thought, well, why not? If we come through this, I thought…perhaps…because you are so like Aisha."

"And I'll tell you a secret," I whispered. "That's why I hit Osric. Because he thought it was a joke, and I thought, just for a moment, that I could imagine being your young wife."

Abdul squeezed my hand.

"But after that," he went on, "I realized that there are other young men who would like you for their wife, young men of your own age." His eyes widened and he tried to raise his head, a sudden look of alarm on his face. "Oh, how selfish I have been, keeping you here!"

"What do you mean?"

"You must get back to the abbey! Wulfstan and Osric! You must tell the abbot what has happened!"

Wulfstan and Osric! How could I forget? I'd been concentrating so much on Abdul!

"And now it is getting dark and dangerous!" Abdul let his head fall back. "How selfish I have been!"

"Stop saying that!" I cried. "You never think of yourself! We both forgot, though I can't believe now that I *could* have forgotten. But it was more urgent to help you!"

"Go now, with Allah's blessing," gasped Abdul. "May He keep you safe on the road."

"All right," I whispered. "I'll be back soon with Brother Walter." Then, in a louder voice, "But promise me you'll try not to die while I'm gone."

Abdul smiled. "I promise I shall try."

I bent and kissed his forehead, then turned and went outside. It had started to rain again but my face was already wet. I patted Chestnut's neck and then Noor's.

"Look after your master," I whispered to the mare. "Chestnut, you come with us. We may need you."

Then I mounted Sorrel and turned my face to the darkening path. First the deserted village, then the woods. I took a deep breath.

"Come on," I urged Sorrel. "Back to the abbey!"

CHAPTER FORTY-THREE

OZ

The wooden wagon jolted my rigid body up and down and there was nothing I could do to make myself even a tiny bit comfortable. All I could see was the wagon roof…except when that old witch Morwen leaned over and peered into my face. I passed some of the time imagining what I was going to do to her when I could use my hands again. I knew it was fantasy, though. So much for being rescued, I thought bitterly.

Sometimes a jolt would knock me sideways into Wulf's body, which was just as rigid as mine. I assumed Wulf could feel it, though neither of us had been able to give any sign to each other, not even an eye movement. Gethin had come into the hall smirking, muttered a few words, and I'd felt the blessed relief of muscles freeing themselves, tingling, loosening.

"Stand up then!" ordered Gethin, and I'd obeyed, only too glad to be able to move my arms and legs. A few more muttered words and the freezing was instant. I was just as rigid as before, but this time in a standing position.

"That's better," sneered Gethin. "You'll fit in beside your friend now."

My friend! Hope had slowly died as I realized that Wulf must be a prisoner, and that neither Abdul nor the rune-stone had been able to stop it happening. Although, he'd said 'friend', not 'friends', so where were the others?

"Ulf!" barked Gethin. "Are you ready yet?"

"Coming, my lord!" called Ulf, and hurried through the door.

"Throw this one in beside the other one!"

And that was exactly what Ulf had done. I'd been dragged outside and shoved into the back of a wagon, with barely time to take in Wulf's frozen expression before my own head hit the floor. *Ouch!* Then the old witch had climbed in after me.

"I told you I had a nice surprise for you," sneered Gethin. "How sweet – two friends together."

"I'll keep a good eye on them, my love, don't you worry," cackled the old woman.

"I know you will, Morwen, but I'll be right alongside. I'd like to ride on and get on with the preparations, but I can't risk losing this precious cargo."

Preparations? What preparations?

"It's a real shame," sighed Morwen, "that you can't just kill them and take the stones. Then we wouldn't have all the bother of carting them around."

"It is indeed," laughed Gethin, "but it doesn't work like that."

Somehow, I didn't find that very comforting. We were reluctantly being kept alive – for what?

"I've put another spell on that one," said Gethin, pointing at Wulf. "So neither of them should come round before we reach home."

"Well, I'll watch them like a hawk, anyway," said Morwen.

She was as good as her word, poking and prodding every few minutes to see if she got a reaction, and then peering into my face with a gloating expression. She was obviously doing the same to Wulf. Why couldn't she let us be? I hated her. If anything, I thought I hated her more than Gethin, though that was a moot point.

The journey seemed endless, the day darkening into evening and then night. After one jolt I wondered if I'd momentarily fallen asleep with my eyes open. Could you do that? I felt empty inside. How had we got themselves into this hopeless position? Ever since we'd first been kidnapped we'd lurched from danger to danger, trying to escape – even from Abdul, who'd turned out to be a good friend. And where *was* Abdul? What had happened to him, *and* to Bron? She was annoying, but she was a good friend as well. Were they even still alive? I supposed Wulf would be able to tell me, if we ever got a chance to talk to each other.

There was a sort of comfort in knowing that he was with me, even though we were captured. Lying there, I could feel his arm touching my own and my mind wandered back to the village and all the times I'd escaped my overcrowded home to sleep in his cottage. We'd always been together, haymaking, learning to read, training as soldiers, then side by side as archers in the battle. The only time we'd been separated was when Gethin's men had captured me, and that was for less than a day.

The wagon-wheels made a different sound, as if they were rolling over a wooden bridge, and then they clattered over stone before creaking to a halt. There were voices: Gethin barking orders and servants answering him and rushing to obey. Someone grabbed my ankles and pulled. I thought my head was going to hit the ground, but it was caught just in time, and somebody's hands worked their way in between my arms and my body. I looked up at a black sky studded with brilliant stars, then they were blotted out and I was carried under a stone arch and down steps into a passageway lit by flickering torches. Footsteps echoed and the air felt damp.

A door creaked open and I was thrown on to some straw, which smelled none too clean. A sharp pain pierced my shoulder as I landed. Through the doorway I could see Wulf being carried past. Then the door clanged shut and there was the grating sound of a key turning.

I was on my own.

CHAPTER FORTY-FOUR

WULF

I stared hopelessly at the stone roof of the passageway. There was no-one in front of us now. A door had shut with an echoing clang and two men had stood aside to let us pass. Oz must be on the other side of that heavy door. If only we could have stayed together!

"This way!" called a voice. "His Lordship's changed his mind. Wants him up here!"

Suddenly my feet were higher than my head. We were going up some steps. The narrow corridor widened into a broad stairway. So many steps, inside a building! The air smelt fresher. There were window slits, through which I caught glimpses of stars. What *was* this place, made of stone like a church, or like somewhere a king might live?

Then we were in a large room with dark green wall hangings and big iron sconces with flaring torches. Gold thread was woven into the green and it glinted in the light of the flames. *I wonder if the hangings ever catch fire*, I thought foolishly. It wasn't something I'd ever thought of before. There were no wall hangings in my home. Then *crack*, my head hit the floor. There was a flash of light, and an instant of blackness.

"Careful, you idiots!" said Gethin's voice. "He'll be no good to me with his skull split open!"

"Sorry my lord," muttered the men who'd been carrying me.

"All right, all right, leave us," said Gethin impatiently, and the two men backed away out of the room, leaving me lying rigid on the floor.

Gethin walked over, looked down at me and burst out laughing.

"I suppose I'd better let you get up," he smirked. "The spell will be wearing off soon anyway."

He muttered a few words and I felt the relief of muscles unclenching, though when I tried to get up my head swam.

"Here, sit down," Gethin gestured toward a carved wooden chair. "Feeling dizzy? That was a nasty knock."

I groped my way to the chair, glaring at Gethin, and sat as upright as I could. I tried to ignore my pounding head and concentrate on focusing my eyes. There seemed to be two of everything. At last the two Gethins merged into one.

"What have you done with Oz?" I demanded. "And what's happening to Abdul and Bron?"

"Ah, the loyal friend. That's what I was relying on. Now which question do you want me to answer first?"

"I don't care, so long as you answer them both!" I said.

Gethin sat in his own chair and made himself comfortable. He lifted a goblet to his lips and took a slow draught.

"Just tell me!" I said. I knew Gethin was playing with me, but it was difficult to control myself.

"Well, as for your two friends whom we left on the hillside," smiled Gethin. "I really don't know, is the answer."

"But you must know!" I burst out. "You stuck that sword right into Abdul! Is he dead? And what about Bronwen?"

"Ah, Bronwen," said Gethin. "Yes, an impressive young woman. She'll be all right, don't you worry. As to whether you'll see her again… well, that rather depends on you."

I clenched my fists on the arms of the chair and Gethin's smile grew broader.

"But as for the Moor, his prospects are not so bright. He may survive, and I am certain your Bronwen will do everything in her power to see that he does. But then again…he may not."

"But how could you do that?" I said. "It wasn't a fair fight!"

Gethin roared with laughter.

"Fair! Fair?" he gasped with mirth. "When was life ever fair? Is it fair that you are sitting in a grand chair, about to be poured a goblet of wine – you would like some, would you not? – while your friend lies on rotting straw in a stinking dungeon? And that, I believe, answers your other question."

I said nothing while Gethin placed a goblet in front of me and lifted the wine flagon. But instead of pouring the wine, he hesitated and put it down again.

"Perhaps not yet," he smiled. "Though I think *I* could do with a refill."

He moved his own goblet closer to me and let the deep, rich liquid trickle into it. I watched, fascinated. My eyes lost their focus again as I stared at the wine, and my aching head eased. *It's like liquid rubies,* I thought, then shook my head. I'd never even seen a ruby. What had put that idea into my mind? Then I looked up at Gethin, smiling at me. And as soon as I focused his eyes, my head started pounding.

"You're messing with my head," I said. "I'm not stupid, you know."

"Indeed," replied Gethin. "I did not think that you were."

A warm, fruity smell wafted into my nostrils. It made me feel drowsy just smelling it. I had to stay awake. *Just keep talking.*

"But why?" I asked. "Why is Oz in a dungeon? What do you want with us?"

"Ah, yes," nodded Gethin. "Really, I am not terribly interested in you. But I very much want something that you have."

"So why don't you take it?" I said. "Take it and let us go. Take Oz's as well. We just wanna get out of here."

But as I said it, I felt a sudden great reluctance to part with the stone. My mum had given it to me. I'd got used to the feel of it round my neck. Even as I thought about it, I could feel a warm tingling where it rested against my skin. It had saved our lives. Then another voice in my mind told me not to be stupid. It had led us into nothing but trouble. Our lives wouldn't have needed saving if all these people hadn't been after it. The first voice spoke again. Gethin was evil. He must be planning some great wickedness, and he needed the stone to do it. Don't let him have it. But how could one boy stop him? said the second voice. Just give in.

Gethin was watching my face closely and I felt sure that he could read my mind.

"Then give it to me," murmured Gethin.

I didn't move. But after all, why not give it to him?

"Why don't you just take it?" I said at last.

Gethin nodded slowly.

"Because then I would not be able to use it for my purposes. It must be freely given."

"Oz took his," I remembered suddenly.

Gethin sat forward in his chair.

"Yes, how exactly did your friend acquire his rune-stone?"

"We were attacked," I said, "and I used my stone to stun this man – he was one of Lord Grimwold's men. And while he was stunned Abdul took the stone from round his neck. He didn't want it and Oz took it. I think he wanted to be the same as me."

"And did he seem at all different once it was round his neck?"

"Yes, he did," I said thoughtfully. "But I don't know…I can't explain how."

I tried to remember what it was that had felt different about Oz, but whatever it was seemed to have faded, or else so much had happened since then that I'd just forgotten about it.

"And has he ever tried to use it?" Gethin asked.

"No, we don't know how," I said. "We don't know the right words." I paused, then went on bitterly, "But why don't you ask *him* about it? Let's invite him up for a drink."

Gethin leaned back again and swilled the wine around in his goblet.

"I admire your spirit, and it's your loyalty to your friend that I am relying on. Because you wouldn't want anything bad to happen to him, would you? There are many amusing ways to kill someone, and none of them quick. So if you do not want to see your friend tortured to death, and of course, die afterwards yourself, you *will* decide to give me the stone. And I shall give you time. You will freely give it to me, let us say… tomorrow evening, during my ceremony. That would suit me very well."

Sitting there facing this man with his aura of power, I knew that I would. There was no way out. I didn't doubt that Oz would suffer horribly if I didn't. But what was the cost? What evil would come of it? I put my elbows on the table and let my thumping head sink into my hands as despair washed over me.

Then I heard a voice – it was my own voice – say, "But why? Why do you want it so much? What are you going to do with it?"

I looked up and Gethin smiled.

"Now...shall I tell you?" he said and took another sip from his goblet. "Well, why not? I should enjoy your knowing exactly what your stone will do...what *I* shall do, with its help. Yes, why not?"

CHAPTER FORTY-FIVE

BRONWEN

My eyes darted this way and that as my horse trotted through the deserted village. The moon was bright, so I could see where I was going, but every black shape seemed a threat. There'd be hardly anyone here. Only a few young men guarding their animals behind firmly shut doors. The rest of the villagers were all in the safety of the abbey. The path had little cottages on either side and one or two of the rough wooden doors were half-open. I urged Sorrel past these, trying not to look inside, imagining squinting eyes, crouching bodies ready to spring out at me.

The clop of Chestnut's hooves behind us was in some ways comforting, in other ways not. Was it only one horse I could hear, or was that someone else following as well? I peered anxiously behind. Then a cloud passed across the moon but I dared not stop. I slowed Sorrel to a walk and found, as we left the last cottage behind and the moon reappeared, that I'd been holding my breath for some time. It came out in a burst that made me jump.

Then I realized where I was…the sheep pens, where three people had lost their lives and Oz had been taken. The ground was more open than it had been in the village, but that didn't make things any better. This was the haunt of Gethin's demons! Suppose they came back! I felt faint. I was so exposed here, but I couldn't go back through that horrible village. I just couldn't. And I had to get help for Abdul! That's why I was doing this!

And with that thought my courage returned. What a selfish coward I was, thinking of myself when Abdul was dying. And who knows what had happened to Wulfstan and Osric. Here I was, not a prisoner or badly wounded, and all I could do was let my imagination run away with me.

I urged Sorrel on and Chestnut obediently followed, always keeping the same pace as the mare in front. *Think of Abdul*, I told myself. *Just keep thinking of him.*

That resolve lasted till we reached the edge of the wood. But it looked so forbidding. Who knew what skulked inside? The night was full of creatures which would never show themselves in daylight. Everyone knew that. Abdul had prayed that Allah would be with me. *Oh God, protect me*, I whispered. *Are you the same as Abdul's God? I think you must be, so please protect me…and don't let Abdul die.*

I walked Sorrel on to the dark of the forest path, where no moonlight showed us the way, and found I was feeling a little calmer. Nearly there now. The abbey was just the other side of this wood and then there would be help…other people, friends, the kindly abbot and, best of all, Brother Walter. I stared ahead into the dark and pushed away thoughts of watchful eyes in the undergrowth, spindly fingers reaching down from branches, twisted shapes lurking behind tree-trunks. I took a deep breath. God was with me. He would protect me.

The trees thinned. Moonlight found its way through the branches. The path came out into the open and there – *oh, joy* – was the massive shape of the abbey looming up into the night sky.

I galloped my horse across the open ground between the wood and the abbey, jumped down and knocked as hard as I could on the great gate.

"Let me in! Let me in!" I yelled. "It's me, Bronwen!"

The little peephole opened and a surprised voice said, "Why, Brother Walter, you were right."

Then Walter's dear, familiar voice said, "Well, let her in then. Don't leave the poor child outside."

A key grated in the lock and one of the great gates swung open a little.

"You'll have to open it wider," I said. "I've got two horses here."

"Two?" said the monk with Walter. "How did you manage that?"

I didn't bother to answer, but led Sorrel inside, with Chestnut following, nose to tail. The monk hurriedly barred the gate again.

"My dear," said Walter and opened his arms wide.

I fell into them, half-sobbing.

"Oh, Brother Walter, you don't know how pleased I am to see you. You must get your things and come with me straight away!"

"You were right then, Brother Walter," came the abbot's deep, strong voice. "You are amazing."

I looked up and saw Abbot Deorlaf striding towards me. I let go of Walter and curtseyed.

"Get up, my child," smiled the abbot. "Our friend here was expecting you, though how he knows these things I never can work out."

Walter nodded. "I believe I am needed, Holy Father."

"Oh he is, he is!" I said. "It's Abdul, your lordship. I'm afraid he's dying. I *know* he's dying, but Walter can save him!"

"And the boys?" asked the abbot.

"They're both captured now! Wulf as well!" I said. "We need your help, my lord! There's this evil man called Gethin…Gethin ap something English. Gethin's a Welsh name, but his father must have been English. He's taken Wulfstan as well as Osric and almost killed Abdul and we've got to rescue the boys, but first we've got to save Abdul!"

"Calm down, my child and catch your breath. Can it not wait till daylight? You need food and rest, and I am unwilling to let anyone abroad in the night-time with all that has been happening."

"Oh no, sir!" I said wildly. "Abdul will be dead by then!"

"Holy Father," said Walter mildly. "I have my equipment here – my salves and everything I need – and good Brother Oslac is fetching us food and drink. I was ready for this."

The young monk scurried over with a basket of provisions and Abbot Deorlaf shook his head and smiled.

"I shall find out what I can about this man Gethin," he said. "Take care then, and may God go with you."

I dropped to my knees.

"Oh thank you, Holy Father," I said. "Thank you, thank you."

"Come, child," said Walter. "Is this the steed I am supposed to ride? He's a little fine for me – and rather large."

I laughed. "He's as sweet as a sweet chestnut, and that's his name — Chestnut."

Walter was helped on to the horse and the gate swung open to let them out.

"Holy Father," he said. "Please send a wagon in the morning. It would be good to carry the patient back here."

"He's in the shepherd's hut on the other side of the village," I said.

"I will, I will," said Abbot Deorlaf.

He made the sign of the cross and, with Brother Walter following, I set off the way I'd just come. But how different the journey was with Walter behind me. It wasn't only that we were both carrying lanterns — the horses could easily be ridden with one hand on the reins. But I felt that nothing could harm me while this saintly old man was with me. No spindly fingers groped from overhead branches, and when we reached the sheep-pens, no thoughts of Gethin's demons troubled me. The open doors of the cottages were just that — doors that someone had left open. And there was the shepherd's hut.

I leapt down and helped Walter off his horse. Then I crept inside.

"Abdul," I whispered. "It's only me and I've brought Brother Walter."

There was no answer. Then we heard laboured breathing. Walter held up his lantern. In the circle of light, Abdul's face was grey, with purple bruising under his eyes. A fine sheen of sweat covered his brow.

Walter looked grave, but knelt down to examine him. The straw bedding was now dark with blood and when the old man tried to move the dressing on Abdul's wound, it stuck.

"It might be best to leave it for now and try to get him to drink some of my herbs."

He unstopped a bottle and poured something into a cup, which he held to Abdul's lips.

"Try to hold his head up," said Walter, and I struggled to support Abdul's head while Walter let a little of the liquid trickle into his mouth.

There was no sign that Abdul was aware of any of this, and the potion dribbled uselessly down his chin.

"Lay his head down again," whispered Walter.

He poured some of the potion on to a small cloth and placed that between Abdul's lips. The lips moved and a faint sound came out. The cloth fell away. Abdul opened his eyes and looked directly at me. His lips curved into a smile.

"Aisha," he murmured. Then he closed his eyes and let out one long breath.

"No!" I gasped.

Walter lifted his hand to make the sign of the cross, hesitated and lowered it again.

"May your God, who is the same as my God, accept your soul into Paradise," he prayed.

I flung myself across Abdul and sobbed.

CHAPTER FORTY-SIX

WULF

"But you must be hungry," said Gethin.

He clapped his hands and a manservant came running and bowed deeply.

"My lord?" he said, looking up, but not standing up straight.

"Supper!" ordered Gethin. "Roast meats for both of us, and be quick!"

The man backed away and nearly tripped over his feet as he ran downstairs.

"I shall tell my tale better on a full stomach," said Gethin. "And you will concentrate better as well."

"I suppose there's no chance of Oz having any roast meats?" I asked, though I knew the answer, so I wasn't surprised when Gethin laughed.

The food – both mutton and beef, served with cabbage, honey-glazed carrots and an onion relish – arrived amazingly quickly. I could imagine what would happen if it hadn't. It smelt…heavenly was the only word to do it justice, and I fervently hoped, as I dug a knife in and ripped mouthfuls off with my teeth, that Oz couldn't smell it down in the dungeons. To have that scent under your nose and not be able to eat would drive anyone mad. Then I stopped guiltily.

"Oz is having *something* to eat, isn't he?" I asked.

"Don't worry, he will not starve," smiled Gethin unpleasantly. "He is being given…*something*, as you put it."

I didn't like to ask what. But, after all, I might as well enjoy my own temporary good fortune. It wouldn't help Oz if *I* didn't eat, and besides, I wouldn't have the strength of will to resist. I ripped off another mouthful of beef. The food seemed to be helping my aching head. Just as well, because this time Gethin did pour me some wine. I had to remind myself to sip it slowly, when I wanted to drink it down in great gulps.

Nothing was said for a while as we both concentrated on eating. At last Gethin licked his fingers and spoke to the hovering servant.

"Something sweet to finish, I think."

"We have apple cake and sour cream custard, if that pleases your lordship?"

Gethin looked at me.

"Does that suit you?" he said.

I nodded uncertainly. What was Gethin playing at, asking me what I'd like?

The next course arrived just as quickly as the first, and the apple cake turned out to be a sort of fruity bread pudding, like one my mum made. I'd somehow expected something fancier. It tasted good.

Gethin sat back and watched as I scraped my dish and licked the last scrap off my spoon.

"Do you like my castle?" he asked.

"I've never seen anything like it," I said honestly.

"They build like this in Normandy," nodded Gethin. "Impressive, isn't it? Useful to have so many rooms on more than one level."

I didn't say anything as Gethin sipped his wine, all the while watching me through narrowed eyes.

"And now you would like to know why I want your rune-stone," he said at last.

I nodded. Though what good would it do to know? I was completely helpless and perhaps it would be better not to know what evil was coming... *if* I gave up the stone. But of course, I would.

Gethin took another sip of his wine.

"My father was English and my mother Welsh," he began. "I have no good memories of my father. I will not bore you with the details of how he treated me, and worse, how he treated my mother. Since his death I have called myself by my middle name, the Welsh one that my mother gave me. Now I think I shall stop calling myself *ap Ordgar*. Though he was my father I would prefer not to be reminded of it. I may call myself *Gethin ap*

Myrddin, after my mother's father. An appropriate name for a magician, don't you think?"

I shrugged. Who on earth was Myrddin, and what had all this got to do with my rune-stone?

Gethin took another sip.

"I have pondered for some time how I could take revenge on my father's people. I had already taken revenge on him, but that did not seem enough."

I stared as I put two and two together. Gethin's father was dead. He had taken revenge on him. Had he killed his own father?

Gethin smiled.

"You have an open face," he said. "I can see the workings of your mind, and you are right. I killed him because he did not deserve to live." Another sip of wine. "But what people could produce such a monster? What revenge could I take on the nation which had nurtured such a viper in its bosom?"

"But you can't blame a whole people for one bad man!" I objected. "Are you telling me there are no bad Welshmen?"

"Be quiet!" thundered Gethin, and his fist came down on the table so hard that both goblets jumped in the air and landed upright, splattering wine around.

I shrank back.

"I suggest you keep your opinions to yourself, unless I ask for them," said Gethin in a quiet voice.

I nodded dumbly, and Gethin carried on.

"Yes," he nodded. "At first I thought how good it would be if we could replay the battle on Senlac hill so that the Normans won."

My eyes widened. Was Gethin actually mad? But I didn't say anything.

"Let the English suffer under a foreign yoke!" sneered Gethin. "But how to turn back time, that was a big problem." He paused. "I am a great and knowledgeable magician, the greatest in the land, but even I struggled to find an answer. If I had had enough of these stones before the battle I could have influenced the outcome, but I only had a few at that time.

232

In the last few weeks, however, luck has been with me. Luck and my own skill. And now I believe I could do it. Turn back time and cause the English to lose the battle."

Gethin rose from his chair and started to pace about the room, while I listened, fascinated. He *was* mad. There was no doubt about it. He was stark staring, raving mad. But did that make him more dangerous or less? I was horribly afraid it might make things worse.

Gethin turned and faced me, then burst out laughing.

"But do you know what, my little English friend," he said. "Now I have an even better idea. I am brilliant! Suppose I could turn back time, not just a few weeks, but hundreds of years. Suppose I could prevent you barbarians ever settling in this country. Now that I have these runes, I see how powerful they can be. Mixed with my own sorcery that is. Suppose I turn back the years to the time of that fool Vortigern. You have heard of Vortigern?"

I started to shake my head, then a faint memory stirred, of listening half asleep to Wiglaf the priest droning on in school. Something about when the English first arrived here. What was it?

"Hengist and Horsa!" I burst out, then shrank back. But Gethin didn't seem to mind.

"You are not completely ignorant then," he said. "Yes, that fool of a British chieftain, that idiot Vortigern actually asked those treacherous brothers over to help him defeat the Picts. He invited the English in! But if I were to turn back time and stop that happening, the English people would not even exist!"

Even to my slightly wine-befuddled mind there seemed to be something wrong with this logic.

"But," I muttered, then stopped and looked at Gethin.

"Go on, go on. Let us hear what the great thinker has to say."

"Well," I hesitated. "Even if you *could* travel back through time..."

"Not just *travel back*," interrupted Gethin. "I intend to roll back time itself!"

"All right then," I said. "Even if you *could* turn back time itself, and even if you *could* stop Hengist and Horsa coming, that wouldn't stop the rest of the English arriving, would it?"

Gethin watched him with a half smile.

"Go on," he said. "Enlighten me."

"Well, it wasn't only Hengist and Horsa, was it? I mean, people were coming over and landing all around the country…Angles, Saxons, Jutes, all the people we call English."

I was amazing myself with how much I could remember of Wiglaf's monotonous lessons. No, *of course*. It wasn't Wiglaf. When we'd got home Oz had asked my mum about it and she'd told us the story, all about how the English first came to be here. She was a good storyteller, too. Oz had said afterwards that only Wiglaf could make such interesting stuff sound so boring.

"I mean," I went on, "how could one man…even a magician, stop all that – all those people coming over in their boats and settling?"

Gethin drew himself up to his full height and his eyes glittered in the flare of the torches. I shrank back again. Had I gone too far? It was time to shut up.

"One man could do it, you insignificant worm," spat Gethin, "because it would not be just any man. It would be Gethin ap Myrddin, come from the future, like a god to save his people!"

He paused and I tried to melt into the back of the chair. *You really are mad*, I thought, but an uncomfortable feeling was growing inside me. I could imagine Gethin on horseback, waving his sword, urging on an army of the British, or Welsh, or whoever they were, against the invading Angles, Saxons and Jutes. Suppose he really could turn back time?

"But that would change everything that happened afterwards," I muttered.

Gethin burst out laughing. "Yes, exactly! That is the whole point."

My head was spinning. Would me and Oz even exist? Would we live over the sea somewhere or would we just not be here?

"Have you heard of King Arthur?" asked Gethin suddenly.

I shook my head.

"You ignorant English!" sneered Gethin. "Arthur was a great warlord. He won famous victories over your people, but I shall be greater than him. My victories will last!"

He closed his eyes and stood, breathing deeply, while I wondered what was going to happen next. Then a slow smile spread across the magician's face. His eyes opened and he looked at me.

"And now I am assured of victory, because of the rune-stone that you will give me. It is a great rune of protection, of which you have barely skimmed the surface. With this stone, freely given to me, I will be invincible." He laughed. "And of course, you *will* give it to me, or else watch your friend die a slow and horrible death. Perhaps we shall start with red-hot pokers thrust into his eyes."

At this point the apple cake threatened to rush back up and out of my mouth, but I swallowed hard and somehow kept it down.

"Why, you have lost a little colour," smiled Gethin. "Oh, there are all sorts of ways to prolong his death. I shall enjoy planning it. But of course, you will give me the stone and deprive me of my fun. A pity, in a way."

I swallowed again, and when I could trust myself to open my mouth without being sick, I whispered, "How do I know that you'll keep your word if I do give you the stone? How do I know you won't kill us anyway?"

"A sensible question," nodded Gethin. "Magic requires oath keeping. Unfortunately, to receive the full power of the rune, I must keep my side of the bargain." He clapped his hands and two servants came running. "Take him to his room!" he snapped.

"Wait!" I said as a new thought struck me.

Gethin looked at me with raised eyebrows.

"Can you tell me why Grimwold wanted my stone? He was English. What was *he* going to do with it?"

Gethin chuckled softly.

"Ah, the unfortunate Grimwold. He was a good magician, but not in my class. I believe he had some mad idea of returning England to its old religion."

I almost laughed. *Mad idea?* I thought. *Not half as mad as yours.*

"But what do I care?" shrugged Gethin. "He is dead. Sleep well, if you can, and think about what I have said. I shall see you tomorrow evening."

And I was taken by the shoulders, hustled along a corridor and shoved into a bedchamber. The door was firmly locked behind me. It was a small room with bare white walls, a narrow bed and a low chest with one candle burning on it – a lot better than Oz's dungeon, but that wasn't much comfort. I sank on to the bed feeling as if I was in a black pit with no way out. Too tired and confused to think, but with a feeling of dread like a rock in my stomach, I stared at the wall.

There was something strange about it. The air in front of it was wavering. Was it the flickering of the candle? No. Something – I couldn't make out what – started to appear and then vanished. I sat up. There was the wavering again, and two short, stocky figures began to take shape.

And then, for the first time since I was captured, a surge of hope rose in my heart.

CHAPTER FORTY-SEVEN

WULF

"We must be mad, doin' this for a human," said Pooka, shaking himself.

"I never met such a load of evil spells protectin' a place," said Mugwort. "I didn't think we was gonna make it."

I fell off the bed and on to my knees, almost crying with relief.

"You have no idea how pleased I am to see you!" I said.

"Oh, I reckons we do," said Pooka. "You owes us one after this."

"Where are Toadstool and Bramble?" I asked. "Are they all right?"

"They be all right," said Mugwort. "They told us about you an' Oz an' they was gonna come with us, but little Bramble, she got scared."

"She were all right till we got to this dirty gurt castle with all its evil spells," said Pooka, "but that were too much for her."

"You can understand it," nodded Mugwort, "after what happened to her sister, an' her seein' it an' all."

"So her an' Toadstool's waitin' a little ways away," said Pooka. "'Cos he wouldn't leave her, o'course."

"So can you take us to them?" I said eagerly. "I mean, can you get me and Oz out of here?"

"Whoa! Hold on, hold on," said Pooka. "How d'you think we be gonna do that?"

"Well, can't you show us how to air-flit? I mean, hold our hands or something, so we can go with you?"

Both the elves burst out laughing, though I didn't think it was very funny.

"Humans can't go air-flittin'!" gasped Mugwort. "If I was to hold your hand, all you'd see'd be me vanishin' an' you left standin' there like a gurt fool."

237

"Well, have you got some other way of getting us out?" I asked. "You have come to help, haven't you?"

My high hopes were starting to fade a bit.

"'Course we have," said Pooka, "But it don't involve gettin' you out o' here. We ain't got that kind o' magic."

"But that's the only help we need," I said dully.

Pooka put his hands on his hips and his head on one side. He looked at me with one of his impossible to read elf expressions.

"That'd better not be true," he said, "'cos that's help we can't give you. But we can help you to help yourself. Leastways, Mugwort here do reckon he can."

"How?" I said disbelievingly. "Just how can I help myself against an evil magician like Gethin?"

"Well, I been thinkin' about your rune thing," said Mugwort. "I knows a bit about them things."

"He ain't just a pretty face, you know," interrupted Pooka, and Mugwort flashed a grin showing his pointed little teeth.

"So have you still got it?" asked Mugwort.

"Yeah, but not for much longer," I said. "I've got to hand it over to Gethin tomorrow night or he's gonna torture Oz to death."

"He be a charmin' feller, ain't he?" said Pooka.

"Can I have another look at it?" asked Mugwort.

When I nodded, he reached out and fearlessly took hold of the stone. I gasped when he held it in his hand with no apparent ill effect. Then I remembered that Pooka and Walter had both been able to do the same. Pooka had said it was because the stone recognized a friend. Mugwort turned it round in his palm and felt the shape of the rune carved on it.

"That be all right," said Mugwort. "What you do is, you give it to him but don't give it to him."

"What?" I said.

"Give it to him but don't give it to him," repeated Mugwort.

"Thanks a lot! That's as clear as mud," I said, exasperated. "I'm really glad you two turned up!"

Pooka frowned. "We can go as easy as we come," he threatened.

"Which weren't very easy," muttered Mugwort, "with all them spells."

"No, don't go!" I pleaded. "It's just…I can't understand what you're telling me to do."

"Never mind that now," said Mugwort. "Can you hold it up so's you can see it, without takin' it off?"

"I think so," I said. "Yeah, look, the bit of leather's quite long."

"Good," said Mugwort. "Now I wants you to jus' look at it and don't think o' nothin' else. Jus' look at the shape o' the rune."

I tried, but nothing happened. After a bit I said, "This is stupid. What's supposed to be happening?"

"Jus' look at the shape o' the rune an' keep your mouth shut," insisted Mugwort. "Jus' let your mind go blank."

I sighed. That was easier said than done. But as I gazed at the rune again, the shape seemed to stand out from the stone on which it was carved. It glowed brighter and brighter, burning itself into my eyes and my mind.

"Thorn," I breathed.

And suddenly the bedchamber vanished and I was in a forest clearing in the dead of night. The trees were tall evergreens, not the broadleaf trees I was used to. In the middle of the clearing was a small bonfire and sitting, warming himself by it, was a man. Although he was crouched down, I could see that he was tall, like the trees. His beard was brown with streaks of grey. He wore a dark cloak, a broad-brimmed dark hat pulled down over one eye and on one shoulder perched a large black bird – a raven. *He must have broad shoulders*, I thought, *because ravens are big birds*. Another raven walked jerkily round the fire, pecking at the ground.

Slowly the man turned and looked at me, and now I could see that beneath the pulled-down hat one eye was closed. You could tell there was no eyeball beneath the lid. He looked at me with his one good eye and I felt that he was seeing right into the centre of my being.

"Do you know who I am?" asked the man.

Of course I did, but the words that came out of my mouth were not what I'd expected to say.

"You are the runemaster," I said.

"You have spoken well," said the runemaster. "I have many names. To you I am Woden, to others Odin, to yet others Wotan. I am Allfather, far-seeing one, taker of the slain in battle, and many, many other names. Some call me the god of the hanged. But you are not here because of all that. You are here because I am the runemaster."

He turned back to gaze into the fire. I stood wondering whether I should say anything.

"Ask," said Woden, looking at me again. "What is it that you wish for?"

I almost asked if he could rescue us, but once again I found myself saying something unexpected.

"Can you help me to stop Gethin doing this thing he's planning?" *And rescue me and Oz into the bargain*, I thought, but I didn't say it.

"Gethin ap Myrddin, as he now calls himself," said Woden, "is doing a deeply dangerous thing. He plans to turn back time."

"So you know all about it?" I said, relieved.

"I know everything that happens on middle earth and in the sky and in the ocean," said Woden. "But that does not always mean that I can change it."

"But you're the king of the gods!" I said. "I thought gods could do anything!"

Woden laughed quietly.

"Would that that were true. We can do far more than humans, but we are woven into the Web of Wyrd, just as you are."

The Web of Wyrd. I'd heard my mum talk about that.

"We are part of everything that is, in all the worlds," Woden went on, "just as you are. We did not make the web, although we can adjust the weave a little. So no, I cannot do anything I like, or I would destroy this Gethin myself."

His one good eye bored into my soul.

"I need *you*."

CHAPTER FORTY-EIGHT

WULF

"Me?" I said. The trees, the fire and everything around seemed to tilt at an angle and then back again. "What can *I* do? I thought it was me who needed you."

Woden smiled, but I thought it was a sad smile.

"Let us say that we need each other," said the runemaster. "If this Gethin turns back time for hundreds of years, he will rip the Web of Wyrd. A few weeks, even a few moons, would not matter so much. The weave would adjust itself. But what he plans will set chaos in motion. You must stop him."

"How am I going to do that?" I asked, beginning to panic.

"Do you see my runes?" said Woden, and I saw a ring of stones just like my own arranged in a circle round the fire. Why hadn't I noticed them before? And there was my own rune-stone in the circle. I felt for the stone round my neck but it was still there.

"I don't understand," I said. "How can my stone be in two places at once?"

"Your stone?" said Woden. "I rather think that it was my stone before it was yours."

"I'm sorry...I didn't mean..."

"Runes are everywhere," he went on. "They too are woven into the Web of Wyrd. But these are my stones, that I carved when I first learned the runes. Nine days and nine nights I hung on the World tree, pierced by a spear, in agony, with nothing to eat or drink, before I won the runes. I looked into the abyss and I saw them. They burned themselves into my mind. And when my ordeal was over, I carved these."

"Oz was right then," I said. "I remembered your story. My mother told me. But Oz said it wasn't the stones themselves that you snatched up

241

from the abyss. He said they were probably in your mind and that you carved them afterwards."

Woden nodded. "It is good to know that people still tell my story, even though this new god has taken over. I have these stones in this world, the world where we are now. But they have their counterparts in middle earth, and your stone is one of them."

"When you say 'middle earth',"I said, confused, "do you mean, like, the world?"

"I mean the world where humans live," replied Woden.

"So where are we now?" I asked.

"In my world, not in yours," said the runemaster. "But we are wasting time. I have a task for you."

I sighed. When was somebody going to let me have a rest?

"You will give your stone to Gethin," he went on, "because you do not want your friend to die."

"You know about that as well, then?" I said.

"I have told you," said Woden impatiently, "I know everything that happens in middle earth, in the skies and under the waves. You will give it to him and you will say whatever words he wishes you to say, but you will still have it, because I will give you the power of this rune in your heart."

So that's what Mugwort was on about! *Give it to him but don't give it to him.*

"When you give it to him," continued the runemaster, "there will be a connection between you, because you will still bear it in your heart. So if he succeeds in doing this thing, going back in time, you will go with him."

"What?"

"You have the rune Thurisaz," he went on. "A great rune of protection which your mother gave you. That makes it even more powerful. She gave it to you with love."

The raven on the ground hopped over to my rune in the circle round the fire. It nudged the stone with its beak.

"Thank you, Muninn," smiled Woden at the raven.

I frowned. "But my rune's called Thorn."

The raven on Woden's shoulder placed his beak in the god's ear. Woden chuckled.

"Huginn tells me you will find it easier if I use the English names, not the ancient names which I gave them so long ago."

"But you speak English," I said. "Why didn't you give them English names?"

"I speak many languages," said Woden. "There was no English language when I learned these runes."

I gave up trying to understand.

"Gethin wishes for one of the runes of protection, either Thorn or Eolh, and soon he believes he will have Thorn."

The runemaster picked a twig out of the fire. One end of it was burning and with that end he drew the shape of Thorn in the air. When he'd finished, the shape stayed there hovering and glowing.

"But I give *you* Thorn so that even when you give the stone away you will keep it and, moreover, you will have the power to remove its protection from Gethin.

"And I will give you Ur, a rune for strength, courage and persistence." Muninn the raven hopped over and tapped Ur with his beak and Woden drew its shape in the air beside Thorn. "These are qualities which you already have, though you may not think it, but I will strengthen them."

"You know what?" interrupted Wulf. "It's Oz you want, not me. He knows a lot more about runes than I do, and he's braver too."

"Is he?" asked Woden. He didn't seem annoyed by the interruption. "More foolhardy perhaps. But to know fear and do the deed anyway is true courage. Now where were we?"

Muninn hopped over to another rune and poked it with his beak.

"Ah, thank you, Muninn," said Woden. "And I give you Wynn, for the first letter of your name, Wolfstone, and because it brings joy and harmony. It is a good rune to work with others, so it is useful in a bindrune."

He drew the third rune and then pulled it across to Ur, so that the two shapes combined. Then he did the same with Thorn, and there floating in the air and shining with triple brightness was a complicated shape containing all three. A bindrune. He pointed the burning stick at the space between my eyes and the bindrune shot into my head, like an arrow hitting its target. I staggered backwards. I felt as if my head was on fire and everything around was dazzlingly bright. Gradually it dimmed and there was Woden, sitting with his two ravens.

Without pausing to ask if I was all right, the rune master went on talking.

"He will use Rad, the travelling rune, and Ger, the cycles of the year. He will reverse them so that the years travel backwards...are you taking this in?" he said sharply.

No, I wasn't. How was I supposed to remember all that?

"What you must do," continued Woden, "is to turn back those runes to their rightful paths. You can do it because you will be there in the same world as him."

"But you could do it!" I burst out. "Don't you go around our world in disguise, like you are now? You could do this much better than me!"

"I used to travel in middle earth," Woden agreed. "But my power in *your* land is waning, now that so few there worship me."

"But what will happen if I don't manage to do it?" I asked desperately.

Woden took a deep breath. "At first the earth will shudder. It will start to revert to the primal chaos from which it was created," he said, showing no emotion. "Everything will unravel and that great and terrible wolf Fenrir will be released from his bonds. The sea will rear up as the serpent Jormungand twists and writhes its way toward the land. Naglfar will set sail, the ghostly ship made of dead men's fingernails. Then will come the final battle between the gods and the giants and monsters. We shall not win that battle. If you do not succeed, Wolfstone, it will be Ragnarok – the end of the world."

I suppressed a hysterical laugh. I could hear Oz's voice in my head. *The end of the world? So no pressure then.*

"Then tell me how to do it!" I whispered, finding my voice at last. "If it's that important, tell me exactly how!"

Woden looked long and hard at me, his one eye boring into my soul, seeing everything there was to see.

"You will discover that for yourself, Wolfstone. Be brave, be strong."

The forest clearing started to fade. I felt as if I was travelling through a cloud, then I found myself once more in the bedchamber. I sat on the floor bleakly, with my eyes closed, Woden's words echoing in my head. *Be brave, be strong.* What about, *Don't worry, I'll look after you?*

Why had it got to be all down to me? And wasn't I supposed to be feeling something from the runes inside me? Some extra courage or something? All I felt now was that it was too much to ask. I just couldn't do it.

CHAPTER FORTY-NINE

WULF

"Where you bin?" said Pooka's voice.

Reluctantly I opened my eyes – my lids felt as if they were weighed down with stones – and saw the two elves looking at me.

"Meet anyone interestin', did you?" said Mugwort. "Meet ol' One-eye?"

I nodded. It was too much effort to speak.

"Well, come on, then," said Pooka. "What did he say?"

"Look, I'm so tired," I managed at last. "I don't think I can do this."

"You'll feel better when you've had some shuteye," said Mugwort.

I collapsed on to the bed and straight away fell into a deep sleep, full of confused and horrible dreams.

When I woke up it was light. The candle had been snuffed out and Mugwort was curled up in the corner dozing. Someone had put a wooden platter and beaker on the floor. Bread and water. The feasting was obviously over. Despite last night's heavy meal, I was ravenous. As soon as I swung my legs over the side of the bed, Mugwort sat up.

"Where's Pooka?" I asked.

"Gone to check up on your friend," said Mugwort. "I seen him too. We had to disappear when we heard footsteps, but I didn't stay long."

"Oz?" I said eagerly. "Is he all right?"

"Not bad, considerin'. He were that pleased to see us."

"I bet," I grinned, tearing off a hunk of bread and stuffing it in my mouth.

"Yeah," said Mugwort. "We had to go thru' the same ol' rigmarole we had with you. He thought we was jus' gonna magic him outta here. A bit disappointed, he were, when he found out we couldn't. But anyways, finish your breakfast. We got work to do."

246

"Work?" I said through a mouthful of bread.

"Oh, p'raps you knows exactly what you gotta do. P'raps you don't need me."

Then it all came back to me. The conversation with Woden, and how vaguely it had been left. How I didn't know what to do at all.

"No, I do need you," I said. "Please help me."

"That be better," said Mugwort. "Now tell me exactly what he said."

I told him the whole thing, from seeing the god by the fire in the clearing to finding myself back in this room. I even surprised myself by remembering the names of the runes Woden had mentioned.

"Rad, you reckon," said Mugwort, "and Ger. That be like this, ain't it?"

He drew on the wall with his finger, then looked around, muttering, for something that would make a mark.

"Ah, this'll do."

Picking up the candle, he used the burnt wick as a pen and drew two shapes on the wall.

"How comes you know so much about runes?" I asked. "Do elves use rune magic?"

"Oh, no, no, no," said Mugwort. "I don't reckon Pooka thinks much to my little hobby. He thinks it got too much to do wi' humans an' gods. We're more to do with the land, nature an' that. We're older'n all this rune stuff. Older'n ol' One-eye."

"Older than the gods?" I said in disbelief.

"Thass not what I said," replied Mugwort. "There's other gods, nature gods an' that, bin around longer than One-eye. We got more in common wi' them. But all these battle gods, we don' have nothin' to do wi' them."

"You mean like Woden and Thor," I said. I was stunned at how much I didn't know. In my mind I'd just lumped all magic together, as something I felt I'd rather stay away from. I had no idea the magical world was so complicated.

"So why are you interested in runes?" I went on.

"I dunno," said Mugwort simply. "Who can tell why somebody be drawn to somethin'? But you know what? We be wastin' time."

"Sorry," I said.

"Now look at these here shapes," said Mugwort. "One-eye reckons our friend's gonna reverse 'em. Like this," and he drew the runes again backwards. "Now I wants you to concentrate really hard, like you did wi' your stone. Jus' look at the back to front runes and don' think o' nothin' else, an' jus' see if you can turn 'em round the right way again."

"What?" I exploded . "How'm I gonna do that?"

Mugwort sighed. "We're never gonna get anywheres if you keeps carryin' on like that. Jus' look at the runes – the back to front ones – an' don't think o' nothin' else. Like you did last night. After a deal o' fuss an' pother that is, an' we ain't got no time for that. Jus' do it."

I knew Mugwort was right. We'd only got till this evening and it had worked last night. Only…last night I'd found myself in another world with Woden. Where was I going to end up this time? But I tried to concentrate on the drawings on the wall and after a while it was quite easy to think of nothing else. I went into a sort of trance and the shapes seemed to float off the wall into the air.

"What now?" I whispered.

"Now see if you can flip 'em over," said Mugwort.

"How?" I asked.

"Dear me, dear me," Mugwort shook his head. "You wants somebody to hold your hand the whole ways. It's a wonder you ever learned to walk with your attitude." He did an impression of my voice which, though not as good as Pooka's, did sound like me. "*Oh mother dear, I've put one foot in front of the other. Now what does I do with the first foot?*"

I collapsed with laughter and Mugwort gave me a big grin.

"Come on, you lummox, let's start again. You got that bindrune inside you to help you. Use your instincts a bit more."

Still smiling, I stared once more at the drawings until they floated off the wall. I stared and stared and somehow my mind emptied, the joke was forgotten, the room vanished. I was alone in space with two hovering shapes and then…I had no idea how…with a lurch in my stomach as if my insides were turning over, I flipped the runes. There they were! The right way round! I blinked, the floating shapes vanished and I collapsed on to the bed.

"Very good," nodded Mugwort admiringly.

For there on the wall was the second pair of runes, not back to front as he'd drawn them, but the right way round.

"You done it!" said Mugwort.

"I feel sick," I said.

"You'll get over it," said Mugwort unsympathetically. "Now you gotta practise. See if you can't get a bit quicker. We don't know how long you're gonna have, an' it'd be best to do it before you starts goin' back in time, if you can."

The air next to him shimmered and Pooka shook himself.

"Greetin's from your friend," he said to me, and to Mugwort, "I heard that last bit, an' I couldn't agree more. Who knows what's gonna happen when you starts messin' about wi' time. He's a gurt fool, that Gethin, plannin' somethin' like this. So clever, all that magic an' knowledge, but a gurt fool." He looked at me. "So if you *can* manage to reverse them things before you starts time-travellin', t'would be better."

"How did you know that's what I've got to do?" I asked. "You weren't here when I was telling Mugwort."

"I got long ears," said Pooka.

A horrible thought struck me.

"But if I do manage it," I said, "what's to stop Gethin just reversing them again?"

"We can't waste time worryin' about that," said Mugwort. "You jus' gotta do what ol' One-eye told you. He do know a lot, that god. I ain't got much time for some of his doin's, but he do know a lot."

"And what'll happen if I don't manage to do it until *after* we've gone back in time?"

I stopped, suddenly hit by the craziness of what I was saying. It was all crazy, all of it. What was I doing here?

Pooka shook his head. "Who knows? Time's a funny thing. We might just get back to where we are now, or it could be a bit in the future or a bit in the past. Or things might be jus' a little bit different. People might be dead who's alive, or alive who's dead. Who knows? But whatever do happen, it be better than the end of everythin'. So you just keep practisin'."

Pooka curled up in the corner and shut his eyes. Mugwort rubbed out the two drawings that I'd reversed and drew two more back to front versions of Rad and Ger. Then, with the sick feeling still in my stomach, I began practising.

By the time the light was fading, I'd become quite good at it, but doubts gnawed at my mind. It was all very well doing this here with Mugwort urging me on, but would I be able to do it when the time came? I could never have put into words exactly what I *was* doing, but I assumed it was something to do with Woden's gift of the bindrune inside me.

Eventually all three of us were sitting in darkness.

"Couldn't you give us a light?" I asked. "Use a bit of fire magic or something?"

"Oh very good," said Pooka. "That ain't gonna look at all suspicious, is it? Here's you, sittin' here wi' no means o' lightin' a candle and suddenly it lights itself. I don't think so."

So we sat in darkness and silence, me worrying all the time about what was going to happen. Finally, to stop myself going crazy, I started talking – anything that came into my head.

"I think this Welsh English thing is mad," I said. "I mean, I'm English and Bron's Welsh and we're good friends."

I didn't mention that I'd like us to be more than good friends.

"'Tis more mad than you knows," replied Pooka. "When all's said and done, humans is humans."

Mugwort nodded.

"T'ain't where you come from that counts," he said.

"Take that friend o' yourn, Abdul" Pooka went on. "If he was to stay here an' have a family, they'd be just as English as you."

"You reckon?" I said.

"O' course," said Pooka. "When all's said and done, 'tis the land that counts."

I desperately wanted to find out more about this strange idea, but I was jerked back to the present by footsteps sounding on the corridor.

"Goodbye and good luck," whispered Pooka. "We hopes to see you soon."

"You can do it," whispered Mugwort. "Remember that bindrune inside o' you." And the two elves vanished.

A key turned, the door creaked open and two of Gethin's servants stood there.

"Our master requires your presence," said one of them.

I stood and walked between them without saying a word. A sense of doom hung over me. At the end of the corridor we started to go down a stairway and I marvelled again at this stone building with its layers of floors. Down we went, down and down. At first I had no way of working out whether we'd been high up and now we were at ground level or whether we were in fact under the ground. But then the stones of the castle gave way to rock walls. I shivered. It felt like some deep cave. We must be below ground. And there, in the rock, was a huge wooden door. Gethin must be on the other side of that door, and Oz.

The time had come.

One of the servants knocked and the door swung open. Standing before me was a figure I'd seen before. A tall, dark haired man with high cheekbones and an air of stillness about him.

"You!" I whispered, as my mind flashed back to the day after the feast. This was the man who had paid Guthrum to give me the letter. The letter that had turned out to be a death sentence. Hadn't Abdul read out something about 'using your English name'? Gethin had an English name which he'd now abandoned, though I didn't know what it was. But the letter must have been addressed to Gethin! And though it had been destroyed and I hadn't delivered it, Fate, or something, had stepped in and made sure that I delivered myself. I let out a deep sigh, almost a moan. After all that, I might just as well have ridden up to the castle, delivered the letter and turned myself in. The man smiled at me and I felt sure that he remembered me as well. He'd seen me watching him from the door of the hut and had smiled that same knowing smile.

"Lead him in, Madoc," came Gethin's voice, and the man beckoned me into the dim torch-lit cavern…and I shuddered with horror.

The walls were hung with animal skulls…horses, goats, sheep and others which I couldn't make out. The magician stood at the back, dressed all in black with the skull of a stag on his head, the antlers spread wide, his face showing beneath the skull.

But that wasn't what made my stomach lurch.

For there, in the middle of the chamber, suspended from the roof, was a figure swinging lifeless, noose round his neck, face turned away from me. He was a boy about my age. He wore a dirty green tunic…like Oz. His head was at a crooked angle on his neck and the hair on that head was fair…like Oz's hair.

Terror gripped my throat, my whole body. I choked and my mouth filled with bile. Then – I couldn't help it – I let out a shriek.

"What have you done? O-o-oz!"

CHAPTER FIFTY

WULF

Gethin stepped up to the hanging body and swung it round. I ducked my head and my hands flew up to cover my eyes. I didn't want to see Oz's face like that. But I had to look. Slowly, reluctantly, I took my hands away and let my eyes travel up the swinging figure. Just before it completed a full circle and hung with its back to me once more, I saw the face. It was the face of a boy about my age, horribly purple and twisted…but it wasn't Oz.

"Bring the boy out!" ordered Gethin.

From behind a black curtain which I hadn't noticed in the darkness, staggered Oz. One arm was gripped behind his back and a dagger was at his throat. His face looked dead white and hollow eyed. Still, I felt faint with relief. But that feeling only lasted a moment before it was swept aside by a hot wave of anger.

Gethin had wanted me to believe that Oz had been hanged! He'd dressed that poor boy in Oz's dirty green tunic and given Oz the boy's patched brown one! And was that the reason he'd hanged him? *Was this Gethin's idea of a joke?* I was convulsed with rage, so incensed that I couldn't speak.

But Gethin spoke, as if he'd read my mind.

"I see you do not appreciate my little joke." He laughed. "But do not worry, the shepherd boy did not die merely to provide me with some amusement. I need a corpse, a hanged corpse, and unfortunately I had promised not to kill your friend…if you co-operate. Ordinarily, such matters as a little broken promise would not concern me. I, Gethin ap Myrddin am above such petty rules. But I have to be certain that nothing gets in the way of my magic tonight. And I thought it a nice touch to find someone, a peasant like yourselves, who resembled your friend."

"He was terrified," croaked Oz in a hoarse whisper. "That boy was terrified."

So Oz had seen it all.

"Keep your mouth shut!" snapped Gethin. "What is that to me?" Then, "Bring me the knife and the bowl."

Madoc stepped forward with a metal bowl and an evil looking knife. Gethin took the knife and Oz was hustled forward and one sleeve drawn back, exposing his arm.

"My stones need feeding," said Gethin. "They cry out for blood."

Then I saw on the ground beneath the hanging boy a wide circle of rune-stones. It jolted me to my senses. This was what I'd got to concentrate on! I tried to quell my fury, forget my worries for Oz. My eyes scanned the circle, searching for Rad and Ger. Some of the stones looked ancient, like mine, but others seemed more recently carved. So Gethin didn't have a complete set of Woden's stones. There was a space left, presumably for Thorn, and I noticed that Eolh, the other rune of protection that Woden had mentioned, was new. How had I recognized Eolh? Was the bindrune teaching me rune-lore? I looked around the circle and as my eyes lit on each stone in turn, its name came into my head. I almost smiled. Perhaps I could do this after all. Gethin needed protection in his mad venture. He didn't have Woden's original Eolh, and that's why he was so delighted that Thorn was going to be his. I'd have to make sure somehow that I removed that protection from him. Woden had said I'd be able to. But how? I'd got to do as Mugwort said, and trust my instincts.

And there were Rad and Ger, already placed in an upside down position. Would now be a good time to begin, or was it too soon? I might not have many chances. Better to risk being too early than to miss the opportunity all together.

Gethin's voice broke into my thoughts.

"Ah, but how could I forget? Thorn. My beloved Thorn." I smiled at Wulf. "Take it off from round your neck."

I obeyed, but the stone felt so heavy!

"Hold it out and say these words after me."

I held it out.

"I, Wulfstan, keeper of Thorn," said Gethin.

I hesitated, then, seeing the knife and Oz's bare arm, I said the words.

"Do entirely renounce my ownership of this rune," continued Gethin.
I repeated it.

"And give it to Gethin ap Myrddin for his sole use and ownership."
I said the words in a low voice.

"And may evil come to my mother who gave me Thorn, if I in any way go back on this decision or try to trick Gethin ap Myrddin, the rightful owner of Thorn."

I stopped. How could I say that? Woden had told me to say whatever words Gethin wanted me to say. Had he known the magician would bring my mum into it? He might have warned me! *Woden, help me!* A tiny glow warmed my stomach – the bindrune giving me reassurance – and slowly I recited the words. But in my head I said, *Mum, forgive me if any harm comes to you.* Oz looked at me amazed.

As I handed the stone to Gethin, the glow inside me grew warmer. Ur and Wynn and Thorn, that I had just given away but not given away, as Mugwort had told me. With a triumphant smile, Gethin put the rune-stone in its place in the circle.

"I take this rune Thorn for my protection, to guard me from all harm," he intoned. Then, with an abrupt change of mood, "Now for the feeding! Give me the knife!"

He took the knife from Madoc and, with one fluid movement, slashed Oz's arm.

"You promised!" I shouted.

"Be quiet!" snapped Gethin. "This is nothing. Do you want to see what I can do if I choose to really hurt him?"

Afraid of angering Gethin now that he already had the stone, I sullenly closed my lips. Oz's face was contorted with pain as Madoc held the bowl under his arm to catch the flow of blood and I started to panic when I saw how much blood he was losing. But in a little while, clearly used to this sort of thing, another servant tied a leather belt tightly round his upper arm.

Gethin held the bowl aloft.

"I feed you with sacrificial blood," he said. "In return, may you do my bidding."

Then he walked slowly round the circle dipping his fingers into Oz's blood and sprinkling every stone in turn, being very careful to see that each stone had its share.

Now would be a good time! Now! Come on, now! I concentrated hard on Rad and Ger – thank goodness they were together – trying to do the things I'd been practising with Mugwort. I had to ignore Gethin, ignore everything else that was going on. I narrowed my eyes, to block out distractions. Slowly the runes began to glow and separate themselves from the stones on which they were carved. Gethin was intoning something again, but I didn't listen. Then a knife flashed in the torchlight and I lost my concentration. The stones went back to how they had been.

Must do better! Forget him! But when Gethin sliced through the rope from which the corpse was suspended, it was impossible to forget what was going on.

The body collapsed on to the floor, noose still round its neck.

"Arise, hanged one!" chanted Gethin. "Arise and speak to me."

It was the runes which were forgotten as, with growing horror, I watched the crumpled body twitch. The limbs jerked. Slowly they rearranged themselves. What had been a shepherd boy was now a thing of unspeakable horror as it raised its distorted face and, in a series of juddering spasms, stood up.

CHAPTERFIFTY-ONE

WULF

The thing stood in the middle of the circle of runes, but it could not stand still. Like a puppet pulled by invisible strings, it jerked its head this way and that, twitched its arms, shifted from one foot to the other, shivering and shuddering in a ghastly dance of death.

I wanted to shrink away, to turn and run, but I was transfixed, as unable to move as the thing was unable to keep still.

Gethin walked slowly round the corpse, inside the circle, with an expression of gloating triumph on his face.

"Speak to me!" he commanded. "Answer my question truly!"

And the corpse spoke.

"What do you wish to know, oh master?" it hissed.

It was not the voice of a boy or a young man. I thought it hardly sounded human at all. There was nothing left of the shepherd boy in that grotesque body.

"Tell me," ordered Gethin, "will my great work meet with success?"

The thing seemed to pause for a brief instant, jerking its head from side to side almost as if it was listening for the answer before passing it on to Gethin.

Then, "There will be great success," it wheezed.

Gethin threw back his head and laughed. A madman's laugh. But hope dawned inside me. An idea had struck me. The magician was so puffed up with pride, so full of his own cleverness and power, that he'd missed the obvious.

There will be great success. But whose? That could just as easily mean my success!

I took heart and tried to ignore the twitching corpse and the circling figure with the stag's skull on its head. *Rad and Ger! Rad and Ger! Must concentrate!*

"So I shall defeat the traitor King Vortigern," Gethin went on, "and lead my people to victory against the barbarians?"

Again the corpse seemed as if it was listening for an answer to pass on.

At last it hissed, "The king will be cut to pieces."

There was more manic laughter from Gethin, but by now I wasn't listening. I was narrowing my eyes to block out my surroundings, staring at the runes and sinking into the trance-like state that I'd learnt while practising with Mugwort. Into the air they floated, two fiery shapes separating themselves from their stones, and I reached deep inside myself for the mysterious power that would reverse them. From the corner of my eye I saw the corpse collapse into a heap. *Distraction.* I almost lost the runes, but just managed to keep them floating in the air. No-one else seemed to be able to see them. Now once again I reached down into my own depths.

Suddenly my insides were wrenched out of me, or that's what it felt like. I gasped and tried to keep hold of the fiery floating runes, but someone else had them! They burned brighter and brighter in their reverse forms and I had to let go. Gethin was chanting, but he was also looking at me with a puzzled expression. Then he broke off his chant.

"You?" he said. "How did you…did you really think you could defeat me?"

With a mocking smile he carried on with the spell and I collapsed like the corpse, in a heap of pain and misery. I couldn't do it. Gethin was too powerful. I'd failed. The chanting grew louder until it filled the cavern. Louder than one human voice, in a language I didn't know. Rad and Ger grew. They pulsed in the air, so bright that my eyes were dazzled and I couldn't see anything else.

Then a wind arose and its roaring mixed with the chanting until they became one sound. I was swept up off the floor of the cavern into darkness and terror. Where was Oz? The storm blew me faster than a horse could gallop. It knocked me through the great oak doors, into trees and rocks, battering me but never letting me grab hold of anything to slow myself down. Weird pictures flashed past my eyes, too fast for me to see properly. Then suddenly the wind dropped me, bruised and shaking.

It died away. I was alone in a moonless night. But where? It seemed to be some kind of moorland and I was crouching by a gorse bush. No, I wasn't alone. Torches flared a little way off. I heard voices. Gethin's voice and other people's. I could hear clearly enough, but I couldn't understand the words.

I peered around the gorse bush and saw the magician, still in his stag's skull headdress, surrounded by people in strange clothes. Their hair stuck up in points. Did it grow like that or did they do something to it? Their arms had curving patterns drawn on them and those arms were carrying powerful-looking spears. Gethin was speaking slowly, but the men were shaking their heads, looking at each other and shrugging. In the torchlight I could just about see Gethin's face, with its impatient frown. One of the men pointed a spear at him. Things didn't seem to be going the way he'd expected. Another man pushed the spear down, so that it wasn't pointing at Gethin. Voices were raised. I wished I could understand what they were saying.

Then in my shaken state I noticed another tiny source of light. A little way from Gethin, outside the circle of torchlight, glowed three shapes. None of the men had noticed them. They were floating a few inches above the ground, quite small, but I could clearly make them out. Rad and Ger, both reversed, and Thorn. My own Thorn, that my mum had given me and that I'd given away but not given away. I felt it tugging gently at my insides. It was the rune which had kept me close to Gethin as the centuries had rolled back with such terrifying speed. Where everyone else was I had no idea – Oz, Bron, Abdul, my mum. Perhaps they didn't exist any more. They couldn't exist. This was the past. I felt dizzy. It was no good thinking about that. I had a job to do, and if I did it well, then everything would be as it should be, back in 1066. I'd been given another chance.

The men marched off with Gethin and, at a safe distance, I followed. The little glowing runes danced along behind the magician, seemingly invisible to everyone but me and, I assumed, Gethin.

It started to rain. I was concentrating on keeping my distance without losing sight of them. The white antlers on Gethin's head were bathed in the orange glow of the torchlight, and it was those, reaching up into the night sky, that I followed. But the torches were guttering in the rain. I ran, crouching, between clumps of gorse, and soon the downpour was so heavy that I couldn't see. There was a smell of sodden earth in my nostrils. I might be in the past but it smelt just the same and that was somehow reassuring. Then there was a blinding flash of lightning, followed almost immediately by a crack of thunder. *Please don't let me be struck by lightning!* But when my eyes recovered from the flash and I tried to peer through the sheeting rain, I realized that I'd lost Gethin and those strange-looking men. I was all alone on a moor in the middle of a thunder storm, hundreds of years before my own time.

They couldn't be far away. But the men knew where they were going and I didn't. I'd have to wait till the storm grew quieter and try to track them. It was the runes I wanted, not Gethin, but they seemed to be following the magician. I very much *didn't* want to meet Gethin himself. Whatever had to be done, I could only do it if that strong, evil magic didn't get in the way. Perhaps I could find somewhere drier to wait it out? Suddenly I was exhausted, weary to my bones.

Just ahead I made out a rock sticking out of the earth. That might give me some shelter if I crouched on the side away from the rain. I crawled over to it, almost too tired to move my arms and legs.

But as I reached it, a little glow warmed my insides. It tugged at me. *Follow me*, it seemed to say. Thorn. *Yes, I will follow you*, I breathed. *Only just let me have a rest.*

And then the moorland shuddered. I jumped in fright but when I landed the tremor was still rippling through solid earth. *What was happening?* The ground, the thing you relied on, the earth beneath you that you took for granted, was shaking. Was everything starting to

260

unravel? I had to act quickly! I had to reverse the runes before it was too late! But first I had to find them. Find them without Gethin seeing me.

Another flash lit up the sky, and then another, throwing shadows on to the rock in front of me. A sob caught in my throat.

For the shadows on the rock showed a man behind me. A man now on horseback. And from his head branched a magnificent pair of antlers.

CHAPTER FIFTY-TWO

WULF

I shut my eyes and waited. It was all up now. The end of me and the end of the world.

"Who are you?" growled a rich brown voice, not quite animal and not quite human. And not Gethin's voice. "What have you done?"

I spun round. Towering above me on a magnificent dark horse sat a figure, a strange kingly figure, human apart from the huge antlers branching from his curly hair. Human, but also animal.

And I knew that he was a god.

Lightning flashed again and showed that the horse was a glossy chestnut and the god was bare to the waist with breeches of some animal hide. His skin and hair were brown, but his eyes were black, with no white around the pupils, like the eyes of a deer.

My breathing came fast and my thoughts whirled. I felt weak with relief that it wasn't Gethin, but also bewildered and...filled with awe.

"What have you done?" he said again.

"I haven't done anything," I gasped.

The horse pawed the ground and thunder rolled. The stag-god looked at me and sniffed the air.

"You do not look like a magician," he growled. "You do not smell like a magician. But this thing that is happening has something to do with you."

"I didn't make it happen," I said, "but I can make it stop...I *think* I can make it stop. If I can find the runes before Gethin finds me."

The thunder was crashing now as soon as the lightning flashed and the rain was sheeting down so hard that I was drenched to the skin.

"This Gethin," said the stag-god, "is he the cause of this? Is he the one who wears antlers in imitation of me?"

"Yes," I nodded desperately, though it hadn't occurred to me that Gethin was imitating anyone.

"I am Cernunnos," said the stag-man. "This Gethin wishes to play at being a god, like me."

"Please...sir...how can I understand you, I mean...what you're saying?" I asked.

"I am Cernunnos," repeated the god.

Not much of an answer, but it looked like all the answer I was going to get. Then I realised that I was hearing the god's voice right *inside* my head, not as if it was travelling through the air to my ears, but as if it were going directly into my mind.

"What has this Gethin done, oh boy who is not a magician?" Cernunnos went on, and his words rolled around inside my skull with a strange echo. I shook myself. Never mind all that. Answer the question!

"He's rolled back time," I said, "hundreds of years."

"Ah," sighed Cernunnos. "I understand. The fool. Why has he done this?"

"He wanted to go back to the time of King Vortigern and stop him inviting Hengist and Horsa and all the English over."

I was beginning to feel we were wasting precious moments, but I didn't want to be rude.

"Vortigern?" said Cernunnos. "Hengist? Horsa? I know nothing of these names." He paused, and in the next lightning flash I could see his expression change, as if he was briefly entering a trance.

"Ah, I see," said the god. "These people are yet to be born." He threw back his head and laughed. "Your friend has overshot himself. He has come too far. The fool thinks it is easy to play with time. And look what he has done!"

"He's not my friend!" I said, but suddenly the earth shuddered again and I staggered.

"Look, can you help me?" I pleaded. "I've got to get close to Gethin without him seeing me."

Without another word Cernunnos reached down one arm and, lifting me up as he might have lifted a feather, sat me on the horse in front of him. In the same moment there was a deep rumble beneath our feet, and the earth split wide open.

The horse leapt across the chasm as if it had wings. I felt the tug of the rune inside me.

"That way!" I pointed, and the horse galloped across the moor. "Not too fast," I yelled against the wind. "They can't have gone far."

Cernunnos laughed. "I see him. Slow down, Fleetfoot."

We skidded to a halt. I couldn't see anything with the rain in my eyes.

"You do not wish him to see you?" said Cernunnos.

"No, but I've got to be able to see the runes," I said. "I can't see anything in this rain."

"It is a wild night," agreed Cernunnos. "I was going to call out my wild hunt, but I think this may be too much, even for them. Come, let us dismount."

He leapt down lightly and lifted me from the horse's back. There was another deafening clap of thunder and it jogged a memory in my brain. My mum, telling one of her stories. The Wild Hunt.

"Are you Herne the Hunter?" I asked, though even as I asked it, I knew what he'd say.

Sure enough, "I am Cernunnos," came the answer. But in the following lightning flash I saw his eyes glaze over for an instant. "Herne the Hunter," he said slowly. "Yes, I think people will give me that name one day. Look, there is your friend."

"Don't keep calling him that," I muttered.

Cernunnos murmured something into the horse's ear and it folded its legs and lay down with its head low. Then he took me by the shoulders and pulled me to the ground where we both lay on our stomachs, though I thought that anyone would be able to see those antlers sticking up.

"Now look," growled Cernunnos, waving a hand across my eyes.

Pacing around some yards away, was Gethin. Whatever Cernunnos had done, I could now see quite clearly through the driving rain. Around Gethin lay motionless figures with strange hairstyles and patterns on their bodies. There was no blood, but they were obviously dead.

"He's killed them all!" I gasped.

Gethin was talking to himself, still in the language that I didn't understand.

"He is mad," said Cernunnos.

"I always thought he was," I said.

Gethin turned and paced the other way and there behind him glowed the three runes, dancing along the ground. Now! I had to do it now! I blocked out my surroundings and began to sink into a trance. The bindrune pulsed inside me. I started to get that strange feeling I always had just before I flipped the runes.

There was an almighty crash and the ground split open. I was looking down into a red-hot chasm and then I was slipping…slipping…into the glowing mouth of the rift, scrabbling to clutch hold of something… anything! A sulphurous smell burned in my nostrils and waves of heat beat up on to my face as my hands scraped against the side of the chasm. Then a strong hand grabbed my leg and hauled me back to the edge. I rolled on to my back and lay there gasping with terror and relief.

"You should be more careful," said Cernunnos.

The horse whinnied and backed away from the chasm and I heard another voice.

"So, it is you again," called Gethin in English, from the other side of the rift. "You are becoming a nuisance. You think that the horned one will defend you, but nothing can protect you from my creatures!"

He raised his arms and started to chant. Slowly, to my utter horror, a black mist rose out of the chasm. Three writhing shapes were uncoiling in the mist, black snakes with red eyes.

All the eyes were looking at me.

"Can't you do something?" I gripped Cernunnos's foot, but he looked uncertain.

"Perhaps," he murmured. "I do not know this magic."

But I did.

The bindrune burned inside me and suddenly I knew what to do.

"By the power of Thorn," I yelled, "I command you to stop!"

Gethin roared with laughter. "Thorn is no longer yours to command!" he chortled.

"Oh yes it is!" I cried. "I take back the gift of Thorn, which I never truly gave away! It will not protect you now!" Then, remembering the words Gethin had made me say, I muttered under my breath, "And may Woden protect my mother."

The snake shapes wavered, as fiery little Thorn separated itself from Rad and Ger and floated across the rift, where it flew into my chest as gently as a bird coming to roost in its nest. I felt it like a sigh of pleasure as it rejoined its other self in the bindrune.

Gethin's eyes widened and he staggered back. He didn't fall pole-axed to the ground, the way the others had done, but his expression changed, his face crumpled and…he looked as if he might cry. He looked like a small, frightened child.

The creatures turned their eyes from me and swung their heads round to face Gethin. He was no longer their master and they turned on him. But as they swayed towards him, he seemed to be seeing something, or someone, quite different.

"No, father, no!" he sobbed. "Don't hurt her! Please, leave us alone."

He held out an arm as if he was trying to protect someone, but the creatures didn't care. Black mist surrounded him, three giant snakes towered over him and then seemed to suck him into the chasm. Gethin toppled and fell, with a last cry of, "Mother!" The mist disappeared with him into the depths.

And I stood on the edge and felt completely empty.

At last I said to Cernunnos, "I never thought I'd say this, but I hope he doesn't go to hell."

"I do not know what hell is," growled Cernunnos.

"If he'd had a different father he might have been a completely different person," I said.

"That is true," said Cernunnos.

"But other people are treated badly and they don't turn out like that," I went on, trying to make sense of it.

"That is also true," said Cernunnos. "And is this thing that you have just done what you were supposed to do? Because I do not feel any change in all this disturbance."

I was jolted out of my thoughts.

"No!" I shouted. "Rad and Ger! Where are they?"

The glow from the depths of the rift had grown brighter, so that the whole scene was bathed in orange. Then behind us we heard an explosion. We both turned round and saw, a little way off, a great fountain of fire spouting into the sky, higher and higher, and rocks being thrown up into the air and landing all around, dangerously close to us. The horse neighed in terror and Cernunnos flung his arms around its neck, trying to calm it down. Then off to our left, another column of fire sprang out of the ground.

"Alas!" Cernunnos cried out. "It is the end of everything! I did not foresee this!"

Oh, where were the runes? Where were they? It was no good! I'd failed and I was going to die and everyone was going to die.

Another explosion.

Then I saw them, on the very edge of the chasm, horribly close to being sucked in along with Gethin. It was hard to make them out against the burning light.

Don't fall in! Please don't fall in! I tried to sink into my trance, tried *so* hard to block out everything else, but it wasn't working. *Trying too hard! Relax. Relax.* But how could I, with all this going on? The runes wavered dangerously close to the edge, but somehow, somehow I calmed myself down. I was going to die anyway, so I should do this one last thing. There was no escape, so just do it. A kind of peace filled me as I accepted my death and gradually I managed to see nothing but the runes, floating in the air. I reached into the depths of my being and then…I flipped them.

There was instant calm. The change was so great that the silence seemed as deafening as the thunder. Then a piece of rock which had landed nearby lifted itself up into the air. It sailed back to the fire that had spewed it out of the ground and now the air was full of rocks returning to their homes and the fires were dying down. It grew darker. Then the chasm at our feet started to grind shut. The split in the earth grew narrower until it was a bright thread which vanished with a crunching jolt.

Cernunnos looked at me and then…he bowed! The god bowed to me!

But before I could say anything a howling wind blew up and grabbed hold of me.

"Well done!" called Cernunnos as I was whisked away. He held up his hand in salute. "Well done, hero!"

"Thank you!" I managed to call back, but whether he could hear me, I didn't know. Then I realised what he'd said. *Hero?* But I didn't have time to think about it.

It was just like before, like being carried along a raging stream of air, buffeted about, with nothing to hold on to and with pictures flashing past that I couldn't make out until…

With a sickening jerk I felt as if I was dumped back into my own body but it didn't quite fit. I had to wriggle around to make it comfortable. And next to me was Oz!

"I did it! I did it! "I yelled. "And Gethin's dead!"

"What?" said Oz. "Who's Gethin? What are you talking about?"

Then I saw that Oz looked different. He was wearing a leather jerkin and on his head was a leather helmet, too big for him. And that must be the strange feeling on my own head. I was dressed the same as Oz. What was happening?

I looked around. We were on the crest of a hill which I felt I should recognize, with soldiers all around. People were shouting and from further down the hill I could hear the clash of metal on metal. It was chaos.

"What's going on?" I asked.

"We've run out of arrows," grunted Oz. "That's what's going on. We'll have to collect some stones and start chucking them."

"But who are we fighting?" I asked, bewildered.

Oz looked at me with his mouth open.

"Have you had a knock on the head, or something?" he said. "Who are we fighting? The Normans, you berk, the Normans!"

CHAPTER FIFTY-THREE

WULF

"Again?" I said stupidly. "But, but we beat them."

"Pull yourself together, Wulf!" snapped Oz. "This is not the time to be having a funny turn!"

And then…with a horrible lurching in my stomach…I realised what had happened. Time had not returned to the present I'd left a few hours ago. It had stopped a few weeks before it should have. Gethin had travelled hundreds of years too far back but I had travelled not quite far enough forward.

My head swam and a green mist floated in front of my eyes. Oz didn't know anything about what had been happening. He didn't know who Gethin was, he didn't know Abdul, he'd never met the elves. Oz, my closest friend who shared everything, couldn't share all these things with me.

An arrow thudded into the ground beside me.

"The bastards!" yelled Oz. "They're getting closer! They're shooting over the shield wall! Come on, Wulf, get some rocks!"

I blinked and started scrabbling around for something I could throw. I'd got to stop thinking and start acting. I could worry about that stuff later. After all, I knew it was going to turn out all right. The Mercian reinforcements would be arriving soon. I could hear horses neighing in terror and men shouting battle cries…and men screaming.

"Come on!" bawled an English soldier in front of him. "Come and get a taste of my axe!"

He was a big man in a mail shirt, wielding a double-bladed axe, but even as he yelled out his defiance, an arrow flew over the top of his shield and struck him in the throat. He fell back and would have flattened me if I hadn't dived out of the way. Blood pumped out of the man's pierced artery and spurted on to my leg, hot and metallic-smelling.

The shield wall in front of us was broken. That hadn't happened before, had it? It must have done. I must have been too confused to remember.

Oz pulled me back and shoved a rock into my hand.

"Here, chuck this," he said curtly.

I pulled back my arm and tried to copy Oz. He was grabbing stones from a small pile and throwing them with a fierce expression on his face that I'd never seen before.

Then a cry went up, a babble of noise, but two phrases stood out. *The king is dead! The king has got an arrow in his eye!* A shiver ran through our troops and Oz turned white.

"It's all right! It's all right!" I said, clutching him. "The arrow only grazes his eye. The king isn't dead!"

Oz turned to look at me as if he didn't know me.

"What are you?" he said bitterly. "Some kind of fortune-teller?"

Desperately, I turned round and crawled back up the hill a few yards, to where I could see the road. This was when the reinforcements should be arriving, the Mercians, their bright banners now tatty, all that was left of the army that had fought the Norwegians in the north. Not that many, but enough to turn the tide of the battle. Where were they, marching and riding, singing their song about Aethelflaed, the Lady of the Mercians? I peered into the distance as far as I could see.

The road was empty.

I heard a voice echoing in my head. It was Pooka's. I'd asked him what would happen if I didn't manage to flip the runes until *after* time had been rolled back.

"Who knows?" Pooka had said. "Time's a funny thing. We might jus' get back to where we are now, or it could be a bit in the future or a bit in the past. Or things might be just a little bit different. People might be dead who's alive, or alive who's dead. Who knows?"

But now I knew. With a terrible numbness, as if I'd died inside, I knew that the Mercians were not coming. We were going to lose the battle.

And then another dreadful rumour went wailing through the troops. *The king has been cut to pieces!*

I heard another voice in my head. The hanged boy, or whatever creature of darkness had taken over his body.

"The king will be cut to pieces."

Gethin had been asking about Vortigern, but it was not the British king who'd be cut to pieces.

It was Harold.

I slumped and laid my head on the ground. I'd failed. I might have saved the world but what did that matter? If *only* I could have turned the runes before time went backwards! I didn't know what would have happened. Perhaps Gethin would have killed me, but the English would not have been defeated by the Normans.

And…if everything was different, then anything could…Oz!

I spun round to see him standing up, yelling dementedly at a Norman horseman who was climbing the hill with his spear poised to throw. Oz had picked up the dead soldier's double-bladed axe and, heavy as it was, was swinging it round in both hands. Then everything happened in slow motion. The Norman drew back his spear-arm and threw, the spear flew gracefully and oh so slowly through the air, and I hurled myself headfirst at Oz. The wind whistled past my ears, the spear got closer, and Oz stood there with his mouth open and a mad expression on his face.

Then it all speeded up. I thudded into Oz, we both rolled over and the spear hit the ground with a thunk, pinning me down by the edge of my tunic, which hung below my leather jerkin. The horse reared up and threw its rider but I didn't wait to see what would happen next. I grabbed Oz, ripping my tunic as I scrambled up and ran, dragging him with me.

"Got to get to the forest!" I panted, and Oz obeyed, seeming to be as much in a daze as I'd been only moments before.

We weren't the only ones running. I could hear the battle going on behind me as the housecarls made a brave last stand, but all around were ordinary fyrdsmen racing to get back to their families. My heart went out to them as they ran. They weren't cowards, but what was the point of getting yourself killed if the battle was lost? A dead husband and father was no good to anyone.

And the Normans chased us. A grey-haired man just ahead went down with a Norman arrow in his back. But it was harder for the Normans when they reached the forest. Me and Oz ducked and dived, grazing our knees and scratching our faces, until at last we couldn't hear anyone following. We found a hollow in the roots of a huge oak tree and fell exhausted, listening to the silence, broken only by our own heavy breathing.

"Thank you," said Oz.

"What for?" I said.

"You saved my life."

"You'd have done the same for me."

"Yeah, that's true," Oz smiled weakly.

I looked at him. "Thank God you look like yourself again. You got the battle madness, didn't you? You were like one of those berserkers they have in the Norwegian army."

"Well, you went a bit peculiar yourself," said Oz.

"I know," I said. "Let's get some sleep."

"Right," said Oz. "We'll live to fight another day."

Exhaustion hit him and he fell asleep as if he'd been drugged. But I lay there, replaying the battle in my mind. I did go a bit peculiar, I thought, but I can never, ever tell you why. Who'd ever believe me? I lay beside my best friend, with whom I shared everything, and felt like the loneliest person in the world. At last I must have slept.

BRAMBLE

And thass how we found 'em, lyin' there sleepin' like two babes in the wood. That Wulf, he had two big tears rollin' down from beneath his closed eyelids.

I leaned forward and put a wreath o' leaves on his head an' we all four bowed our heads and then Pooka says his bit.

"We come to honour you for what you done, an' p'raps also to help you."

"He be so sad," I says, "and yet he saved the world."

"He be blamin' hisself," says Mugwort, "'cos when the Web o' Wyrd restitched itself, it weren't in exactly the same pattern."

"An' yet," says Toadstool, "without him it might not have bin able to restitch itself at all."

"An' he've got another trouble," says Pooka. "This here Oz an' him have bin like twins, but now they can't be, 'cos Wulf do remember everythin' an' Oz don't know nothin' about it all."

"What about that herb, sweet forgetfulness?" says Toadstool. "We could squeeze some o' that in his eyes."

"My thoughts exactly," says Pooka. "Only we don't have none around here."

"I knows a bank where sweet forgetfulness grows," I says, hoppin' up and down. "'T'ain't that far away. Shall I get it?"

One nod from Pooka an' off I goes. 'Tweren't far, 'cos I were air-flittin', and I were back in no time with this little grey plant in my hand.

"Trouble is," says Mugwort, "we don' wan' him forgettin' *everythin'*, only the last few weeks."

"Trust me," says my Toadstool. "You knows all about them rune things an' I knows all about herbs. I'll put just the right amount in his eyes."

I give him the plant.

"Good girl," says Toadstool. "Thass the one."

He crushed it in his hand an' then he leaned over and squeezed a few drops on to each o' Wulf's eyelids, while Pooka crouched down and whispered in his ear.

"This time now be real. Forget the rest. That were a different future, but for you it didn't happen."

"I'd want him to know, though," says Mugwort, "that he done somethin' really great."

"Oh, he will," says Pooka, "but he'll know it in his heart, not in his mind."

273

We stood quiet for a while, lookin' at the two sleepin' boys. Then we wandered off into the forest.

"But these other humans," I says. "Won't they wonder what's bin happenin'? I mean, you're gatherin' nuts late in the autumn, an' then all of a sudden there's a great jerk an' the summer's hardly over an' you're gatherin' berries. Surely they'll wonder."

"That ain't how it seem to them," says Pooka. "To them it be as if none of it happened. It be the same wi' air-flittin'. They jus' can't do it. They ain't as close to everythin' around as us elves." He shook his head.

"'Tis a good thing Ol' Stag-head were there," says Mugwort, "when he went back all them years."

"Thass the bit *I* don't remember," I says.

"Thass 'cos you wasn't born yet," says Toadstool. He stood awhiles an' thought. "I weren't very big myself. Your sister Thistle were there. She were runnin' around, a little elf-maid." An then he done a lot o' blinkin', 'cos he still got very sad thinkin' about Thistle.

"'Course, none of them humans was born then," says Pooka.

I sighed an' shook my head.

"Such short little lives they got," I says.

"So you wouldn' expect 'em to remember that bit," Pooka went on. "But you mark my words, they won't remember none of it, like that Oz. Weak in the head they are, humans. Weak in the head."

CHAPTER FIFTY-FOUR

BRONWEN

Yesterday was chaos on Lord Aelfric's estate. We had news that Lord Aelfric and his brother Guthrum had both died bravely trying to defend the king. Lady Rhiannon was laid low with grief and I felt I had to take charge. With the Normans marching up from the south this was no place for a mother and baby to be and I told her so.

"We have to go back to Wales," I said, "and quickly. Just gather a few things together, any valuables you can't bear to leave, get a cart and go. You'll be much safer with your own family."

Sniffing and red-eyed, Lady Rhiannon agreed. But there seemed such a lot to be arranged and it wasn't until today that we were on the road to Wales. It isn't exactly an empty road. People are travelling in both directions, on foot, on horseback and in carts, like ourselves, but more of them are headed north, away from the Normans. Once we'd settled the baby, Lady Rhiannon thought she might be able to sleep for a bit, so I sat next to the driver.

I was horrified at what had happened but, though I'm ashamed to admit it, also secretly joyful. We're going home to Wales! I'm going to see Nain! I looked around curiously at the other travellers on the road.

And then time stopped. For a moment I was in that strange in-between state that happens to me sometimes. It's always as if someone's trying to tell me something, but so often I can't work out what it is.

There was a rider, dressed all in black, on a magnificent black horse, coming in the opposite direction, heading south. I could only see his face and hands under his outlandish clothing and they were dark too. He looked at the cart and our eyes met. He looked startled, and then as if he were trying to remember something. We held each other's gaze all the while he was riding past.

And then the moment was gone. I shivered and I was back in ordinary time. *Don't be silly*, I told myself. He caught your eye because he was just so foreign looking. But I knew that wasn't true. That man seemed important to me. I'd have to ask Nain about it. It's been difficult, these last three years, coping with these strange feelings without my grandmother to help me.

But now I'm going home.

ABDUL

I was heading south just now, riding my precious black mare to the coast, where I hope to get passage to France – for both of us. I would never leave Noor behind. My good friend Godwin was killed in the battle and after years of travel, it's time to go home. There's nothing now to keep me here and Cordoba beckons. Of course, it might not be easy at the moment to find a suitable ship, but I am not a poor man and money opens many doors. Nor am I unduly worried about travelling alone in these troubled times. I am an experienced fighter, and the mere look of the curved scimitar at my side is usually enough to make an attacker think twice.

And then I saw the girl.

What was it that made me momentarily check Noor? I couldn't take my eyes off her. Surely I knew her?

But of course. She reminded me of Aisha. I sighed. She was uncannily like my beloved dead wife. Her skin was fairer, but her features, her expression, everything about her was so like Aisha. And she looked back at me as if she recognized me too.

I slowed Noor and watched the cart until it was almost out of sight. Then I turned and continued on my way with longing in my heart. I was remembering a dream, the most beautiful dream I had ever had. It had seemed more real than reality. I was walking in a garden, sweet with the scent of roses, holding Aisha's hand. A stream murmured along beside us and a gentle breeze cooled the air. In the dream, I had felt a sense of bliss. There was no other word to do it justice. I had never been so sorry to wake up.

I am sure this was a reminder from Allah. I have not been so observant with my prayers lately, but that is going to change. Nothing must prevent me from rejoining my beloved in the Paradise that awaits all true believers. From now on, wherever I am, my religious observance must come first.

I am urging Noor to a canter. First we have to reach the south coast, then find a ship, and finally will come the long ride south, home to Andalusia.

STIG THE SHEPHERD BOY

I watched hungrily as my mum dished up the evening meal, a special treat, lamb stew. The lamb had been born dead, so I smuggled it home for dinner. I wasn't at all sure the lord of the manor would allow this, but I hoped he wouldn't find out.

Lord Sigelac, or Lord Gethin as he calls himself nowadays, is a funny character. Actually he's creepy. He rebuilt his father's hall and turned it into this amazing fortress made of stone. But now he's disappeared, and I hope he never comes back.

"Still no news?" asked my mum, putting a bowl of stew in front of me.

"Nope," I said, dipping some bread into the broth. "And I hope the only news we ever get is that he's dead."

"Stigand!" my mum tutted. "Don't say such things! What has he ever done to you?"

"It's not what he's done," I tried to explain. "It's…I dunno. It's when he's riding past and he gives me this funny look, as if he's planning to do something nasty to me and he thinks it's a joke. He gives me the shivers."

Mum roared with laughter.

"Don't be ridiculous! What nasty thing could he be planning to do to you?"

"I dunno," I said. "But I hope he never comes back."

BRAMBLE

I s'pose you wants to know what happened to us elves. Well, a whiles after that, me an' Toadstool had a baby. A beautiful little thing she were an' we called her Thistle. 'Cos believe it or not, 'tis Thistle come back to us. Leastways, thass what me an' Toadstool believes. That sort o' thing do happen, you know. What goes around comes around.

So Mugwort made her a little necklace, a little wooden disc on some plaited grass.

"To keep her safe," he says.

But Pooka, he weren't very pleased. Oh no.

"Whass this?" he says, takin' it from Mugwort. "Whass this shape burnt on to the wood?"

"'Tis a 'th' for Thistle's name," says Mugwort, all innocent like.

"'Tis one o' them rune things!" says Pooka. "In fact, 'tis that very same rune shape that Wulf had round his neck! You must think I were born yesterday!"

"'Tis only for the first sound of her name," says Mugwort. "Thorn for Thistle. 'Tis writin'. You can write wi' the runes. It don' have to have nothin' to do wi' magic."

"Writin'?" says Pooka. "Thass human stuff. Thass a kind o' magic in itself, but it ain't *our* sort o' magic. An' rune magic is from ol' One-eye. It ain't got nothin' to do wi' us. Jus' 'cos *you're* interested in it, you don' wanna go givin' it to an elf baby!"

"It were useful, though, weren't it?" says Mugwort. "We wouldn't none of us have still bin here if I hadn't a known somethin' about the runes!"

'Course, Pooka couldn' argue wi' that.

An' not only that, but none of us wouldn' have bin here if it wasn't for Wulf. He saved the world, did that Wulf, an' us elves have always give him great honour for that. There was dark times to come for the humans, terrible dark times, but us elves jus' kep' out o' the way. An' after a hundred years or so things got a bit better. 'Course, thass a long time for humans, but 'tis only a blink of an eye for us.

But backalong, we didn' know none o' that. We jus' knew that Wulf had saved the world an' we had a beautiful little elf maid. I sat and cuddled her and felt so peaceful an' happy.

"Ain't it funny," I says to my Toadstool, "how things do turn out."

He stroked her little downy head.

"'Tis that," he says. "'Tis that."

WULF

The sun woke me up the next morning, the autumn sun peering down at us through the branches. I squinted back up at it. And I smiled. It was the morning after the battle, the battle that we lost. But I smiled. I felt light, unburdened. I knew that when I'd gone to sleep everything had seemed really bleak. So why did I feel so different now?

The king was dead, our great leader, King Harold. But somehow even that didn't seem quite so terrible this morning. This was just the beginning. People would rally round someone else. The Normans weren't going to have it all their own way! I sat up and brushed some leaves out of my hair.

I had the strangest feeling that I'd done something wonderful. I looked down at Oz. Of course…I'd saved Oz's life! I'd always felt Oz was braver than me. I'd wished I could just jump into things without thinking, like him. But now I knew that, when it came to it, I could. In my own way, I was just as brave as Oz. And there was something inside me, like a warm glow round my heart, telling me that I could do anything if I put my mind to it. Why was I feeling like this after such a defeat? It was a puzzle.

Oz moved, yawned and opened his eyes. He looked around in surprise before reality hit.

"Shit. We lost."

"Yeah," I said, and then wondered what else to say. I couldn't exactly say, *never mind, it doesn't matter that much*. It *did* matter, and I was still trying to work out why I didn't feel worse about it.

"I was having this wonderful dream," said Oz. "We were in this massive hall having a victory feast and getting drunk, and the king made a speech saying how great we all were. But the funny thing was…you remember they said he got an arrow in his eye? Well, in my dream he was wearing an eyepatch. And then I woke up. What a joke."

279

"Yeah, but listen, Oz. It's not the end. People aren't gonna just lie down and let the Normans walk all over them."

Oz sat up. "No, you're right. We ought to go and find some group that'll fight them. I mean, two experienced archers like us…anybody'd be glad to have us in their army. Oh and, er, thanks again…for doing what you did. I suppose I owe you one now."

"Nah," I grinned. "Don't worry about it. But we ought to go home first and check our families are all right. Let them know we're still alive."

"And we especially ought to thank your mum," said Oz.

"What d'you mean?"

Oz shifted himself so that his back was against the tree trunk.

"Think about it," he said. "Just think about how lucky we were. I know it was very brave of you and all that, to leap on me and knock me out of the way of that spear. But if we'd fallen a couple of inches short, we'd both have been skewered by it. Don't you think we were just a little bit lucky?" He held up one hand with the thumb and forefinger almost touching. "Just a tiny bit?"

"And your point is?" I said.

"I reckon," said Oz. "You know what I reckon?"

He paused. I raised my eyebrows.

"What do you reckon, oh wise one?"

"Well, that thing your mum gave you. That rune-stone that was supposed to keep you safe. I reckon it worked."

I put my hand under my tunic and felt the stone, with the shape of the rune etched into it. It felt warm to the touch, as it did sometimes.

"Yeah," I said. "You might be right."

ACKNOWLEDGEMENTS

Jo thanks her Friday writing workshop, all published authors, for their support and inspiration: Penny Joelson, Angela Kanter, Vivien Boyes and Derek Rhodes. Special thanks to Angela for proof reading and editing, and both Penny and Angela for their enormous help with publishing. Thanks also to Reena Patel for her amazing art work, and to Helen Hart and the staff at Silverwood Books for their support and professionalism.

ALSO BY JO BARNES

Odd Fox Out
Have you ever had a chance meeting which changed your life?
That's what happens to Edgar Sharpeyes when he is a small fox cub...

ISBN 978-1-80042-247-6
Available in paperback and as an ebook

www.ingramcontent.com/pod-product-compliance
Lightning Source LLC
Chambersburg PA
CBHW030529030726
47495CB00004B/911